Cradled in the Arms of Cassy

By Matt Egner
Copyright © 2015, Matt Egner

Copyright © 2015 by Matt Egner. All rights reserved.

Cover copyright © 2015 by Matt Egner.

This is a work of fiction. Any resemblance to actual persons living or dead, businesses, events, or locales is purely coincidental.

Reproduction in whole or part of this publication without express written consent is strictly prohibited. The author greatly appreciates you taking the time to read his work.

4

Table of Contents

Preface 11
DAY ONE – The Office 13
    Chapter 1. My Arrival 13
    Chapter 2. Nice to Meet You 17
    Chapter 3. Getting Groceries 25
    Chapter 4. Dinner and Dancing 31
    Chapter 5. The Shortcut 41
DAY TWO – Camp 45
    Chapter 6. A Good Breakfast 45
    Chapter 7. Off To Camp 51
    Chapter 8. Taxi Driver 57
    Chapter 9. Unpacking My Gear 61
    Chapter 10. The Outhouse 65
    Chapter 11. Planning the Day 69
    Chapter 12. Strumming a Tune 73
DAY THREE - Evening Songs 77
    Chapter 13. Early Birds 77
    Chapter 14. Report Writing 81
    Chapter 15. Lunch with Laura 85
    Chapter 16. Filing 93
    Chapter 17. Pickup 97
    Chapter 18. Admiring a Bikini 103
DAY FOUR - The Gossan 107
    Chapter 19. Coffee 107

- Chapter 20. A Little Pyrite 111
- Chapter 21. An Old Showing 115
- Chapter 22. Religion 119
- Chapter 23. Play 123
- Chapter 24. Plenty Fast 129
- Chapter 25. Sulphide 133
- Chapter 26. Nicknames 137

DAY FIVE - Rain 141
- Chapter 27. Sleeping In 141
- Chapter 28. Administration Work 147
- Chapter 29. Whisky 151
- Chapter 30. My Theory 157
- Chapter 31. Dessert 161

DAY SIX - Blueberry Island 169
- Chapter 32. A Note 169
- Chapter 33. West Grid 173
- Chapter 34. My Justice 175
- Chapter 35. Caribbean Swim 179
- Chapter 36. Bath Time 183
- Chapter 37. Embrace 189
- Chapter 38. A Mystery 193

DAY SEVEN - The Rock Ledge 197
- Chapter 39. Laundry 197
- Chapter 40. Paddle 201
- Chapter 41. The Rescue 203
- Chapter 42. Connecting 207
- Chapter 43. Raftology 215

- Chapter 44. Really?...221
- Chapter 45. Relax..225

DAY EIGHT- The Sad Poet..231
- Chapter 46. Goodbye 231
- Chapter 47. The Bombshell News...237
- Chapter 48. Moose Crossing..243
- Chapter 49. Poetry 249
- Chapter 50. Luncheon 253
- Chapter 51. Willows..257
- Chapter 52. Up a Tree...261

DAY NINE - The Confession 265
- Chapter 53. Recliner...265
- Chapter 54. The Mine Geologist...271
- Chapter 55. My Confession 277
- Chapter 56. Camp Visitor..281
- Chapter 57. Advice 287
- Chapter 58. Fishing Trip 293

DAY TEN - The Last Sunset 297
- Chapter 59. Food Fantasy...297
- Chapter 60. Management Skills 301
- Chapter 61. Chores 303
- Chapter 62. Sneak up...309
- Chapter 63. Camp Love 315
- Chapter 64. Dear Thora..317
- Chapter 65. Come on! 321

Dedication

The author would like to thank all the geologists he knew and worked with from Newfoundland to B.C. for helping inspire the content of this story.

Preface

Geology, the study of physical earth, is a profession like few others. Economic geology is the side of earth science that deals with ore minerals, and economic geologists search the ground for ore deposits. This profession entails spending protracted periods of time far off in the remote wilderness.

This is not a simple romance, it's a love story. It may fill your soul, or it may break your heart. You will descend into a world few people know anything about, yet a world in our own backyard populated by a special breed of people coping with hardships most have never experienced. This, our most natural world, is where basic human nature can expose the extremes of both joy and anguish, hope and dismay.

DAY ONE - The Office

Chapter 1. My Arrival

I've been sitting on this bus for hours as It wound northward through the spruce forests of Manitoba. I'm Titus Weatherby. That's a pretty posh name for a guy living in a prospector tent. As they say, you can't judge a book by its cover, or in my case, by its title. I am a simple man living a simple plan; make it to the next day unscathed.

I'm an exploration geologist. I work from job to job; sometimes for a week and sometimes for a year. You take whatever comes along. I just spent three months on a drill job searching for nickel near Thunder Bay with The Golden Lake Mining Company. It wasn't so much a mining company, but yet another junior exploration company staking a swath of bush and weaving a good story to sell shares. It's usually a great deal for the company, and always a losing proposition for the unsuspecting shareholder.

Anyway, my job is to scour the ground for minerals, or in the last case, log the core that comes up from drill rigs. In a way it's quite exciting. You never know what you're going to find, on the surface or underground. I have seen core with beautiful, coloured rock, incredible wavy folds, massive zinc and copper minerals, and in one case, a sprinkling of gold. Now, you would think that was something to celebrate, but strictly looking at core is like taking a few words from a speech out of context. Core is a one dimensional view of a three dimensional world.

You have to understand the rocks to appreciate the mineralization. Take that gold I found; it was in a stretch of core that persisted for about fifteen feet. Wow, you say. If a zone of rock fifteen feet wide is sprinkled with gold, then there must be an ore body down there worth mining. That would in fact be so, if the drill cut across the vein. But in this case the drill followed the vein, a vein that was only a couple inches wide. In essence, there wasn't a great deal of gold. That, however didn't stop the mining company from displaying all fifteen feet of gold vein at conventions and shareholder meetings. That probably netted them a million dollars of new investment.

Sometimes I wonder how these promoters sleep at night, and then other times I wonder what it would be like to sleep in a luxurious bed with thick feather pillows and clean cotton sheets. I rarely get to sleep in a real bed. Usually, I have to build a makeshift bed of logs, attach a piece of plywood on top and then cover it with a thin foamy. I shouldn't complain, at least I'm not lying on the ground.

The spruce trees whizzed by. Up ahead I could see a sign that read 'Flin Flon' and the bus slowed down to take a left off the highway into town. Then emerged the common signs of populace; a Canadian Tire, an Esso gas station, a park and a few houses. Finally, we pulled into a convenience store and stopped. The driver, a middle aged portly man in a grey uniform and drivers cap, stood up and ceremoniously announced that we had arrived in Flin Flon.

About half the riders got up and departed the bus. I assumed the other half were going on up the line to

Thompson or Lynn Lake. It was a nice summer day; sunny with dry air. I stretched and waited for the driver to unload the bags underneath. Mine looked about normal for these northern towns; a canvas backpack and a big heavy sleeping bag. I picked them up, nodded to the driver and walked across the street to a diner. I'm not sure why I did that. I have no idea where I'm going. I have an address, but no map. I looked up and down the street, like that was going to give me a clue. I could start walking deeper into town, but what's the point of that if I don't know the way. I turned to the diner and walked in.

"Hello", I addressed a young lady at the cash. "Do you know where Drury Road is?"

"Yes, it's about four blocks down the main road and then two blocks west. Where are you going?" she asked.

"The Cliff Mines office at 427 Drury."

A voice behind me said, "I'll take you."

I turned around to see an older gentleman waiting to pay his lunch bill. "Are you sure?" I asked.

"Yeah, it's no problem. That's not far out of the way for me," he said.

"Thanks. I appreciate that." I stepped aside to let him pay his bill. He slapped a twenty down and waited for his change.

"Come on, I got my pickup truck right out front here," he said.

I followed him outside and over to a gold coloured Dodge that had seen better days. I tossed my gear in the back and hopped in the cab with him.

"My name is Ron. What's yours?" he said.

"Titus. Good to meet you, Ron." We shook hands. "What do you do?" I asked.

"I'm the resident geologist for the district. I know all the mining companies in the area. I take it you're looking for Barry Denisen," he said.

"Yes, that's right. He hired me for a three week job on Schist Lake," I replied.

"Ha ha ha, three week job, eh? I hope you're prepared to dig in for a while. I know what they have planned for that property. I bet they have enough work for six months," he said. "Have you worked up here before?"

"I did an eight month stint over in the Athabaska and lots of work near Pickle Lake. I'm just coming off a job northwest of Thunder Bay. Mostly I've worked around Timmins," I said.

"Hmm, so you know what it's like. Pretty good bush around there. Make sure you take a boat ride over to the East Arm. Gorgeous clear water over there." He rambled on a bit about the rock structures and old mines. He'd be a great guy to know if you wanted to prospect the area. The truck bobbed along over the frost heaved roads. It only took a few minutes to reach the company office. "Here you go. Best of luck to you," he said with a grin.

I smiled back at him. "Thanks. And thanks for the ride. Glad I didn't have to lug my gear across town." I hopped out, grabbed my gear from the truck box and thumped the side of the truck. I gave him a wave and he drove off.

Chapter 2. Nice to Meet You

There I stood in front of a rather small, one story brick building, wondering if I had just been caught up in another long drawn out exploration project. I had already been out in the bush for three months without a break. I wasn't keen on another six month stretch. I didn't really have much choice now. I was here. I opened the door and walked in.

Six people were standing around a large table staring at maps. A stout man with a big black beard and straggly hair looked up toward me. "Hello. Titus?" He asked, obviously anticipating my arrival. Who else would show up with a backpack and sleeping bag?

"I am," I answered.

"Come on in. If I knew when you were coming I'd have picked you up at the bus stop. Looks like you found your way here OK. How was the bus ride?" he asked.

"Not bad, slept most of the way," I answered. "I just got out of the bush two days ago, so enjoyed the comfort of a cushy chair and down time."

"Well, hope you enjoyed it. We're off to the bush again in the morning," Barry said. "We're just looking over the maps here. Let me introduce you around. Over there is David. He got here two days ago from a job in Noranda with Bridgeway Exploration." I looked across the far end of the table at a tall, slim fellow in his early thirties. He had orange hair, freckles and a broad, rather devilish grin.

"Hi David," I said. "How ya doing?"

"Good," he replied. "Nice to meet you."

Barry continued, "That's Kyle. He's been with us for two months already." Barry pointed to a slight, tough looking guy across the table. He had mid-length, wiry hair and a rugged narrow face with thin lips and a pointed chin. No smile, just a nod of the head. I nodded back, taking note to watch my step around him.

"This is Laura," Barry pointed to the woman beside him. She was probably mid-twenties, long brown hair with an average, though attractive face and tall, sturdy body.

"Hi Laura, nice to meet you," I said, and gave her a little wave. She responded with a weak smile and a wave back.

"And this is Cassy," Barry nodded to the girl beside him.

How do I describe her? She had shoulder length, straight blonde hair that was cut with bangs across the forehead. She stood about five feet five inches tall. She had icy blue eyes and pale clear skin. Her face was very attractive, in a plumpish way. She had a figure any man would stare at. She was not skinny; she was far more robust. Her breasts were overly large for her stature. She wore a T-shirt that was fully filled out with what looked like two grapefruits. Her torso was a tight trunk that seamlessly merged into perfectly filled denim cut-offs. Don't get me wrong, she was not the image of a playboy bunny, just beautifully shaped in an honest, country girl way.

"Hi," she said, with a wide, bubbly grin. "We talked over the phone."

"Oh, that was you." I said. "Hi. Good to meet you." I shook her hand like we were a couple of business partners.

"And that's Cassy with a 'Y', by the way," Cassy stated, emphatically.

"Why?" I asked.

"That's right, a 'Y'," she repeated.

"No, I mean why a 'Y'? I would expect an 'ie'. Isn't it ordinarily with an 'ie'?"

"Well, I'm not ordinary," Cassy blurted out with a grin.

"So I shouldn't say normally an 'ie', because then you would have to explain you aren't normal, right?" I kidded back with a smile.

Cassy laughed and explained that throughout her whole life she wrote Cassy with a 'Y', correct or not and she wasn't going to change it. Anyway, it made her unique. An interesting character trait perhaps, but completely trivial in the context of our first encounter.

Barry cut in, "Cassy's the project manager. She's been here three months working on another property and I asked her to take on this one."

What the fuck? She couldn't have been more than twenty five. The first thing that went through my mind was that Barry was giving her more than responsibility, if you know what I mean. I'm twenty nine and I've never seen a project manager under thirty five; most are over forty. No fucking justice! Well, who cares, just get through this job and move on.

You know what? I'm not going to assume anything about her. Barry definitely looks like a weaselly son of a bitch. I got him pegged. But Cassy seems OK. In fact, Cassy looks remarkably innocent and naive. Of course, I have never been good at first impressions. I should have learned by now not to trust my first impressions because I'm often wrong. It's like orientation; you might think you know the right way through the bush, but without the aid of a good compass, you could be going in any direction. Actually, my intuition in the bush is better than my ability to read people. After a couple days, I may completely revise my impressions. Or not.

"This is Titus," Barry told everyone and waved his hand toward me. "So tell us about that last job you were on, Titus?" Barry asked.

"Dull job. Mostly swampland. I spent three months looking at anorthosite core. Shitty camp too. We were on a lake so small it was nameless. I think the moose used the lake as a shitter. It was a miracle the plane could land on it."

"You're in luck here. We're on Schist Lake, one of the nicest lakes you'll ever see. The East Arm is crystal clear and looks like the tropics. You'll setup camp down here," Barry pointed to a small bay near the bottom of the lake on the West Arm.

It was a big lake, actually three lakes connected by a tiny inlet where the train line crosses. I have no idea why they would call it one lake. The arms all converge near the south end. Down the Northwest Arm was a point of land jutting into the lake. The train line followed the east shore of the Northwest Arm. It was a complicated shoreline with a number of islands scattered around.

"You'll be mapping a few lines to the west side of your camp, and on the east side all the way over past the train tracks. There are some reported massive sulphides from old reports, but no clear locations. That's what we want to look for." Barry swivelled the maps around, looking for something. "Here, look at the structure. It's similar to the Trout Lake Mine. We'll do some geophysics over the area this winter, but it would be good to see if we can map the folds and spot any mineral before then."

"We're just planning a few weeks of mapping now," Cassy added. "So we'll get in and get out quick. Take samples of every outcrop, regardless of what the rock type is. I suspect we'll mostly see greenstones, but there are some pyroclastics too. We've got two boats at the dock at the top of the lake. The road doesn't go any further down the lake, so we'll have to take everything in by boat."

Cassy was busily pointing to different parts of the map. Every time she stretched out and leaned across the table, I had the most vivid view of the lower part of the left cheek, and her breasts draped over the table. It was a nice distraction, however this sort of thing is better avoided when in a camp. I both wanted to see her form and avoid it. I moved closer to the table to focus on the maps. Laura, across the table, was fully dressed in work clothes, she may have been just as attractive as Cassy but hid it well, as most geologists tend to do.

Barry added, "We've cut lines here, and over here." He pointed to the claims on the map. "They're at hundred foot intervals; should be lots of outcrop in the area, very little swamp. Take a few rolls of Mylar with you and draft at the camp. Cassy will bring them into town occasionally. There's not much more to it. Any questions?" he asked, flipping his shaggy hair around.

Everyone looked around at each other. David trumped up, "When's dinner? I'm starving!"

"David, you're always starving. It's only three, you know? Why don't you show Titus where he can put his gear and get him a foamy for tonight," Barry said.

David waved me into another room which looked like a fairly big lounge or living room. There was a chesterfield, Lazy boy chair, TV and stereo. "You can put your stuff anywhere there's room. We're sleeping on the floor." David went to a storage room and brought out a rolled up foamy and gave it to me. "Here you go."

Par for the course, I'm afraid. Mining companies don't like spending money on the comfort or privacy of geologists. Dump them all in a shabby room to sleep on the floor, then pack them off to a bush camp. Can you imagine if they sent an accountant on a business trip and asked him to sleep on an office floor? There is an element of respect lacking in the mineral exploration profession, but sadly I have become accustomed to it.

I tossed my gear down in a vacant corner near another foamy along a wall. No one else had come into the room, so I sat down and rested against my foamy. Tomorrow will be a full day. I never liked camp setups and hated camp tear downs. Lots of lugging and hard work. I much preferred walking through the bush and looking at rocks.

You may ask how I ended up in this profession. Well, I grew up in a middle class home. My father was a cold hearted business man; my mother, emotionally detached. In retrospect, they were perfect for each other. I, the only child, often felt abandoned as my parents worked late or played host to their many shallow friends.

I took refuge in the forest that spread out beyond the end of our street in suburban Kitchener. I wandered the woods long enough to know every tree, creek and knoll. I became interested in rocks when I found my first fossil; a trilobite. After that, I scanned every rock I saw and spent endless hours at the library cataloguing my collection. That attachment to the forest and my interest in rocks led me to study geology at Waterloo.

I assumed that my early years as a geologist would naturally lead to a senior job at a mining company and a formidable future. My assumption was not based on fact. I would soon learn that most corporate leaders were not geologists, but lawyers and accountants. Geologists were expected to serve the company in the field, and not earn sacrificial compensation or loyalty beyond the life of any project. This reality should have sunk in soon after leaving school, but it did not. I am a stubborn sort. I am a believer.

Chapter 3. Getting Groceries

I wondered if there was a kitchen in this place, with a fridge, full of food. I was hungry. I probably should have grabbed a bite at that diner. I got up and rummaged around the place, checking out rooms. There was a bedroom with a single bed and simple, maple dresser. Someone was using it. Another door led to a storage room filled with camp gear that could be loaded out through a garage door. Another room was indeed a kitchen with sink, oven, fridge, etc. I opened the fridge. It was half filled with beer, condiments, and pop. Next to the bedroom was a full washroom with a bathtub. That would be handy after coming out of the bush. I circled back around to the office.

"You bored?" Barry said.

"Getting hungry," I replied.

"I sent David and Laura out to get groceries for the camp. They might be a while. The store is only a couple blocks away if you want to go help them. You can grab a snack there. We'll go out for dinner when they're all done. Otherwise, grab a beer from the fridge and relax," Barry said.

"Alright, I'll go down to the store and help them out," I replied. I saw Kyle stretched out on his foamy, a banjo propped up behind him, and Cassy was nowhere to be seen. Not much reason to sit around this place. A walk in town would be nice anyways. I walked out the door, then popped my head back in. "Which way is it?" I asked. Barry pointed, I waved and nodded a thanks.

It was a typical small town with slat board buildings and lots of trees. Outcrops of greenstone bubbled up in round hills that roads and houses avoided. I strode along slowly, purposely wasting time to enjoy this moment of urban life. I saw the store ahead and walked through the front doors. It was an old, small grocery store. Perhaps the mining company had some kind of deal with them. I looked up and down the few aisles until I spotted Laura at the meat counter.

"Hey," I announced, coming up behind her.

"Hey, what are you doing here?" she asked.

"I was bored. Didn't want to hang around the office. I sat on a bus all day," I replied. "What are you getting?"

"Burger, steaks, chicken. Anything you want in particular?" she asked.

"Nope, that all sounds fine. Did Barry give you a list or are you just winging it?"

"Yeah, I have a list. But we can get anything else we want. We're just getting a week's worth. Cassy will get more for the next week," Laura said.

"Where's David?" I asked.

"Fucked if I know. He was supposed to be getting lunch supplies, but I haven't seen him in a while. How long does it take to get bread and mayo?"

"I'll go look for him. Anything you want me to get?" I asked.

Laura pulled her list out of a back pocket. "Can you get drinks? We need cases of pop. Oh, and get cleaning supplies, for dishes."

I agreed and left to get a cart. Then I walked around looking for David. I found him down an aisle talking to some old man. You could tell David was in the wrong profession. He was definitely a people person. He'd have made a great salesman. I left him to finish playing social gadfly and went looking for the drinks.

Didn't take me long to fill the cart with cases of ginger ale, pop water, coke and sprite, then find the cleaning supplies. I grabbed the most expensive ones they had. I was not in the business of saving a stingy mining company a few loonies. They were saving enough cash on my living conditions. I tossed in dish soap, towels, washcloths, a couple buckets and scrubbers. I went an aisle over and grabbed some toothpaste and soap. I think the mining company can spring for that. I wanted to wander around picking out more stuff. It was fun shopping with someone else's cash.

David came up behind me. "Hey, what are you doing here?" he asked.

"Oh no, what are YOU doing here?" I replied and then smiled. If I wasn't mistaken, I had David pegged as a practical joker. "I got bored, and Barry told me to come help out… what did he say? Oh yeah, 'go help out that fuckup David'. Paraphrasing, that is. By the way, your cart is empty. I thought you were supposed to be getting lunch stuff."

"Oh shit! That's what I was supposed to get. I forgot what Laura said. I better get it." With that, David rushed off with his empty cart. I went back to the meat counter but Laura was gone. A quick search and I found her nearby getting butter.

"Did you find David?" Laura asked.

"Yes. He was fucking around, talking with people. He's getting the stuff now." A moment later, David came flying around the corner and down the aisle where we were picking out milk and eggs.

"All done!" David exclaimed with his hands outstretched and a grin on his face. Laura just rolled her eyes and ignored him. I gave him a smile back in acknowledgement of his stunt.

"Sorry David, I already told her you were fuckin' the dog," I told him.

David laughed, "I don't care."

We caught up to Laura who had moved further down the aisle. I yelled up to her, "What else we need?"

"Fruit and snacks," Laura replied. "David, can you get snacks? I'll get fruit." David dashed off like a kid and I followed Laura. God knows what antics David will pull. At the fruit section I grabbed oranges and apples and Laura picked out several bunches of bananas. We headed toward the checkout and David caught up to us there. Took a hell of a long time to scan and bag up all those groceries. Laura signed the bill for the company and we loaded it all in the back of the truck.

"Can we stop at the liquor store?" I asked. "I want to get a two-four."

"We already went there. Barry actually bought it for the camp. Never seen that before," Laura said. She jumped into the truck and cranked the engine. David and I sat in the passenger and middle seats and we rolled off toward the office. Minutes later we were unloading the groceries and filling the fridge and freezer.

"You guys took your time," Barry said.

"Yeah, I slowed them down. I demanded the butcher make special cuts for us." I said. I think Barry actually believed it at first. His expression was almost incredulous. Then Laura turned and gave me a disapproving frown and shook her head. Barry smiled and snickered. I don't think he has much of a sense of humour though.

First rule of bush camps, protect your crew. Actually that may be the second rule, at least in my rule book. First rule is keep your ass clean. Second rule, backup your crew like family. I got lots of camp wisdom. I once wrote some insights in my geologist journal that I thought were worthy of sharing, though never knew who would ever benefit from it.

- Consider everyday a golden opportunity.
- Frankum tastes bad but turns a lovely shade of lavender.
- Catching a fish means eating something fresh for a change.
- Do not wear rubber boots from December to April.
- Naming unknown lakes after body parts in Cree is fun.
- The compass never lies, but it's not always right.
- A gun is a tool that can save your life or take your life.
- Top camp tip: Always, always, always keep your ass clean.

I'm sure each one of these tips had great meaning at the time I thought of it. My first job was in Timmins when I was only twenty years old. We were camped on the shore of some unknown lake in early May. It was still cold and ice formed around the edges of the lake each night. After about seven days, I developed a severe irritation around the anus because we had no shower or bath. The lake water was icy cold and I didn't think to clean myself properly.

This was when I learned what my top camp tip would be. I was so uncomfortable, I took a bucket, warmed the water on a fire, then walked into the bush and gently washed the inflamed zone. It was quite painful, and still took a couple days to heal. It was a miserable few days trying to walk through the bush and just as painful to admit my irritation to the crew. After that episode I made sure, no matter how rough the camp was or how cold the weather, to clean my ass regularly. This is one of those simple facts most people who shower daily would never have to worry about.

Back to the crew, we were, by virtue of our circumstance, a newly formed family. We would all have our quirks and characteristics, but we would accept that and appreciate what each has to offer the group.

Chapter 4. Dinner and Dancing

"OK gang," Barry said, "let's go eat. How about the Tin Roof Diner?" As if we really had much say in where we would eat.

All were, not surprisingly, in agreement. Barry drove and the girls sat up front with him. The rest of us sat in the truck box. It took about ten minutes to get there. It was a white clapboard building with a blue metal roof. The dusty gravel parking lot seemed overly large for this size of a diner, but Flin Flon was not stingy on space. I hopped out and scuffed my feet as I walked up to the door. Barry held the door open and we all filed in.

"Got a table for six?" Barry asked a lady at the cash.

"Sure. Just a minute and we'll push a couple tables together," she replied, and disappeared into the dining room. We stood silent for a minute until she returned and guided us to a table setup for six. Only Barry and Cassy looked like they lived in this town with their casual clothes. The rest of us looked like we were already in a bush camp. I suppose there were lots of others in this town that looked like that. I certainly didn't feel out of place, like I would if I was in Toronto. We walked into the dining room and over to our table which was not set, just vacant and clean. A moment after sitting down another waitress came by and laid paper place mats and cutlery down in front of us.

"What can I get you all to drink?" she asked.

I raised my voice first, "What do you have on tap?"

"We only have bottled beer, sir. We have Canadian, Blue, Carlsberg and Coors Lite."

None of those appealed to me, and I am sure that was apparent from the expression on my face. But I had to pick. "I'll take a Carlsberg," I said, somewhat disappointingly. I don't know what Barry thought of me ordering a beer, but that didn't bother me. I thought I'd start things off and that way others would feel comfortable ordering a beer. Let's see how this plays out.

Around the table, one by one, everyone ordered a beer, even Barry. Either I was a trend setter or they would have anyway. I guess I'll never know. There was a pile of menus on the table. I snapped one up and started reading. I wonder if they had anything deep fried. Well, I was in luck, pretty much everything was deep fried. I bet if they could invent a method for deep frying pasta, these diners would serve it. I really didn't know what I wanted. I'll make up my mind at the last second. Everyone was asking each other what they were going to have. I kept my face buried in the menu so they wouldn't ask me, but to no avail. Cassy, who had sat beside me, asked what looked good.

"I don't know. You eaten here before?" I asked her.

"Yup. Nothing's good," she said and laughed. "I like the perogies."

"Hmm, I hadn't thought of that. I usually pick fish and chips when I don't know what I want. Do you like fish and chips?" I asked her.

"Yeah. I know what you mean. They're a good standby."

"If I get the fish and chips, would you take some? I'd like to taste your perogies." After saying this, I immediately thought it sounded inappropriate, and I snickered to myself.

"Sure. Have you had perogies before?" Cassy asked.

"Nope. I don't even know what they are," I said, and laughed out loud.

My beer came. I reached for it and held it up in the air in front of Cassy. The glass bottle was sweating and I could feel a few drops of cold water run down my arm. She got my message and lifted her beer. We clinked bottles.

"Cheers," I said to her and she smiled at me. Then I stood, held my beer out over the table. "Hey, a big thanks to Barry for bringing us together. Thanks, Barry." Everyone clinked bottles and said cheers. I was not just a scientist. I was also a good actor and insincere schmuck. I didn't give a rat's ass about Barry, the arrogant bore. But I can play the game. Barry grinned with approval.

I sat back down. I was tempted to look over at Cassy and smile, but I didn't. I couldn't tell if she respected Barry and looked up to him or if she was just a very grateful and loyal employee. Either way, I wasn't going to judge her or share my impression of him. For some reason, I had taken a dislike to Barry.

I heard lots of chit chat around the table, the loudest voice coming from Barry, the voice of authority. I don't doubt he'd had lots of experience in the bush and running projects, but that shouldn't make you a loudmouth. I'll focus on getting through dinner. Tomorrow I'll be out in the bush."

Barry stood up. "Let's play a little game while we wait. Tell us your most embarrassing moment in a bush camp. I'll start. I was on a platinum project near Thunder Bay. We built a shitter with plywood. We thought we did a great job, and situated it on a small hill right behind camp. Well, I was the first to use it. I sat down and a second later the damned thing shifted, toppled forward and rolled down the little hill to camp. It wasn't far and only rolled a couple times, but the door swung open and I looked up at several faces looking down on me as I lay there, pantless. As soon as they saw I was OK, they laughed so hard I thought they were gonna pee themselves. So let this be a lesson to you. Don't place the shitter on a hill and make sure it's secure." Barry sat down and said, "Over to you, Kyle."

Kyle looked a bit dazed and searched for a thought. "I was on a big job up in the territories and we were sampling stream beds by helicopter. The VP of something came into camp to check the property out. We all stayed up one night and got drunk. The next day he wanted to go out in the field, and so me and him and another geologist went for a ride in the helicopter. We were sailing along over a plateau and as soon as we hit the drop off the helicopter rose about a hundred feet and I lost my cookies. Puke flew around like shit hitting a fan. I bet that exec was wishing he'd stayed home."

"Alright, I got one," said David. "I was in a hell hole drill camp in La Ronge, way back in the bush. We had about 10 drillers, a camp cook, and me. The camp cook was this ditzy chick with obvious emotional problems. But she took a shine to me. Well a couple weeks into the project the manager of exploration came in to see how things were going. I don't know if the camp cook was trying to make me look good or what was going through her head, but as we all came into the kitchen tent to eat, she ran over to me and planted a kiss on my cheek. She said 'I'm so glad you're back' and then left the tent. I was as surprised as anyone, but the look on the manager's face was one of complete shock. I just smiled and shrugged like I didn't know what was happening. I'll never know what that guy thought."

Laura smirked. "Fine, I got one too. I was in a mine up in northern BC. They hadn't started mining yet, but there were lots of drillers and miners and a couple geologists. We were all in the oversized dining tent getting our meals. I was one of the last to be served. I was walking over to a table and a mouse ran by. I screamed like a schoolgirl, dropped my tray and jumped up on top of a table. I then realized, as everyone silently stared at me, that I was a field geologist. How could I be afraid of a stupid little mouse? I explained that it was just a reaction, and of course they all laughed at me, as they should have. I got back down and cleaned up the floor."

My turn. I can't say I have a lot of embarrassing moments, but I won't relate the most embarrassing ones to them. "I was in a camp near Chapleau looking for shear zones in the Swayze belt. We actually had a cool little cabin on the shore of a small lake and a decent dock out front. We were taking the boat across the lake to do some mapping. It was late May. So everyone was in the boat waiting and I was the last one out to the dock. I tossed my pack in and then stepped out onto a middle seat. No one was holding the dock. The boat started to drift away and I was half in and half out. I had nowhere to go. I slowly did the splits and yelled some form of obscenity. Not only did my pants come undone at the seam, but I fell ass first into that freezing water. Thankfully it was only a couple feet deep and I scrambled out as fast as I could. Yeah, everyone in the boat was howling with laughter. There you go, I'm a klutz," I finished with a smirk.

Cassy was last to go. I'm sure everyone expected an anecdote in which her tits popped out at some awkward moment. That was the obvious scenario.

"Alright, this is embarrassing," she started. "I was in a camp near Red Lake. There were six of us, three girls and three boys. One night I was lying in bed and I ripped a huge fart. Not only loud, but toxic. I don't know what I ate but it obviously turned into some noxious gas. I couldn't control it. I farted again and again. The other two girls couldn't stand the smell and left to sleep in the kitchen. I don't blame them. I was dying of the smell too. I kept farting for about an hour. Every time I did, the boys would yell out a score; '7, come one, you can do better' or 'that was a 9' and 'I think they heard that one in Pickle Lake,' and so on. They nick named me 'Gassy', which stuck for the rest of the project."

There was great laughter at this one. David looked over to Laura and said, "Better get an alternate bed set up in the kitchen, just in case."

I added, "Better not have any open fires in camp, for safety sakes." I gave a grin to Cassy, who grinned back.

"And let's make sure Titus has an inflatable duck around him whenever he gets into a boat," Cassy shot back. I laughed.

The plates all came. No shortage of food on them. My fish and chips looked like every diner's fish and chips. It came with a dish of sauce and a spoonful of coleslaw. Cassy's came with her perogies, a good helping of corn, a small salad and a wee dish of sour cream. "Here," I said to Cassy, "stab one of these fish." She did, and plopped it on top of some perogies. Then she lifted her plate and pushed half the perogies onto my plate.

"Take some sour cream. Makes the perogies taste better," she said and scooped out a dollop which dropped on my plate. I just happened to notice that no one else was sharing food. It was in fact uncharacteristic of me to share food, especially with someone I just met. For some reason it just felt OK with Cassy.

"What's in them?" I asked.

"Usually potato and cheese, but sometimes bacon, ham, chives, or other things. I've even seen dessert perogies filled with cherries," she answered.

I tasted one. "Wow, this is good!" I exclaimed. "I've had Chinese dumplings before. They're a bit like this, but not as heavy. These will really fill you up."

There was idle chit chat around the table as people got to know each other. The diner was filling up and there was a hum of chatter in the air. I learned that Kyle was actually the son of an executive at CP Rail, David had a Master's degree, Laura grew up in Winnipeg, Barry was divorced and Cassy played competitive soccer as a child. Me, I told them I played the guitar, or used to. I was in a band in high school. We thought we were pretty good. I started with the electric guitar but later took up the acoustic so I could just strum and sing along. I wasn't a big fan of country music, though if I could change a country song to a folk song, I'd play it.

We wrapped up dinner fairly quickly and piled into the truck. Barry took us to a bar not far away from the office and told us we could walk back whenever we wanted. It was pretty much like the diner, but with plain tables and chairs and a dance floor. I don't like bars. Music is always too loud, beer too expensive, and there's nothing to do.

We sat there for about twenty minutes, yelling to each other over the noise. A nice looking girl with short hair came over and asked me to dance. I nodded yes, but didn't want to. I hate dancing. I feel foolish swinging and swaying with my arms flailing about. I'm sure I looked completely unnatural. We danced for one song and then I stood and chatted with her for a moment. Her name was Lola, or so she said. I imagine there's not much for a mid-twenties girl to do in a mining town. I reached out and touched a ring on her finger, then held it up to look at it.

"What's this for?" I asked her.

"This is my birth stone, garnet," she answered.

"That's a nice ring." I fumbled with her fingers as I inspected it. She started this, asking me to dance. I was just enjoying a private, somewhat intimate moment with her. But this wasn't going anywhere. I had to go back to the office and bug out to the camp tomorrow, so no point in pursuing her. I told her I had to get back to my friends, but hoped to see her again. I don't know if she believed that or if she just knew this was the end.

I went back to my table. David grinned at me. Laura leaned over and called me a man-whore. Kyle was out trolling around, asking girls to dance, it would seem. I sat there watching him get shot down over and over. He even asked girls who were clearly there with a boyfriend. I was sure he was going to get the shit kicked out of him. He was relentless. I did not want to get into a fight defending some blockhead who was annoying women in a bar. Eventually he came back and sat down with us. I leaned over to Cassy and said, "How long are we gonna stay here?"

"I'm ready to go," she answered.

I asked the others what they wanted to do and they all wanted to stay longer. Laura knew the way back to the office, so Cassy and I decided to leave. It was near dark as we walked down the street toward the office.

Chapter 5. The Shortcut

"Want to take a shortcut?" Cassy asked.

"Alright. You're not going to get me lost, are you? That may become my most embarrassing moment, stumbling through town, asking strangers where I live." I laughed.

"Follow me, and don't stray or you'll be bunking with the alley cats tonight," she said.

We climbed a rounded outcrop at the side of the road, and then another, heading up a dark hill. We climbed all the way to the top where we finally reached a water tower. I turned and looked out over the town. I'm sure if this was a city it would be a beautiful site. But this small town encircled by mines was... uninspiring. Still, I appreciated the vast view of lights. Cassy turned and came back to where I was standing. "Not a bad view," I said, "though not a lot to see." We sat down for a moment, picking up pebbles and tossing them down the hill. "You like Flin Flon?"

"Not especially, but it's not bad. Better than a lot of other towns."

"Yeah, some towns are just shit," I said. "What do you think of Cliff Mines? Doesn't matter what you say, I'm only here for a few weeks." I wanted her real thoughts.

"It's OK. Barry likes my opinions. He brings me out of the bush and to the office often enough. Barry's been in and out of town a lot. He's in the process of moving here from Kirkland Lake. He's getting divorced, so settling that."

"Oh, I thought he was already divorced. That's what Barry said." I looked puzzled, but frankly didn't care.

"I don't know," Cassy said. "He tells me a lot, but I try not to get involved. What about you? Seems the ladies like you. No wife or girlfriend?"

I grinned. "No time for that. I'm never in one place long enough. You looking forward to this project?"

"Yeah. It's a pretty simple one. Three weeks of mapping and then a few days in town cleaning up the maps and writing a report," she replied. "What do you have planned after this?"

"I haven't had a break in months. I'd like to get a dose of civilization. I think I'll visit my parents in Kitchener and then hang out in Toronto for a while. I have to go there to look for another job anyway, cruising King Street and banging on doors. I don't know what I have planned, actually. You know, there's a bar on Queen Street West where bands play. I love that place. And there's a cafe on Gerard where they serve the best banana splits," I told her.

"Sounds nice. I've never been to Toronto, or Montreal. Actually I've never been east of North Bay or west of Calgary. All my work has been in Saskatchewan, Manitoba and Northern Ontario. I've visited Calgary though, and of course I know Winnipeg well," Cassy said.

"You ever left the country?" I asked.

"Oh yeah," Cassy replied. "When I was a kid we used to go down into the States to shop now and then, but just North Dakota."

"I went to Mexico two years ago, between jobs," I said. "I just spent a week, but it was incredible. You can't even imagine the colour of the ocean. I spent half my day either lying under a coconut tree on the white sand beach or snorkeling. I did some sightseeing too. I went to town and saw some Mayan ruins. But mostly I just relaxed and soaked in the beauty and warmth. I really want to see Europe one day."

We talked and tossed stones for a while longer before resuming our brief trek over the basaltic hill that led to Drury Street and the office. I took a long shower when we got back, enjoying the hot water and clean smell of soap. In the mirror I saw a lonely man with disheveled hair and unhappiness in his eyes. Seeing myself age over these past few years was like watching a plant grow. You never see the changing, just the change.

I got dressed and left the washroom. In the living room, Cassy sat against a couch pillow on the floor, reading a book. "All done?" she asked.

"Yup, it's all yours," I replied.

Cassy got up and took a small bundle with her to the bathroom. I had no pillow to fluff, just my dirty old sleeping bag. I opened it up, undressed again and crawled in. A minute later I was fast asleep.

DAY TWO - Camp

Chapter 6. A Good Breakfast

I had a restless night. Maybe those perogies were a bit too heavy or the fish a bit too deep fried. Oh, and then there were all those fries; why did I eat all those fries? I don't usually sleep well the first night in a new place anyhow, and being enclosed in a silent room after months of sleeping with night air, distant frogs croaking, rustling animals, raindrops and wind, it was eerie.

So I tossed and turned; my thoughts constantly turned on. I slept on and off. I have no idea when the others got home, they were just there in the morning. I felt tired but awake when the room began to illuminate. It must have been quite early. I heard Cassy rustle and I looked up to see her walking into the kitchen. A few minutes later I arose, dressed and went to see what she was up to. The stove was littered with pans, greased and warming.

"You making breakfast?" I asked.

"Yes. We don't have time to go out," she answered.

"Awesome. I'll have two eggs, over easy, soft but not runny, sausage, hash-browns and black coffee; strong." I spoke slowly and deliberately without any sense of humour. Cassy looked at me like I was a jerk. Then I smiled and nudged her.

"That all sounds good. You're in charge of the sausages and coffee. I like my coffee with milk and don't scorch my sausages!" she barked.

"Alright, Cassy with a 'Y'. Which is my pan?" I asked.

"Take the back one there," she said, pointing to a pan on the back right burner.

I tossed a glass of water in the oiled pan and then dumped in two packs of sausages. I rummaged through the shelves looking for coffee only to find it was right there on the counter beside the coffee maker. "Did you sleep well?" I asked.

"Yeah, you?"

"Not really. Too quiet. I needed some background noise. Not really looking forward to setting up camp today. Such a shitty part of the job."

"Yeah, I know, eh? Especially for just a few weeks. If we can get it done quickly, then we can relax this afternoon and maybe do a bit of fishing," she said. "You like fishing?"

"Yeah. Maybe sometime we can take the boat out and troll around. A lake that big will have hot spots, and they might be hard to find," I said. The sausages were turning white in the shallow bed of boiling water. I rolled them around to cook the other side. The coffee was dripping in the glass flask. "Oh, shit, I forgot the toast." I grabbed the bag of bread and snatched a handful of slices. Cassy grabbed a bunch more and we both lightly buttered them and then put them in the oven. "Twelve slices ought to cover us," I said.

Cassy was a chipper person. A lot of people are not so cheerful in the morning. She bounced around in the kitchen and joked with me as we cooked. I heard a noise in the other room and looked to see Laura up and dressed. "Hey," I said to her, in a pleasant tone.

She "hey'd" me back with a mumble. When she came into the kitchen, she remarked on the smell of sausages and eggs.

"Can you set the table?" I asked her and she responded with an affirmative uh-huh. Laura was definitely not a morning person. There was no effervescence in her attitude nor bound in her step. The dishes clinked and rattled as she firmly spread them out on the table.

Lastly, we doled out all the food; two eggs, two toast, two sausages, and coffee to each. That was a small breakfast for a big work day, but there were bananas, oranges, and more bread for toast if anyone wanted it.

Cassy poked her head in the living room and shouted, "Breakfast is ready," hoping the others would heed the call. Personally, I didn't care if they got up or not. Then again I wasn't in charge of the project. My job was to take orders like a good soldier. I grabbed a seat and started eating, as did Cassy and Laura. A few minutes later, a very tired and perhaps hungover Kyle made it into the kitchen followed by a smiling David, and lastly our fearless slob, Barry.

"Nice breakfast, guys!" David exclaimed with enthusiasm. Good God, another cheery morning person. That's OK, better than a grump, though normally you can just avoid grumps. The cheery ones are too talkative. You really just want to veg out in the morning and not interact so much. But this is our first morning together, so I will be cheery.

"David, how are ya today?"

"I'm absolutely fantastic, Titus. How was that foamy I gave you last night?" He said with a wide grin.

"David, you give the best foamies!" I answered and David laughed.

"Kyle, you feeling OK today?" I asked. He wasn't eating much. He just looked dazed and distant.

"Yeah, I'm fine," he answered without looking up. I decided to just move on.

"Laura, dare I ask how you are?" I could tell she was in no mood to play, but I wanted to have a bit of fun with her.

"Are you gonna be like this every fucking morning?" she asked, bluntly.

"No, I promise. Just this morning," I shot back with a smile.

I didn't ask Barry. He hadn't said a word all morning. He just sat there picking at his food and sipping coffee. I wouldn't want to spend time with him in a camp. We finished up breakfast. I whispered to Cassy "Tell David he has to do the dishes."

Cassy looked uncomfortable delegating such a lowly task. She just frowned at me, jumped up and started clearing the dishes. I grabbed a wash cloth and said, "Hey David, would you mind drying for me?" He didn't answer, just grabbed a towel and stood there, waiting for dishes to come his way. Cassy nudged me. I looked at her and she said thanks.

I goofed around with David as we did the dishes. Barry asked the others to start loading gear into the truck. I assume Cassy went with them to direct the flow because I didn't see her around. That was fine with me. We really didn't need a bunch of people sitting at the table sipping coffee and watching us do the dishes.

Chapter 7. Off To Camp

When we were done, we went to the living room to gather our gear and take it out to the truck. Seemed everyone else had already packed up. Didn't take that long to fill the truck. It would be a tight ride down to the lake. Cassy drove with Laura and Kyle up front. David and I squeezed into the back seats of the king cab. It was a tight fit. Not a lot of leg room, and pretty uncomfortable flying down a bumpy, gravel road. I was happy to get back out.

The road terminated at a large dock. This was an old mine site, the headframe still standing. I wanted to go look in the tailings dump, but there was no time for that. I love finding chunks of massive sulphide. Any sulphide will do. David and Kyle tossed gear to others on the ground and then we packed what we could into the boats.

It would take a couple trips. Cassy stayed back with the truck and we drove the boats down the lake, about a twenty minute ride, to the last small bay where we dumped the gear at a small sandy beach. Kyle and Laura drove the boats back to the truck and David and I started cutting poles for the tents. They had to be good, solid poles about fifteen feet long.

We looked for spruce and balsam. These are good to use, though the sap is ultra-sticky, especially from balsam. We had three tents, so we needed to cut eight logs per tent. We just had axes, so it was a slow process, not that the trees were big, but all the limbs had to be pruned. By the time the others returned, we had all the poles cut. With the gear all laid out, we started stretching the prospector tents out wide. Then we put the poles in their respective places; two at the front, two at the back, one ridge pole along the top, one along each side and a final pole at the back to act as a tripod. Sometimes it's good to use a tree already standing so you don't need that final pole at the back.

David and I worked on a tent together. We laid the back poles out, the logs overlapping at the end of the tent. I wrapped twine around the poles, lashing them together, then did the same with the poles at the front. Next we laid the ridge pole on top of the tent and tied the top of the tent to it. Then came the hard work; lifting the back end up, a little at a time. We were lifting three poles and a heavy canvas tent. Thankfully it was not raining. That would have added a lot more weight.

We each had a pole and the back end slowly rose, occasionally stopping to get a grip and rest. At last, the tent back was three quarters up. David held it in place while I strapped the third pole on, then we hoisted it all the way up. We went around to the front and raised that end. Almost done. The side poles were strapped on which pulled the tent walls outward, giving lots of room inside.

These were big ten foot by twelve foot tents. We checked it out to make sure it was stable. It was a wee bit wobbly, so we tied a few ropes on and secured them to nearby trees. By this time, everyone was in camp. I saw the other people working on the other two tents. This is when a camp starts to look like a living community. I went back behind camp and started cutting more trees. I chopped seven more, trimmed the limbs and dragged the poles to the beach. I hopped into the boat and then with the butt end of the axe, I drove two small poles into the sand about a foot off shore. I then went another seven feet or so out and drove another two poles in.

Laura came down to the beach. "You want some help?" she offered.

"Sure, can you lash one of the small poles across those stakes?" I asked. She cut some twine and tied a cross pole in place. "Hey, can you toss me a small pole and the twine?"

First, she threw the roll of twine, and then slid the small log through the water to me. I thought that was pretty nice of her, so not to splash me. I lashed my crossbar in place. "OK, if you push a long pole out, we can lift it in place on the cross bars," I said to her. It went on and we tied it down. Then the next, and next, and next, and next. At last we had a crude dock where one boat could sit on one side and the other boat on the other side.

"Can you test it out? I don't have good luck with docks," I said, smirking.

Laura gingerly stepped up on it at her end and gave it a little kick, then walked slowly to the end and back, bouncing up and down. "So good, even you should be safe on this one," she joked with me.

I tied up the boat and carefully stepped onto the dock. Solid. "Not too fucking shabby," I said to Laura. "Maybe I should take up a career as a master dock maker. If I had a PhD, I could be called Doctor Dock. That's a good reason to get a Doctorate, right?"

"We could call you master something, and something comes to mind," she said.

"Very funny," I countered. We walked up the bank to the camp. The others had finished erecting the tents and setting up the kitchen. Kyle and David had carried the barbeque about fifty feet out behind the camp.

"OK," David said, "who wants what tent?"

The boys looked at the girls and the girls looked at the boys. "I don't care," said Laura.

"Alright, we'll take the far one and you can have the middle one," David continued. The tent closest to the beach would be the kitchen. They were all the same and all beside each other.

"I've cut enough poles for today. Anyone else want to do it for the beds?" I asked. Kyle agreed and disappeared. There was a pile of gear near shore, just up from the beach. It was all our personal stuff. We walked over to rummage through it. There, amongst the packs and sleeping bags and foamies was an old guitar. "Hey, whose is this?" I asked.

"That's an old guitar someone left behind with other gear, long before I got here. Barry said it was there for years in the storage room. It's a bit broken at the back, but I strummed it and I think it's OK. I thought you might like it here in camp," Cassy said.

Geez, that was nice. What a thoughtful thing to do, and such a surprise. "Wow, thanks. I love it," I said, picking it up and testing the strings. "I'll see what I can do about that gash at the back." I brought it and my sleeping bag up to the tent, then retrieved my backpack and foamy. The plywood boards could wait until the poles were cut and the bed frames built.

It was nearing noon, so we unpacked most of the food and began making sandwiches. We made an extra one for Kyle who we could still hear chopping trees out back. Laura lit the camp stove and I got water to boil. I would have looked pretty foolish if I fell off the dock getting water, so I was especially careful. As I approached the tent, I called out to Kyle to come for lunch. Inside, we all sat on folding chairs and chatted.

When Kyle arrived, we ate. We ate well. Lots of hard work meant a good appetite. We must have sat in there and ate for an hour. Of course there was no lack of chit chat too. We discussed our favourite foods. Mine was spaghetti, with rose sauce and extra Gouda cheese on top. Laura liked a good old T-bone steak on the barbeque. Kyle agreed with that. David was all about the ribs. Cassy had to think for a minute and then went with roast turkey. Well there wasn't much controversy over this conversation. As such, we talked about holidays and meals. Cassy abruptly hopped up and said she had to go to the office but would be back with the crew tomorrow. She didn't have anything to take with her.

Chapter 8. Taxi Driver

"Can someone take me to the truck?" Cassy asked.

"Sure, I'll take you there," I said. That was better than hanging around camp and building beds. We walked down to the dock and got into the boat. I had to back it out slowly because there were some weeds in the water and it was pretty shallow for the prop. Once out a ways, I swiveled the boat around and opened up the throttle. We flew down the lake past rocky points, beaver lodges, loons and white pelicans. The big dock neared and I slipped the boat gently alongside. I got out and walked with her to the truck where we stood for a while.

"What do you have to do in town?" I asked.

"Barry told me to come back today, not sure why, but I think he wanted that last project wrapped up. I haven't finished the report for it yet." Cassy said. "Anything you need from town?"

"No, I'm OK. That guitar was very thoughtful; a nice treat. Thanks." I think Cassy blushed a little. She seemed lost for words. "Have a beer for me tonight, eh?"

"You got beer in camp," she said.

"Yeah, but not cold beer," I said.

"Well, dig a hole, put some ice in it and bury a few beer, ya big baby! I'm coming back to camp tomorrow. I'll bring some more ice and we can have a cold beer together, OK?" Cassy needled me. I just smiled at her. "Can you come pick me up tomorrow at four?" Cassy asked.

"Sure, I'll be here. But if you forget the ice, you're swimming back to camp," I teased her.

"Deal. Have fun tonight with the mosquitoes. Keep an eye on the camp, eh?" she said.

I nodded. Cassy climbed into the truck and started the engine. I stepped away and let her back up. She stuck her head out, looked back at me and gave a wave. I waved to her and watched as the truck sped off down that dusty gravel road. I stayed and watched until the truck was gone. I was sure I was going to miss her, even for a day. She was the only one I had made a connection with. Actually, on most jobs, I either never make a real connection with someone or it takes weeks. I suppose I might still gel with David or Laura. It was highly unlikely I would connect with Kyle.

There was something about Cassy that made me comfortable. There was an ease of being around her. We often looked at each other to share an unspoken moment, like we had the same thought at the same time. Cassy had a bubbly character with a gentle temperament and a sweet, considerate nature. I still don't know how she became a project manager. She doesn't have the strong personality needed to lead a group of misfit geologists. But I liked her. I'll watch out for her and help whenever I can. Three weeks will fly by.

I sat on the roadside dock, not quite ready to leave, and watched the dragonflies whiz around over the water, hunting for bugs. Sure would be cool to fly like that. Wonder what their society is like, if they like, love and live together the way we do. Maybe they choose their friends and mates, or maybe they just hook-up as they go. Whatever they do, it seems to work pretty well for them.

A few lily pads rested on the surface of the water, their white flowers open to catch what was left of the late afternoon sunshine. I watched as small fish meandered by, weaving in and out of the pike weeds near the sandy bottom. Eventually I decided to ride the boat back to camp and be social.

Chapter 9. Unpacking My Gear

I coasted up to our small, hand fashioned log dock and tied up the boat. Kyle was sitting outside his tent with his banjo, picking at the strings and composing a rambling melody. Laura sat on the ground nearby, her back against a tree watching me come ashore.

"Hey, did you miss me?" I yelled.

"Who the fuck are you, again?" Laura joked.

"That sounds good, Kyle," I said, standing for a minute to listen.

"Thanks," he replied. "Gotta get your guitar tuned up so we can play together."

"Yeah, I'd like that. Where's David?" I asked.

"In there," Laura nodded to the tent.

"I'm in here, trying out the bed," David yelled from within the tent.

I poked my head in to see the beds. They made mine for me too, and laid out my sleeping bag. Dammit, I should have asked Cassy to get me a pillow. "These look good." I said, placing my hands on it and shaking a bit to see how stable it was. The beds were only two feet off the ground, but that was fine. Any distance off the ground is still off the ground. I sat on the edge reconciling the fact that I would only be in this place for three weeks. Who knows where after that? This was a nice camp. I wish they could all be this good.

I grabbed my pack and began removing much of the stuff inside: clothes, telescopic fishing rod and small tackle box, my toiletries, a little camera, sandals for around camp and a rain coat. That's it; not a lot of earthly possessions. I wonder what most twenty-nine year old professionals have; a house, a car, a wife? I find myself thinking of these things more and more lately. It didn't used to bother me that I had nothing because I was in a big adventure, building my experience and tracking to a great career. I guess the world changes as we age.

"What do you like to do when you're back home, David?" I asked.

"Well, I haven't been home in two years. But if you mean when I'm in civilization, I like going out, you know, to pubs, parties, golf, sailing," he said.

"You know, I definitely could see you sailing and playing golf. What got you into this wild world?" I asked.

"I don't know. Geology just sounded interesting I guess. Didn't bargain for the bush life though. Now I'm kinda stuck in it. I grew up in Vancouver, so I saw myself as some junior mining company exec wheeling and dealing. I might try an MBA sometime, see what that does for me," David said, definitely sounding far more sober than I had ever heard him sound before. I suspect he thinks about his career choice just as much as I do.

"How old are you?" I asked.

"Thirty-three, going on fifty."

"Ha ha ha. Trust me, you do not have the character of a fifty year old. Maybe you should try sales or marketing?" I told him.

"I don't even know how to apply for something like that. How does a guy with a science degree and loads of bush experience walk into a company as a salesman?"

"David, if anyone can do it, you can. You have a gift with people, especially strangers, just chatting away with them. I think you could sell yourself," I suggested. I saw him thinking about that, but clearly he was, as many of us are, rather frustrated and depressed about our chosen careers. It's very hard to dig yourself out of a deep hole. Speaking of that, "Hey, did anyone dig a shitter?" I asked him.

Chapter 10. The Outhouse

"Oh shit, that's right, we gotta dig one and shelter it for the ladies. That sounds like a good job for Laura and Kyle," David said, loudly.

"I heard that!" Laura yelled back, and we both laughed. I didn't want to sit around so I got up and went looking for the shovel. It was leaning up by the kitchen tent. I grabbed it and wandered off behind camp about fifty feet, though not near the barbeque, and started digging a hole in the soft peat moss. Once you hit the tree roots you really slow down, and then hope you don't hit rocks.

I had a good enough hole dug. David came out to help. I asked him to get me a piece of fluorescent trail tape. When he returned, I tied it to a stick and then lashed the stick to a tree beside the hole. We gathered up a few leftover logs from the cut trees and made a makeshift seat. There, it looked complete.

"Hey Laura, the shitter's done." She and Kyle came to see it. A new shitter always needs an inspection, and often a ceremonial dump.

Laura looked at it, smiled and said, "What the fuck is this?"

"It's the perfect shitter. Look, you sit down, raise the red flag to signal that it's occupied and then relax till it all comes out," I said, straight faced.

"Ummm, what do you need the flag for if everyone can see you sitting on the shitter?" she said, nearly laughing. She knew it was a joke.

"Alright, can you bring us a small tarp?" I sighed. I went down to the kitchen and grabbed an old water bottle. I filled it up at the shore. I also grabbed a bar of soap and brought it back up to the outhouse. It's always nice to have water on hand to clean up.

Laura came back with an army green tarp and we draped it around the nearby trees to make a cover. "Swanky, eh? Now you and Cassy can pee in privacy." Guys just look for a tree or bush or anything to point at and go. Truth is, after being in a camp for a while, the ladies often don't care and will just pee in plain sight. This is always the case above the treeline.

"OK, get the fuck outta here, I gotta take a shit. First come first served." I said. I'd been holding those perogies way too long. The mosquitoes were motivation enough to move it along quickly. No splash in this toilet, not even a thud with that soft peat moss in the bottom. I reached for the… dammit! I forgot about the toilet paper.

"FUUUUCK!" I yelled. "Can someone bring me some toilet paper?"

I heard roaring laughter down at the tents. A minute later a roll of toilet paper came flying up past the shitter and I had to wobble my way over to pick it up. "Thank you!" I yelled to whoever tossed it. Another job accomplished. I went to the kitchen where we kept a bowl of water and soap and cleaned my hands. Give it another couple weeks and this kind of hygiene will disappear. Ain't no cleanliness nor godliness in a bush camp.

"Have a good laugh?" I asked, back at the tents.

Laura said, "Have a good shit?"

It was all healthy fun.

"What do you think Cassy's doing back in town right now?" I asked.

"Oh she's probably in the office right now, looking at maps. She seems studious. But, in about an hour from now she'll be at a diner with Barry, enjoying a good meal. Then she'll be out at a bar, probably with Barry. Anyone see a pattern here?" Laura said.

"You think they're fucking?" David asked.

I really wanted to stay out of it. The thought of Cassy with that slimy Barry kind of upset me. I don't know if it was because it showed what a creep Barry was or because it bothered me that Cassy would be with him. No one answered, but there was definitely a feeling they were screwing.

Chapter 11. Planning the Day

"What are we having for dinner?" I changed the subject.

"We should use up the chicken first. It won't last long. I can get the barbeque started," Kyle said, and disappeared to get the charcoal. The rest of us stayed on the ground in front of the tent. I remembered the guitar and went into the tent to look at it. I came back out and inspected the back. The gash wasn't that bad, maybe two inches long and quite narrow. I put it down by a tree and then walked around the tent to examine the balsam poles.

There were sap leaks where the trees were cut. I checked around for a birch tree and pulled a small sheet of bark off. Birch bark is composed of many layers. You can peel the layers apart making several thinner sheets. I peeled it down until it was just a couple layers thick and I trimmed the size to match the gash. Next I used the knife to scoop some sap off the logs and wipe it on the bark. Once it was covered enough I pressed it against the back of the guitar. Not sure how long it would take to dry; a day, a month, a thousand years. As long as it stuck, all was OK.

I sat back down on the ground with Laura and David. I could smell the thick aroma of burning charcoal wafting through the trees. I checked the strings. They weren't in the best shape.

I slowly began twisting pegs to tighten the strings and listen for the tones. One by one they gradually hit their proper notes and a simple strum revealed a pleasant sound. I formed cords with my left hand while picking and strumming with my right hand, trying to remember basic melodies. I'm sure it sounded rough as I fumbled through it, then found my groove with 'Carefree Highway'.

The day had been long and was drawing to an end. I stopped, laid my head back against the tree and closed my eyes. I think Laura went to the kitchen and took the chicken up to the barbeque, then made a salad. I can't say for sure it was her, but a short while later I opened my eyes and she was gone, but David was still there, reading a book. I heard the clanking of a spoon against a metal pail and Laura calling for dinner. It was all I could do to pick myself up and drag my weary feet to the kitchen. The makeshift table was set with plates, each with a hunk of chicken and a big salad. I grabbed a pop water from a box on the ground and opened it.

"This looks great. Did you make the salad, Laura?" I asked.

"Yes. Kyle did the barbeque." Nice of her to give him credit.

"I know. Smells fantastic, Kyle," I said.

"Thanks," Kyle replied.

The chicken was drenched in barbeque sauce and sprinkled with salt and pepper. The salad was a mix of lettuce and tomatoes topped with a white dressing. Standard fare; nothing fancy. This was a typical bush meal. Conversation always involved the one thing we do most and the one thing we do least, shit and sex. None of us are well versed in current events.

"Is there anything else we need to do?" David asked.

"I don't think so," I replied, looking around at the others for input. No one spoke up. "I guess we better pull the map out tonight and decide what we're doing tomorrow."

I found the claims map with lines drawn on it. These are lines that were cut through the bush in a grid pattern one hundred feet apart and picketed with a location all the way along. At any place on this grid out in the bush you know exactly where you are and can use that as a guide for mapping and sampling. Line cutters often do this work in the spring before the leaves are out. Sometimes they'll even cut down big healthy trees, unfortunately.

We rolled the map out on the table and looked it over. The grid ran right behind camp, stretching west for a few kilometres and east for several kilometres, all the way to the rail line. There were a few isolated grids as well.

"Since it's our first day, how 'bout we pair up and take a few lines each. I'll go to the far south east grid. You want to come with me, Laura?" Laura nodded. "We can take the boat down this river and walk the rest of the way from here." I pointed to a place on the map. What do you guys want to do?" I looked up at David and Kyle."

"Maybe we should go to the far south west and start from there. We can walk from camp. That OK, Kyle?" David asked. Kyle nodded in agreement. I don't think he cared where he went. He didn't strike me as a leader, just a follower.

I pulled out a stack of clear sample bags and plunked them on the table. I snatched up about ten bags. When everyone else had finished taking some, I put the rest back in a box. We each grabbed a small book and pencil and some sheets of paper for our clipboards. There wasn't much else we needed for mapping. Everyone knew the drill. We had all mapped a thousand outcrops in the bush before.

Chapter 12. Strumming a Tune

"I'm bushed. I'm gonna go read for a while and then hit the sack. I'll see you in the morning." I said.

Despite being nine o'clock at night, it was still light. The days are long this time of year. In early July, there is still a slice of light on the horizon at eleven o'clock. Regardless, you have to get a good night's sleep. Seven o'clock in the morning comes all too fast. I took the supplies to my tent, made sure I had my hammer and compass ready and filled my pack for the morning. I stretched out on my bed with a novel in hand. Surprisingly David and Kyle came to the tent as well. I suppose we were all tired from the day's work. I felt bad for Laura, alone in her tent.

"Hey Laura," I called out.

"Yeah?" She replied

"We're not sleeping yet. Wanna come over here for a while?" Without answering, she popped her head in the tent and looked around.

"OK. I'll get a chair." She left and came back within a few seconds with a folding chair. "What are you reading?" she asked.

"Havana Storm, by Clive Cussler. You want one? I brought a few with me." I sat up and swivelled around to pick up a sample bag I used to hold personal things. "I've got, The Hammer of Eden by Ken Follett, Command Authority by Tom Clancy, and Jurassic Park by Michael Crichton. Any of those sound interesting?"

"Sure, I'll take Hammer of Eden," she said.

I tossed her the book. "How 'bout you guys?" I asked. They both declined, as they already had books in hand. This was a lively night; all four of us in the tent, reading. The front side of the tent, a white canvas, was taking on a rich pinkish colour. I stood up and opened the flap to have a look. The sky was streaked with lines of orangey pink clouds much like the pattern of bear scrapes on a tree. The lake was calm and a few birds still called to each other.

It was a peaceful, quiet night on Schist Lake. In one day, we had transformed this tiny wild bay into a small community. Civilization springs up where we make it. Wild is only a relative term. I stepped back inside and lay down on my bed. This time I picked up the guitar and very quietly picked the strings. I wasn't playing any particular song, just making a tune.

"How long have you been playing guitar?" Laura asked.

"I started when I was fourteen. I saw another guy at school play. He was really good. So I begged my parents for one and then learned a few cords from a library book. The rest I learned just from listening. I can hear a song now and figure it out on the guitar within minutes." I picked a few notes as I talked. "Do you play?"

"No. My mother made me take piano lessons when I was eight, nine, or ten. I never was any good, and I didn't want to play. I kinda feel bad about it. I complained a lot. She was musical. I guess she just wanted something for us to enjoy together."

"Never too late to start up again. You could surprise her." I said.

"She died when I was sixteen," Laura said.

"Oh, sorry. I didn't know." I stopped picking. I'm never comfortable with these situations. I tend to change the conversation quickly.

"It's OK. That was a long time ago. I was pretty rebellious. I guess I still am. I doubt she would have liked that I became a geologist. My dad's OK with it, though I'm sure he wishes I was in a more stable job, and closer to home."

"Where's your dad?" David asked. He had been quietly listening.

"He's in Winnipeg. He was a sales rep for a seed company. He would drive all over the prairies in the summer. I didn't like that. I dreaded spring because I knew he'd be on the road soon and I'd only see him on weekends until fall. Now look at me, travelling just like him; even worse, all year. I guess it's good I don't have kids." Laura snickered.

We sat there quietly for a bit while I gently strummed the guitar. A few minutes later, Kyle was snoring.

DAY THREE - Evening Songs

Chapter 13. Early Birds

I had awoken very early. Dawn comes at four o'clock and the birds just assume the entire forest is ready to rise. I was not. I looked at my watch and turned over to sleep some more. At seven, David's little alarm clock tinkled and I rubbed my eyes. I did sleep last night, but I had rich, imaginative, if not weird dreams. I seem to recall a huge, derelict house and inside were many rooms. I lived there and could not get out. It was shaky and I worried it would fall over, I was not alone, but don't recall who was there with me. It was a lonely feeling. Outside was a desolate landscape of dead grass, rocks and leafless trees. There must be meaning in this, but damned if I could figure out what. That was only one of many vivid dreams. I wish my dreams could be more hopeful and optimistic, but they never are these days.

I slipped out of my sleeping bag and pulled my ragged work pants on, then my shirt and smelly socks. To finish my ensemble, I slid my feet into old boots, tied them up, capped my head and went to the kitchen. I wasn't that hungry. I seldom eat much first thing in the morning. I do like coffee though. Maybe I like the smell more than I like the taste, but that duo of senses is a powerful mix in the morning. I started the stove up and put the full percolator on the heat, then added the grounds to the top basket. Everybody loves the convenience of a drip coffee maker, but you can't beat the aroma of percolating coffee. I like a rich blend for strong coffee, but I do not like French roast. For some reason it bothers my digestion. I started making my lunch, a banana sandwich, when David arrived. I looked over at him and said, "Hey." That's all I could muster this morning. Not a happy, good morning guy am I.

"Yo! How'd you sleep last night," he said, in a perky tone. A damned annoying perky tone.

"Alright. Stupid birds woke me up this morning," I replied.

"I slept right through till the alarm," he said.

Laura was next in. She never said a word. She looked grumpy. She was grabbing at lunch stuff, tossing things around, seemingly quite unhappy. I'll assume she is not a morning person. I just went about my business. I finished making lunch, threw the sandwich, an apple, pudding cup, spoon, and chocolate bar into a sample bag, then filled a small thermos with apple juice.

The coffee had perked long enough. I turned the stove off and filled a tin cup with the lovely dark brew. I took it black. That's how I learned to drink it at a drill camp one winter. I sat back in a chair and held the coffee, blowing steam off the surface. It was entertaining to watch how the others coped with morning. David was quite cheery. He was a good sleeper. Laura was clearly a moody person, grumpy in the morning. Kyle, who had stumbled in later than anyone else was clearly half asleep. I could imagine him like this anywhere. I made a mental note to avoid talking to Laura in the morning, so I wouldn't piss her off. Kyle, I would be careful with at any time. David, I had no fear of.

"Have some coffee, Laura. Whenever you want to go, let me know," I told her. She did not reply. I found that somewhat amusing, like when a five year old gives you the silent treatment.

"Hey," David said, "what did you make for lunch?"

"Banana sandwich." I answered.

"Really? That's it? We got lots of cold cuts."

I looked down at the pile of cold cuts. It did look tempting. I know I'll be hungry at ten and then again at noon. "hmm, maybe I should make a brunch sandwich," I said.

"Now you're talking," David said.

So I did make a good, hearty sandwich with pastrami, tomato, mustard and mayonnaise. Why the fuck not, eh? Banana sandwich can be my quasi breakfast. I stuffed the second sandwich in my sample bag. Now I could just sit and enjoy my coffee along with the others. I was tempted to close my eyes and nap a while, but that would only make me sleepier. I had to stay awake. Cassy's probably in a hot shower right now or sitting in the kitchen with a plate of bacon and eggs. Some people have all the luck.

I was about halfway through my coffee when Laura said "I'm ready." I guzzled the rest of my coffee, washed the cup in a pail of water and put it away. I just needed to put my lunch in my backpack and I was ready. I came out of my tent, my pack on my back, my hammer in my hand and a smile on my face.

"Let's go," I summoned Laura. We trudged down the small bank to the boat, threw our stuff in and pushed off from the dock. I backed us out, turned and we ploughed off through the water to the east. I gave the boys a wave. We didn't have that far to go, just around the corner and down a small river that would eventually connect to another big lake. I maneuvered us careful through this small inlet until we found our start. Laura jumped out and tied off the boat. From there we needed to walk about one kilometre to the next grid.

Chapter 14. Report Writing

Every morning in town is the same routine for Cassy; a hardboiled egg, one slice of dark toast, coffee, and a banana. Cassy is a creature of habit. Change does not come easily. As such, Cassy was sitting at the table in the office kitchen watching steam roll up from the pot on the stove while the aromas of burnt toast and coffee filled the air. She looked particularly tired this morning; not typical for her. She seemed deep in thought, but truthfully her mind was elsewhere, it was in the camp, flitting between simple thoughts and mindlessness. She saw everyone chatting, laughing, and having fun together while she sat quietly, alone in town.

She was also picturing Titus with his mild manner and gentle voice. She recalled the moment they said goodbye at the dock. He was genuinely thankful for the guitar. It made her feel good that he appreciated what she had done. She thought he was a really nice guy. He was certainly handsome. A small smile came across her face as she thought of him and his sense of humour. She wondered if he was thinking of her at this very moment. Then she shook that thought off. Of course not. What a ridiculous thought. Well, in any case, she'd be back out at the dock at four and would see him, and soon after all the others in camp. That was something to look forward to. Cassy was happy to give up these creature comforts for the social life in the camp. And she had to face the fact that she did like being around Titus. He was fun.

Barry emerged from the bathroom with a towel around his waist. "Morning," he almost grunted as he walked past her, poured himself a cup of coffee and continued to his room.

There were certainly times when Cassy felt a little uncomfortable around Barry. He talked about his divorce too often, and then there were these somewhat suggestive moments. He had never come right out and asked for anything, but his availability was clearly communicated. You could potentially draw a conclusion that employing Cassy as a project lead and his divorce may be an invitation to a relationship. Cassy may have been naive, but she was not devoid of morals. Cassy had no personal feelings for Barry. From the other room, Barry called out, "I'll be there in a minute."

"OK," Cassy called back. She jumped up and got plates, a mug for herself and cutlery. She had made extra eggs and toast. The food was assembled on plates and her coffee poured before Barry entered the kitchen again, this time dressed.

Barry sat in his chair and stretched with a loud "Ahhhhhhh". He then dug into his breakfast. With mouth full, he said, "Can you finish that report today? I want you to get that and the map filed with the ministry."

"Yup," Cassy answered.

"And I have another job for you. I want to to stop by the assay office and take a load of samples in. They should have results from that last batch. If so, pick that up and we can look them over. I want to start thinking about where we can drill this winter."

"OK, no problem," Cassy said. "Any word from the head office about making me a permanent employee?"

"No. Not sure what they have in mind. I put in a good word for you," Barry replied.

"Just wondering if I should look for an apartment," she said.

"You don't need to," said Barry. "I'll put another bed in the bedroom and you can stay there. It'll save you money."

"Thanks, but I'm fine on the chesterfield for now." It sounded like one more step to a soiree with Barry. "You have any more trips coming up?"

"Yeah. I'll go to Vancouver on the thirteenth for a few days, then I'm going back to Kirkland Lake a week after I get back. So you'll have to run everything while I'm gone. I also have to take a trip up to Lynn Lake soon for a couple days to see a property. You should come too. Might be good for you."

Cassy didn't answer, she just looked pensive and changed the subject. "We're picking up a lot of properties, eh? Seems like the company is doing well."

"Guess so. I heard we had a shit load of financing this year from a private equity firm. I don't know details though."

Cassy began clearing dishes off the table and washing them. Barry left the room with his coffee.

Chapter 15. Lunch with Laura

Laura and I were deep into the woods at the grid we selected to map. We chose to follow two lines and meet up at the end at noon. It wasn't a particularly long segment to map, but there were plenty of outcrops and good potential for old mineralized zones. It was great bush. For the most part it was a mix of mature poplar, birch and jackpine with an understory of tall, deep green ferns. The smell was rich with chlorophyll. Mature forests are usually the best place to work, the only exception is when it gets too mature and there are blowdowns. Then you're constantly trekking over a twisted mass of big trees on the ground, like the setup for the game pickup sticks. Another problem with blowdowns and thick young growth is visibility. You don't see bears and they may not see you. No one wants to unexpectedly meet a bear and not be able to escape.

I could hear Laura's hammer now and then off in the bush somewhere. She could potentially be very close to me if she just happened to wander toward my side of her line investigating some outcrops, or I wander toward her. I had seen lots of interesting stuff, tore strips of moss and dirt away from many outcrops looking for hidden treasure, and bagged my share of samples.

Around ten in the morning I sat down in a peaceful spot under a big poplar tree and unwrapped my banana sandwich. It was quite warm and the air was still. I savoured the taste, washed down with some juice. It was tempting to eat the chocolate bar or pudding, but then would be disappointed later in the day. I didn't waste much time there. I continued wandering the bush, making notes and mapping until I reached the end of the line. I wandered north along the baseline until I reached Laura's line and sat down, waiting for her. She arrived about fifteen minutes later looking hot and tired.

"Don't tell me you're worn out already?" I asked.

Laura smiled, "It's frickin hot, man!"

"I heard you wailing away on some outcrops," I said. "I thought for a while Thor was out here with me." I laughed. "See anything juicy?"

"I don't know, maybe," Laura said, slyly.

"Intriguing. I'll show you mine if you show me yours?" I laughed.

"I don't want to see your rocks, buddy!" Laura retorted. I see the morning moodiness dissipates through the day with her. She was cheery enough now.

"Funny. Why don't you tell me about this mysterious, possible something you might have found?" I asked.

"Well, it's not a massive sulphide, but... it might be some specks of native copper in a gabbro dyke," Laura hinted. "I can't really tell, because it's so small, but has the right copper colour and sheen." She reached into a side pocket on her backpack and pulled out a small rock. I reached out and she dropped it into my hands. I used a magnifying glass and inspected the grains. To me they looked something like chalcopyrite, but weathered to a deeper colour.

"I don't know. I can't tell. I guess an assay will help." I told her.

"What did you see?" Laura asked.

"I saw some gabbro, some greenstone and a possible conglomerate. I found a little shearing and some pyrite in quartz veins. Nothing obvious. Great folding here though. I even saw some chevrons," I said. "Sit down and take a load off."

Laura pushed her pack against a tree and sat down, leaning back. Then realized it was lunch time and pulled her food out. This is actually the best time of the day. At breakfast you have to pack a lunch and then you have a full day of work ahead. At dinner you're pooped from all the walking, and you have to cook dinner. After dinner there's plotting and sample prep, and then bed. OK, bed ain't so bad, but lunch is best. You get to settle down and relax for a while. You get to eat without prep or cleanup. And it's warm, peaceful and comfortable. The worst days are those that are grey and drizzle just enough that you can't justify a rain day, but you know you're going to be wet. I hate being wet. This was a particularly good lunch. Not only was it warm and calm out, but I had company to eat with. Whether we talked or not, we were not alone.

"What did you bring?" I asked her.

"I don't know. I just grabbed some meat and made a sandwich. I think it's bologne. Doesn't matter. At seven in the morning I don't think straight. How about you, what do you have"?

"Pastrami. And I don't care either. Any cold cut will do. As long as I have lunch. I should have brought a pop. I'll be thirsty later today," I answered. "In camp last night, you told us about your dad being away. Why did choose the same thing? Seems like you didn't like it when you were a kid."

"Maybe he and I are roamers. I'm sure he could have found another job that kept him at home. Maybe he needed to move around. I kind of feel like that. I don't know if I'll change as I grow older. Maybe I'll want to settle down and stay home," she explained.

"You know, it's hard to find a girlfriend, or boyfriend in this job. You don't think about that?" I asked, leading this conversation into personal territory.

"I meet guys; lots more guys in geology than girls," she said.

"Yeah, but they're all transient, like you." I tried to understand, but maybe there was no good explanation. Maybe this was one of those mysteries that can't be explained, like women attracted to abusive men, or addicts that know it's destructive but keep using. It's a conundrum.

"Look at you? What's are you doing out here in the middle of the wilderness eating a pastrami sandwich and talking to me? You must have a story buried in you," Laura tried to dig into my life now.

"Maybe. I've never reflected on why I fell into this lifestyle, but could be there's something in the way I was brought up. I didn't get a lot of attention at home. I had whatever I needed, but was alone a lot. Maybe I subconsciously gravitated to field life because I was alone."

Laura was staring at me. Was she feeling pity or sympathy for me?

I continued, "But I'm not too happy now. So maybe it was all for nothing. Maybe I've completely misinterpreted myself. Actually, I really enjoyed the first five years out in the bush, but not the last three. I'm getting more disappointed with my life with every job I take."

"Not too happy here?" She asked.

"Well, I like this camp fine. I'm enjoying my lunch date with you. But frankly I'd like to sleep in my own bed at night. I want my weekends off, and I'd like to have lunch at a nice bistro in the city, or any nice town. Know what I mean?" I asked.

"Yeah, I do. I'll have that someday, I hope." Laura answered. "I still like to wander. I don't know what I'd do if I 'settled down'." She made quote symbols with her fingers. "I could try getting a government job in Ottawa, or Winnipeg, or in a town like Flin Flon. It's not so bad here. There are some nice areas with nice homes. Have you seen the ones up at the head of the lake? They're like little mansions, and right on the water."

"No, I haven't seen them. Maybe I should boat up and have a look, eh? They aren't near the dock, are they?" I asked.

"No, up the Northwest Arm. The water and trees are beautiful, too. The only bad thing is the train. It passes right by there. But I think it only goes twice a day and it moves slow, because it's just leaving the train yards in town," she explained.

"Sounds like it's worth a visit, then," I agreed. "I actually like trains. I don't mean model trains, but the real sounds and sights. Something romantic about rail, I suppose."

"Aha, so you're a romantic?" Laura asked, raising her eyebrows.

"I think anyone who enjoys being out in the bush is, at heart, a romantic. Aren't you?" I asked.

"I don't know. Maybe about some things. Not so sure about boys," she laughed.

"You never imagine some handsome man rescuing you?" I teased.

"Ah... no, not really," she replied.

I didn't know if I believed her. I thought all women fantasized about princes and candlelight dinners, and roses. Well, what the Hell do I know about women? I'm a man. I have occasionally guessed wrong and got burned by my intuition. So clearly not all women are the same. That's what makes all this relationship stuff so complicated. If we only knew what others really thought and wanted, we wouldn't get into so much trouble. I have had great luck in the past. I do have a pretty good ability to read women. Where I fail is when dating turns into love. Then my radar gets foggy and I mess up.

"You ever been in love?" I asked.

"Wow! You sure ask personal questions. I don't know if I was in love, but I had a boyfriend in University." She replied.

"How long did you go out?" I asked.

"One year. Is that long?" Laura said.

"Yeah, I think so. I never dated anyone that long. I think the longest I stayed with someone was four months. I didn't really take relationships that seriously back then. Well, except for one girl. I liked her a lot. Just didn't work out. What happened to your boyfriend?" I asked.

"He wanted someone else. I mean, he met someone else. I guess he got tired of me at the end of the school year. I probably should have known. We did drift apart. Don't know if it was because he was chasing someone else or if we just lost interest in each other. Really wasn't a surprise when I found out. I wasn't broken hearted. How 'bout you, what happened?" Laura asked. She smiled, embarrassed by her interest.

"Well, it all started off great. It was my last year of University and I got a two month contract up in Timmins. I sent a letter to her every two weeks with the food drop, and got a letter back from her. I kept writing, but she said less and less in her letters. Then one day I didn't get a letter. No more letters. When I got out of camp and back to town I called her. She just wasn't talkative, and I knew it was over. I took another job up in Kap and that was the end of things. That was the beginning of the great decline in my personal life. Of course, if things had been different, I probably wouldn't be here now, with you. See, my loss is your great fortune." I smiled at her.

Laura tossed a stick at me and said, "Jerk!" We both laughed.

Chapter 16. Filing

Cassy had been busy in the office all morning staring at maps, drafting in outcrops with strikes and dips, rock types, sample numbers and geography. She spent time sitting at the computer writing the results of exploration and then printing up the report. With map and report finished, she drove to the regional geologist's office to file it.

"Hi Ron," Cassy said, as she walked in through the front door to the regional office of the Ministry of Natural Resource and Mines.

"Hello Cassy. How are you?" Ron greeted her.

"I'm fine, thanks. Been keeping busy?" She asked.

"It's been crazy this year. Wish we could get more people here to process all the work. Copper's a good price. Everyone's out looking for it. Hey, I met a young fellow said he was working at Cliff, just a couple days ago. Said his name was Titus. Know him?" Ron asked.

"Yes. He just moved out to a camp on Schist Lake. I'm heading out there later today."

"Seems like a good kid. I liked him. I'll bet he does a good job," Ron said. "So what can I do for you?"

"Oh, I have the report and map from the Broughton property. I want to file for work done. I think this should keep the claims for a few years. I have the forms here too," Cassy opened a file and handed the paperwork over, then the map and report.

Ron perused the report and said, "This looks good. Your name is on it. Barry asked you to write it?"

"Yup," Cassy replied. Ron must have wondered what was going on between Barry and Cassy. It was natural to be suspicious under these circumstances.

"OK, good. I'll file this and apply the credits. You should see the results online. Are there any copper or zinc numbers in here?" Ron asked.

"Yes, but only some. We still have a lot of samples in for assay. They aren't fast these days. I'm supposed to pick up more this afternoon. There were some good numbers in a few samples. We plan a drill program this winter. That should give us a better view of the potential. We'll file that with you too when it's done," Cassy answered. "Hey, if you feel like a break, come on out and see us at Schist Lake. We're down at the south end, in a small bay on the West Arm."

"As tempting as that sounds, I don't know if I'll have time. How long you plan to be there?" Ron asked.

"It's just a three week job; mostly looking for shear zones and sulphides," Cassy replied.

"Hmm, last I talked to Barry he said that property got lots of cash, and you know how big it is. Don't know why you'd only spend three weeks mapping it. Maybe he's going to drag it out. Found anything big elsewhere that trumps this property?" He asked.

"Not that I know of, and I think I'd have heard. But who knows. I just do what I'm told, eh?" Cassy laughed.

They said their goodbyes and Cassy left for the assay office where they handed her a brown envelope with results. She wouldn't open it till she got back to the office. Feeling accomplished with her report and chores, Cassy took her time going back to the office. She stopped at the grocery store and grabbed some treats, ice and bread for the camp. Then she saw a roadside stand selling local corn, so she bought a couple dozen. It was getting close to two o'clock and soon she'd have to leave for the dock. Back at the office she loaded the ice into the freezer and discussed her meeting with Ron.

"Watch out for Ron. He's a nosey guy. Don't tell him anything more than we put in the claim reports," Barry told Cassy. Barry wasn't the most social fellow. Of course, any results not published are in fact private and confidential, but it's a good idea to be friendly and open with the regional geologist, even if you don't give details.

"OK," Cassy said, feeling a little intimidated by Barry's attitude. "Here are the results from the assay lab. I haven't opened it yet. Not sure how many they've done. They said they are really busy now."

Barry ripped the envelope open and sat down at the table. He stared at the papers for a moment, flipping pages. "Well, they only did about a third of the samples they have. Looks like we have some good numbers. Let's check the map." They pulled out the map they had for Broughton and checked the coordinates for the best samples. "Here, it says a mafic shear with quartz veins. Do you remember this outcrop?"

"Yes. It looked interesting. Definitely sulphide in the veins. It was a pretty wide zone too. Look, there is a shear over here," Cassy pointed to another location nearby, "so it continues. Any numbers on this outcrop?"

"No, we haven't got those results in yet. Shit! Why couldn't they have gotten those done? I bet we get good numbers there too," Barry mumbled.

"I'm going to get ready. I have to go soon. I told them to pick me up at four," Cassy said.

"Alright." Barry didn't even look up from the map at first, then said, "oh, I want you to come back to the office on Monday, OK? Can you bring in samples and give me a progress report? I want to know if you find any of those old gossans."

"Sure," Cassy replied. She was a bit shocked. That seemed pretty soon, only a few days at the camp. But she thought nothing else of it. She left the room and went to the bathroom to take a shower.

Chapter 17. Pickup

Laura and I cruised back into camp around three thirty. We dumped all our samples up at the tents and then dropped our packs in our tents. "What should we have for dinner?" I asked her.

"Ummm... pork chops?" she answered with a question.

"Sounds fine to me. We have lots of broccoli. Maybe we can boil that," I replied.

"Alright," Laura answered.

"I gotta go get... what the fuck was her name? Oh yeah, Cathy, right?" I said, unconvincingly.

"You're so full of shit. Funny how she asked you to pick her up," Laura said.

"As I recall, I was the only one that offered to drive her to the truck," I replied.

"Ah yes... that's interesting too. Not sayin' nothin'," Laura quipped.

"Ha ha ha." I gave her a fake smile and headed off to the boat. The route was becoming very familiar. The sights were the same and the time to destination my usual 20 minutes. I docked the boat. No sign of the truck yet. I wandered over to the headframe and kicked at a few of the rocks lying around. They were a drab green with a few veins. I picked away at the rubble, looking for darker, rusty rocks. I found a few with nice patches of sulphide, then a few with massive sulphide; nice samples. I picked up a large rock and dropped it on the massive sulphide to crack it open. It took a couple blows, but I finally broke it. Inside was a nice clean face of chalcopyrite. It was a beautiful sample. I bet if you collected some blocks of this and cut slabs, you could sell them as specimens.

I walked up higher on the tailings pile and looked at more rocks. Behind me I heard a vehicle coming down the road. I turned and saw the truck. I felt excited. I didn't expect that. I was happy to see Cassy again. I slid down the pile and waited for her to park. With a smile, I walked over as Cassy swung the door open and hopped out.

"Hi," she said, in her bubbly voice. "How ya been?"

"Really really good!" I emphasized good. It sounded completely fake. "So much has changed. I cut my nails last night... that's about it. What's new with you?"

Cassy was nearly laughing, clearly enjoying this silly banter. There was something relaxed and genuine about these conversations. "I missed that silly look on your face. It's like a combination of Jim Cary and Jimmy Durante. You must get into a lot of trouble, don't you?" Cassy suggested.

"Probably not as much as you'd expect. I fly under the radar. Good to see you. I'd give you a welcome back hug, but, you know, you're my boss." I told her.

"I'm not your boss, Barry is. I'm just the project lead, your team captain, your social committee director. Would a boss bring you... fresh corn on the cob?" Cassy said, grabbing an ear of corn from a bag in the back of the truck.

"Holy fuck! Get over here, you," I said, wrapping my arms over her shoulders and around her back, pulling her in close. She sunk in deep and completely relaxed. If I was not mistaken, she was melting in my arms. I held her a few seconds, then stepped back. "Welcome to Schist Lake, and thanks for the corn. You always surprise me with your thoughtfulness." She gazed into my eyes as I spoke to her. "What else did you bring with you?"

"Well, I didn't forget the ice, if that's what you're getting at," Cassy said.

"Ah yes… you're the best. Should we throw this stuff in the boat?"

"Yup," Cassy replied.

We hauled the goods down to the dock and tossed them into the boat. "Want to sit for a bit?" I asked. We sat on the dock near the boat. "How'd it go at the office?" I wasn't really asking innocently. I was looking for clues about what might be going on with Barry. I wanted to judge her tone and words.

"It was fine. I got my work done in the morning, visited your old buddy Ron, and then got assay results," she said.

Ron… who was Ron? I searched my head for that name. Who do I know in Flin Flon? Who do I know that might be working up here? "Ron. Ron Who?" I asked.

"The regional geologist. He says he met you," Cassy replied.

"Oh yeah. He gave me a drive from the bus depot to the office. A really nice guy. You know him?" I asked.

"Yes. I see him now and then. He seems to like you. What do you do, go around making good impressions on everyone?" Cassy said, laughing.

"What can I say, people like me. Who wouldn't like jim Durante?" I stated, smiling. "How is good old Barry?"

"He's fine. I hardly saw him today. Last night, after you dropped me off, I went straight to a diner and ate. I didn't want to rummage through a fridge looking for grub. Then I went to the bar just to veg out and have a drink. That was your fault. You told me to have a cold beer for you. By time I got into the office, the lights were off and I flopped on the chesterfield. I had another beer," Cassy said with a laugh. "So, to sum things up, I had no fun. I was looking forward to coming back to camp."

"Well, thank God you're back. The camp needs its fearless leader, and I need someone to have a beer with. Seriously, I'm afraid Kyle might be a wild man after a drink, and David might become emotional and blubber about his feelings, and Laura… well, not sure she could resist me if she was drunk," I said.

Cassy hit me. She knew I was joking, of course. "What did you all do today?"

"Laura and I went to that far southeast grid and took a couple lines. Kyle and David went to the far southwest end of the main grid. I haven't talked to them. I came to get you as soon as I got back to camp. Lots of good outcrop. The bush is excellent too; easy to walk." I rambled on a bit about the rocks and land.

"Let's get going. I'm pretty anxious to see what the camp looks like. I don't think I saw the final product. Did you make a bed for me?" Cassy asked.

"Of course. The camp looks good. We're having pork chops for dinner, with broccoli. I will request we cook up some of that corn tonight too. By the way, I threw some beer in a hole with ice so it would be ready when you got there. We know how to welcome our VIP guests," I said.

"Hey, I'm no guest. VIP maybe, but not a guest. That's my home now too," Cassy reiterated.

I gave her a big, broad smile. I hopped into the boat, shuffled to the back and then Cassy jumped in and untied the bow. We moved off and sped down the lake to camp. As always, twenty minutes later we arrived at our own small log dock.

Chapter 18. Admiring a Bikini

Cassy looked happy to be back here in camp. The smell of barbeque meat wafted through the air and smoke lifted through the trees behind the tents. Kyle was sitting in a chair out front of his tent, picking away at his banjo. You could hear it a hundred metres off shore. Laura was standing nearby. David wasn't around. He was either cooking the pork or in the tent fucking the dog, as usual. I shouldn't say that. He's a good guy and always eager to work. Just seems like he's always lying on his bed. Maybe a bit of depression cooking inside him.

Cassy didn't get quite the same welcome from the others that she got from me, but it was amicable. I think Laura was happy to have another woman in camp. Kyle said hi, but you could tell he didn't care if she was here or there. I went back to the barbeque to see what was going on. David was splashing sauce on the meat and turning some of the chops while holding a beer.

"Hey, how's it going?" I asked David.

"Good. How was your day?" He replied.

"Not bad. Had a nice walk and a good lunch. Fuckin' starving now though. That looks fantastic," I told him.

"Thanks. Did you get a beer?" he asked.

"Not yet. I just got back. Had to pick up Cassy. By the way, she brought us fresh corn on the cob."

"Fuckin' A. Go get some and we'll throw it on as soon as I get the meat off. Almost done here," David said.

I went back down to the boat and carried the corn up to the kitchen tent. Looks like they already made the broccoli and it was just waiting. I brought five ears of corn out to David, who was chatting with Cassy.

"David, look at the size of this corn," I announced and showed him the ears.

"That looks beautiful. I'm just stacking this meat in a pile toward the back here to keep it warm and then we can put the corn on," David said. He did just that and the corn sizzled as it touched the iron grates. The smells were killing me. I would have drooled if my mouth was open. I left them there briefly while I went to the pit and grabbed a couple cold beer, then returned to the barbeque.

"Here," I handed a beer to Cassy. "Can't let David drink all the beer himself; fuckin' guy." I twisted off the cap and clinked my can to David's and then Cassy's. "Cheers, guys."

We sat outside and ate dinner together. Everyone was amply jovial. A good meal can do a lot of good for a weary worker, and a laugh can do wonders for a hungry soul. After dinner, Laura and I cleaned the dishes. Sometimes that's the best job because your hands get a good soaking in warm soapy water. When we were done, I stepped outside to enjoy the warm, calm evening.

I saw Cassy sitting on the end of the dock in a black and white bikini. I leaned up against a spruce tree and watched her. She sure was pretty. She turned and looked up at the camp and saw me. Not sure why. It was as if she sensed me watching her. I did not shy away. I smiled and gave her a little wave. She smiled and waved back. I was tempted to go down and sit with her, but thought I'd give her some space. I went into my tent and lay down on the bed. David was in his bed too, reading. "Thanks for cooking dinner tonight, David. It was done perfectly."

David looked over at me and said, "Thanks, man. It was no problem."

I read a little too. After a while I heard Laura and Kyle talking outside the tent and a few notes from the banjo. I picked up my guitar and joined them outside. After a few minutes we were all assembled and David lit a fire in the pit we had. "Hey Kyle, you know Bluebirds by Wilderness of Manitoba?" I asked.

"Yeah, I can play that," Kyle said. I strummed the harmony while Kyle picked his strings. I lead in with the words and then others joined where they could. We sang songs for about an hour. I showed Cassy how I fixed the back of the guitar. She seemed quite impressed with my ingenuity.

"Too bad we don't have a piano out here for Laura." I smiled at her.

"You're lucky you don't," Laura replied.

We had a good evening. We ate, laughed and sang. Before it got late, we all crashed. Snug in my bed, I closed my eyes and tried to picture a green lawn next to a driveway with a parked BMW. I wanted to be able to drive around my old neighbourhood and show people I was a success. Moments later I was sound to sleep.

DAY FOUR - The Gossan

Chapter 19. Coffee

Day four on the job started bright and early. I usually hate bright and early, but today I was quite happy to get up and get going. I didn't know what this day would bring, but I felt good about it. I checked my watch. It was only six forty, too early to get up and yet too late to go back to sleep. I lay on my back and stared up at the top of the tent. A wasp flew by slowly from the front to the back, cruising along the top ridge. I watched him; back and forth several times. It was almost mesmerizing. He was elegant and controlled, seemingly aimless until, with great precision and veracity, he snatched a fly. He landed and systematically stripped the fly of all appendages. A wing fluttered down, then another. The wasp devoured the body and licked its fingers, then cruised the crease at the top of the tent for another victim.

I checked the watch again; six fifty. I couldn't stay there any longer. I got up and put my clothes on. I kept my toothbrush in a cup by the bed. I grabbed it and stepped out of the tent into the morning sunshine, followed the path to the water, and bent down to dip the brush in the lake. A dab of toothpaste and a few slow strokes brought a fresh cleansing to my mouth. I wasn't in a hurry. The view was beautiful. The sun sparkling on the small ripples up the lake dazzled my eyes. The warmth and serenity of this place, in a moment like this, must have been felt by many others over the past several thousand years.

Those people must have loved and cherished this land.

I heard a rustling up at the tents and turned to see what was going on. Laura emerged from her tent and went into the kitchen. I heard lots of thumping and sighing. Might be good to give her some room. No reason to tease a tiger. I went back up to my tent, checked my gear and took my pack outside.

When I heard the noise dissipate in the kitchen, I tenderly entered. Laura was stuffing food into a sample back. I went about making my lunch. Didn't take long for others to follow. David brazenly walked in and said good morning. I quickly returned the greeting so he'd leave Laura alone. She just might bite him if he pestered her. It was kind of a routine morning. I was surprised though that no one else had made coffee. Of course it was only the third day out. I'm sure after a week someone will start making it daily. Might end up being me.

The last person into the kitchen was Cassy. She still looked half asleep, a little dazed, and somewhat confused. I smiled and whispered to her, "rough night?" She half smiled back.

"Could have used a few more hours," she replied.

"Anything I can do to help you get ready, just let me know," I said.

"Could you make coffee?" She asked. And there it is. The morning coffee routine starts. Mornings will be a bit slower from now on. People will take a bit more time to wake up and get going, with the help of java.

"Sure," I told her, and assembled the coffee pot, lit the stove, and started the percolation. I must admit, it smelled great. I'm sure most everyone will want some. That's quite alright with me. I have no problem vegging out for a while in the morning. It's completely unproductive, but I waste plenty of time out on the line and in the evening, so why not in the morning too. I watched as Cassy made her lunch and ate some bread with jam.

"Alright, who wants coffee?" I asked. Not a soul declined. Everyone sat rather quietly caressing their mugs and sipping at steam off the top. There is no variable in this routine equation; spring, summer, fall and winter, this is a morning constant. As the coffee is drained and people wake up, a restlessness starts.

Cassy pulled a map from the side of the tent and opened it on the table. "How about Laura, Kyle and David, you guys take some lines over on the west grid. See how much you can get done. I expect there is lots of outcrop there because it's hilly. I'll take Titus to the east where the rail line is and we can search that area for some of these old reported gossans. I have rough sketches of where they were found, but that's all. We'll have to root around for them. Is that OK with everyone?"

All were fine with that as noted by their quiet nods. I suggested we bring a good grub hoe and a shovel in case we need to dig. It's unlikely a gossan will just pop out at us in a big outcrop. That would have been too easily spotted by others. These old showings date back eighty years or so. Sometimes you just have to plunge a grub hoe in the ground here and there and hope to hit some rubble. That's the kind of thing most people walk right past because it's covered in leaves and dirt. How these old timers found some of these showings is a mystery.

We grabbed our gear and plodded down to the dock where the boat gently shook in the tiny ripples. "Looks like it's gonna be a hot day," I said to Cassy.

"Every day seems hot this month. I don't ever remember such a long stretch of heat before. I kinda wish it would cool down. I work better when it's cool," she replied.

We stepped into the boat and backed out. We were off to the same area we were in before, but with less walking. Not even sure there was a grid in this area. I lowered our speed so I could talk. "Hey, is there a grid where we're going?" I asked.

"Nope. We'll have to tie into the train tracks and ground features. I got some orange tape to mark any showings." Cassy raised a roll of tape to show me. I resumed a higher speed and found a good landing spot along the shore by the train tracks.

Chapter 20. A Little Pyrite

Kyle, David and Laura walked single file through the bush. They all had the same thing on their minds; lunch, that magical time to settle down, eat and maybe snooze a bit in the hot weather. David led the way, holding his compass out and guiding the trio to the grid. In his head, he counted every step, estimating how far they had walked and still needed to go. Kilometre after kilometre passed in this great forest until they reached a picket with the numbers 1200W 300S written on the flat part of the sharp top. They needed to get to the baseline that was 0S and then they could follow that to the end of the line where they could pick east west lines to follow. David and Kyle already did the last lines, so they started where they left off.

The travel lines were equally littered with outcrops. The rounded hills were predominantly mafic volcanics cut by dykes and sills of granite. Pyrite wasn't uncommon, but copper and zinc minerals are rare. This was a regular day in the bush. Just because the good ore minerals weren't being seen didn't mean this was a waste of time. All information is important, like the folds, the rock types, minerals, faults, and shears. The forest echoed with the clanking of rock hammers. It probably disrupted the daily calm within the woods, though the birds weren't phased at all.

David was whacking away at a small outcrop when he dislodged a block which contained a quartz vein that held strings of chalcopyrite, a copper sulphide mineral. He whacked some more, looking for more veins. He kicked around at the base, digging up the dirt to find hidden parts. He noticed some stains and chipped away at it until he hit a nice block with lots of sulphide, probably pyrite.

"HEYYYYY YOOOOO!" he called out, hoping someone would hear.

"Heyyyyyy yoooooo," he heard back from somewhere out in the woods.

"I found something!" David yelled. A few moments later, Laura came trudging through the woods to see him.

"Hey," David said, "that was fast."

"I wasn't far. I didn't get that far in the bush. Lots of outcrop over there. What's up?" Laura asked.

"Look at this," David passed her the rock.

"Holy shit! Nice find. Is there a lot?" Laura asked.

"Well, not visible. I got one piece with quartz veining up top, and this was down under the ground. There might be lots, but we'd have to tear this outcrop apart and maybe dig down to rubble. I'll get some soil samples around the base."

Kyle was nowhere to be seen or heard. Who knows where he went or what he was doing. He's out in the woods, alone. There's a reasonably good chance he's leaning up against a pine tree with his pants down, shaking seeds out of the cones. Laura and David hacked at the outcrop some more and looked around at nearby outcrops hoping to find an extension of the ore minerals. They intended to meet down at the next cross line for lunch, so they packed up their samples and headed down the line. They could backtrack and finish later. After about fifteen minutes, they arrived at the cross line and wandered over toward Kyle's line. There he was, sitting by an outcrop in an extreme state of relaxation.

"Kyle! Wake up. It's lunchtime." David yelled to Kyle. Laura laughed. Kyle smiled in response. "You haven't eaten already, have you? We just traipsed high speed through the bush to get here."

"No, not yet," Kyle replied. "What took you guys so long?"

"We found some decent sulphides in an outcrop," David said. "You find anything?"

"No, nothing," Kyle replied.

David and Laura plunked their packs down and pulled out their lunches.

Chapter 21. An Old Showing

Cassy and I trod through the ferns under the big poplar trees as we approached the first gossan site. I looked around and didn't see a heck of a lot of outcropping. "How good is this research for old showings?" I asked.

"Not good. It's pretty sketchy what was found and where. I just went by some rough drawings and old notes from the 1920's," Cassy replied.

"Nearly a hundred years, eh? That's a lot of time to cover them up. I'll bet there's been forest fires and maybe logging since then. These trees are only about fifty years old. The odds are against us." I said. "So where exactly should we start poking around?"

"OK, as best as I can guess, right where that outcrop in front of us is the place, but, without any good features here, it could be within a hundred metre radius," Cassy suggested.

"Might as well call this point zero and work our way out. Is this the best gossan you found in the old notes?"

"No." Cassy answered. "It's just the first along this path. Maybe we shouldn't spend too much time on it if we don't find something."

"Alright," I replied. "Why not tie some red tape around a tree here and we can work our way out. If we find nothing, we can just move on."

I really didn't want to waste time beating up rocks for what might have been a few specks of pyrite. Cassy tied the ribbon to a tree and I started digging around the outcrop with the grub hoe. I pulled moss and lichen off, knocked some loose blocks around and dug up earth here and there. Cassy worked the other side of the outcrop, about forty feet away. I was seeing nothing.

I yelled out, "Cassy Cassy Cassy, how's it goin' in Tallahassee?" I heard her laugh.

It took a moment, then a reply from the other side of our tiny mountain, "Rocks rocks rocks, north of Halifox."

"Are you kidding me? That's the best you can come up with?" I yelled over.

"Yes!" Cassy called back.

"Better work on that! See anything good?" I asked.

"No, nothing. You?" Cassy replied.

"Nothing good. I'm going to branch out. I'm only pacing a couple hundred feet, then I'm giving up on this lame duck. You coming with me or going the other way?" I asked.

"Going the other way. Your criticism has deeply hurt my pride. I need some time!" she jokingly called back.

"Fine then, abandon me. But if something happens to me out there in the wilderness, all alone, you'll have to live with that."

"I think I can live with that," she yelled back.

"Harsh!" My condemnation actually sounded real.

"Don't be such a big baby! Next you'll be asking me to hold your hand when you shit."

The thought had crossed my mind, or a variation of it. "Well, now you're just being silly. OK, I'm leaving. Farewell... call me!" I teased.

I looked out around my side of the hill and wandered off. If this gossan was found that long ago, and they obviously put effort into it, then maybe it wasn't an outcrop above ground, but something low, now covered by debris. I scanned for depressions. It wasn't uncommon in the old days to blast with a bit of dynamite. So maybe I should look for holes.

I wandered, now and then thrusting my grub hoe into the ground to see what I could pull out. Being a low, flat area overgrown with ferns meant a lot of moist soil. You could dig a long ways before hitting rock in much of this area. I found a few small outcrops, but they were barren. I found what looked like a sinkhole, which was pretty much impossible as these rocks were not sedimentary or calcareous. It could have just been a softer metamorphic zone, like an ultramafic that eroded. I started digging into it and soon pulled out rubble.

There was no mistake, this rubble was rusty. I slammed a few pieces with my rock hammer to get a clean face. It had strings of quartz vein and small pyrite crystals in it. I hammered away at blocks and dug it up as best I could. I couldn't be sure that this was their showing or if it just had weathered down because of the rock type. I grabbed a sample and moved on.

I scoured the ground and then circled back to point zero. Cassy wasn't back yet, though couldn't be far away. I stood up on top of the outcrop and looked around. I heard some banging off to the left and looked, but couldn't see her. I dropped my pack and took a whiz off the edge of the outcrop, then wandered toward the distant banging. As I drew closer I could see her blue shirt moving about.

"Hey, you find something?" I called out.

Cassy stood up straight, turned and looked back at me. She waited till I got closer. "Hey. No, not really. How about you?"

"I found a bit of pyrite in some quartz veins. It did stain the rocks, and it was in a bit of a rubbly pit, so maybe that was their showing. Looked pathetic, but got a good sample. We'll see if there's anything there. I didn't have any tape. Maybe as we move on we should mark it," I told her. "How far to the next one?"

Cassy pulled out her map. "I'd say about five hundred metres, up by the train tracks. Why don't we boot it there now and then have lunch."

"Ah yes, lunch. You do know that is the single most important thing in my day, right?" I raised my eyebrows.

"Really? So you're in this for the free bread and bologne, huh? That sounds rather selfish. Haven't you heard? There's no free lunch. You have to work your ass off to get an Oh Henry around here, mister!" she said with a smile.

Geez, she keeps feeding me great innuendos to rattle around in my mind. "Who found the pyrite? Huh? Huh?" I goaded her on.

"Yes, you did." Cassy replied.

"Good, I want my reward. Let's get to the tracks and have lunch!" We both chuckled and walked off to my showing, to flag it, and then continue another half click to the train tracks by the water.

Chapter 22. Religion

The trio on the west grid sat slumped against their packs, their lunches in hand. It was quiet for a bit while they fed their hunger. They later discussed what they brought and compared sandwiches. Kyle hated tomatoes but loved ketchup. There was no rhyme or reason for that. David disliked mayonnaise on a sandwich, but liked white salad dressings made with mayonnaise. Laura ate everything.

Laura asked, "Don't you find it weird that people all like different things? I mean coyotes all like the same meat. Moose all eat the same buds. Blue Jays all eat nuts and robins all like worms, but people are so picky with what they like. You'd think we'd all have the same tastes."

"Maybe we did, back a million years ago, when we all starved and there was no variety. But now we've developed such a complex diet, and we don't starve, so we can be picky," David responded.

"A million years ago?" Kyle said, surprised. "God made us, and he made each of us unique. That's why we have different tastes."

Laura and David looked at each other. David said, "Kyle, I never pegged you as a religious guy."

"What, I can't believe in God?" he answered.

"Well sure, but seeing you get piss-faced and hit on girls at the bar just doesn't seem to fit the Jesus image. Except of course for those preachers who secretly go out at night, smoke crack, and pay hookers."

"I can believe in God and still get shit-faced on occasion. All part of my uniqueness," Kyle said, smiling. "How could you not believe in God?"

"Ahhh, science?" David said in a rather smug way. "How did you get a science degree if you don't believe in science?"

"I believe in science, though I dispute some of it. I know mathematical equations make sense, and I understand the chemical components of rocks, the geometry of crystals and tectonic forces. I just dispute how and when it all started. Have you ever read the bible?" Kyle asked David.

"Actually, yes," David answered. "When I was young I had to go to church. I was taught all those ridiculous stories. I guess I believed them until I was a teen, then I started to doubt it. All of it. How come God never talks to me?"

"I don't hear voices either. That doesn't mean he doesn't exist," Kyle went on.

"So what are you, catholic, protestant, in the middle, or something else?" David asked.

"I'm Protestant. We protest a lot, I suppose. A Protestant Irish family. We hate the Catholics. I don't know why. I was just told to hate them. I don't really hate them. I guess that's something you have to grow up around, like my grandparents did. I don't believe in Catholic's weird ideas though; all that robe and chalice stuff, and confession to some guy. Like I'm gonna tell some stuffy old man about who I screwed or what I did wrong. None of his fucking business!" Kyle said.

Laura laughed. "You know, this is a pretty intense topic. If we sit here and debate this we won't get any work done today. Can we postpone this for a drunk session?"

Both David and Kyle smirked. David trumped up, "I don't take any of this seriously you know. I like debating it, but only because it's interesting, not because I have deep beliefs."

Kyle added, "Wish we could get drunk tonight. I want to end this thing!" He laughed. "Well, actually I just wanna get drunk." And Kyle laughed at himself again. This was the first spark of life anyone had really seen in Kyle. He had lacked any personality until now. Maybe he is just slow to warm up.

Chapter 23. Play

Cassy and I arrived at the rail tracks quickly. I loved this place. Why do I love trains so much? I don't know. There's just something about being able to travel deep into the wilderness and see what no one can see. It's so remote. Same as fly in camps. You are so far away, it's like a world from thousands of years ago. This is where the moose and bear reign. This is the real wild country. I'm sure the moose and bear don't appreciate trains passing through their home, but at the same time, they aren't disturbed by trains like they are cars, because trains don't stop and annoy them like cars do. The trains just keep on going.

It was a beautiful sight. The train tracks passed along the edge of the lake and the river connecting other lakes. That's where we were, at the point where the lake ends and the river begins. If we walked south we'd follow along the river. If we walked north, the lake would open up and eventually we would see our camp from a distance. At the side of the tracks was a gravel bank that sloped sharply down toward the shore. There was lots of room to follow the shore without much danger from the tracks.

Because the tracks and sides were cleared of trees and brush, blueberries and raspberries grew in abundance. The blueberries were huge, almost the size of grapes, and plants bulged with fruit right now. It was still early for raspberries, but a few were ripe in sunny locations. We walked along the tracks for a hundred metres or so until we came to a nice place where we slid down the gravel bank to the rocky shoreline. We sat side by side and lay back against our packs.

"What did you bring for lunch?" I asked Cassy.

"Peanut butter and honey sandwich," she answered.

"You're kidding, right?" I expressed indignation.

"What's wrong with that?" Cassy asked.

"It's fucking disgusting. That's like spaghetti and fish balls, or beer and ice cream. My mother made that for me once when I was in school. I came home and told her I'd stop loving her if she ever made that for me again! Seriously, that's gross."

"Well, I disagree. I think it's delicious. Here, try some," Cassy pushed it in my face.

"Aww, get that stinky shit away from me. Are you trying to make me puke?" I said, making an awful face. Cassy just laughed at me.

"What are you eating?" she asked.

"Salmon, with lettuce, tomato and mayo. Boom! That's a sandwich, or as I call it, a manwich. Wanna try some?" I shoved it in her face. Damned if she didn't snag a big bite out of it! I did not see that coming.

"Yeah, not bad. Thanks. See, I'm not picky like you... snob," Cassy said, smiling a devilish grin.

Oh, she got me good. All I could do was stare at my disfigured sandwich, frown and nod. She won this round. It didn't faze me. I consumed my sandwich and enjoyed it. After we ate I noticed she didn't have much else in her lunch bag and I asked her, "Do you want a banana?" I held it out for her.

"You sure?" she replied.

"Yeah, I brought lots of grub. Go ahead." I looked at her eyes and smiled. She took it from my hand. I reached into my bag and pulled out a box of smarties and ate them. Now and then I put a few smarties in my hand and reached out to Cassy. She took them, like I was feeding a raccoon at a petting zoo. I enjoyed sharing with her. It made me feel good, and I liked it when her fingers touched my hand.

"Hey, you never told me what you had for dinner when you were at the office. You just said you went to a diner. Tell me all the details," I begged.

"OK. First off, they had a special, linguine something or other," she started.

"Whoa whoa whoa... what do you mean something or other? That's not details. What did it smell like, look like, taste like?" I asked.

"It was white, and creamy. I think it had herbs in it, like basil or tarragon, and sausage. The noodles were a bit stiff, but I liked it. The plate was big and deep and I had trouble eating it all, but I did. Oh, and it came with garlic toast. Then I had apple crisp for dessert, with ice cream. How's that sound to you?" She smiled.

"Sounds like you enjoyed every mouthful, and telling me all about it, too. You couldn't have snuck a wee bit of toast out for me? I miss herbs and spices. Salt and pepper's fine, but there's so much more. I can cook, you know," I told her.

"I know," Cassy replied, "I remember breakfast. You fry a hell of a sausage." Cassy was having fun with me. That was a total tease.

"I can do better. I can bake bread and cook pasta and make all kinds of great foods. I learned when I was in University. I remember watching this show about Chinese stir fries. Heat a wok, throw in the chicken, then veggies, then create the sauce and add it. Done. That was my first real attempt to cook and I loved it. And wouldn't you know it, I ended up in bush camps where I can't get fancy. I wish I had a real kitchen." Cassy listened, but didn't respond. I think she was being respectful. She understood I was having a serious moment.

We finished our lunch and threw the packs on. The next showing was back down along the tracks about three hundred metres. We picked blueberries as we walked. There was an old hydro line running down along the tracks, obviously not used anymore. The wires were gone, but the poles were still there.

"Hey, look up the pole. See the glass insulators? Try and hit them," I said. We picked up stones and flung them up at the glass knobs. There were a lot of misses. Finally a stone pinged an insulator.

"Yeah!" yelled Cassy. "Take that!"

"OK, settle down. Lucky hit," I replied. We continued pinging the glass insulators far longer than we should have. Then we collected a few insulators from poles that had fallen down ages ago. At one point I stopped and leaned against a pole, watching Cassy collect insulators. She was adorable. She was innocent like a child and at the same time very smart and mature. I was so drawn to her. I could stare at her all day.

What was it about her that gave me this feeling? I hadn't dated in a long time, but could not remember ever feeling this way about a girl before. I craved her. I wanted to be close to her. Everything about her made me feel good, from her smile to her smell. There is no way I can ignore this any more than a thirsty man could ignore water or a hungry man ignore food. That's how I saw her right now, as if I was a hungry child on a hot summer day looking at an ice cream sundae. Well, maybe there was more to it than that.

We continued down the track, playing and acting silly. I put the grub hoe between my legs and pretended to ride a horse while Cassy clapped for me and yelled 'ride 'em cowboy'. We played baseball with an orange and a stick until the orange blew apart. It must have taken us an hour to walk three hundred metres, but we laughed and acted like kids all the way. It's just part of the job, the way I do it.

Chapter 24. Plenty Fast

"This is it. This is about the right spot," Cassy said, looking at her map. "Look, see how the river bends? That's here on the map," she pointed out. "So the showing should be between the river and the tracks." That was about fifty feet.

We started digging around. Cassy began whacking at rocks. I figured it wouldn't be in an obvious outcrop or we'd see a good rust stain. So I dug around with the grub hoe. With every slice into the ground my temperature rose a degree. Soon, standing under the hot sun I was roasting like a Swiss Chalet Chicken.

I dropped my grub hoe and pulled a drink out of my pack. It felt good. I needed the fluids. I took my T-shirt off, walked down to the river edge and dowsed it, then rung it out over my head, letting the cool water drip down onto my chest and back. I turned to see Cassy about thirty feet away, watching me. I was standing tall, my arms stretched up. I know I looked good. My shoulders are broad; my arms and chest strong; my back slightly arched and my stomach muscles rippling. I am pretty well tanned from a summer outside. My pants sagged slightly, exposing a slim pale band of skin. I wouldn't doubt that I'd lost a bit of weight with all this sweating.

"How can you stand this heat?" I asked her. "It must be thirty out here." The deer flies buzzed around my head and I waved the shirt at them. When it's hot, they become relentless, thriving in the sunshine.

"I know, eh? Why couldn't copper mines be shaded under big pine trees? There isn't even a breeze today.

Let's take a break," Cassy said. She looked around and found a sharp outcrop to sit against, offering a little shade. I soaked my shirt again and patted my chest to cool down, then walked over and sat beside her. There wasn't much shade, and I may have sat rather close to her, close enough that our arms touched. We drank water and sighed.

"I think two o'clock sun is the worst," Cassy started. "Noon might be highest, but not the hottest."

"Yeah, and by two you've suffered longer and you're ready to die. By four, you can slow down and head back to camp. Just the same, I like the heat. What I hate is the cold. I don't like being wrapped up in a coat. I would have done well to be a surfing instructor in Tahiti," I said.

Cassy looked up at me, "Yeah, I can see that. I don't know where I fit in."

"Are you kidding? You'd be a great Bay Watch lifeguard," I told her and smiled.

"Actually I'm a great swimmer. I've just never swam in the ocean. I'd probably be scared of sharks, and waves, and lobsters. So many dangerous things in the sea." Cassy joked.

"Well, you have to be fast; out swim the sharks, jump the waves, and dance past the lobsters. That's all there is to it," I said.

"I'm plenty fast enough," Cassy said. She held a stone in her hand in front of me. I snatched at it and she closed her hand. She was fast. I looked over at her, raised my eyebrows and looked back at her hand. Again, she opened her hand. Once again I snatched, but not for the stone, for her hand. I grabbed it and pulled it in close, prying it open with my other hand as she attempted to secure the stone. It was an epic struggle, but I won and held the stone up high above her. I laughed maniacally. She grabbed my arm and tried to pull it down. My muscle bulged under the strain.

"Sure, you win, arse pickle!" she said, smiling. She slid her hand down my arm and felt my bicep. "That's quite the muscle. You didn't get that from just pinging rocks."

I held my arm straight out and then flexed, and she examined the muscle. It tickled, and felt nice. I saw her glance at my chest.

"No, I started working out in high school. I still do. I like sit-ups, push-ups, punching bags and weights. I have to use a log or rocks for weights out here, but that's OK. It makes my hands stronger. Usually I do a half hour in the morning and a half hour in the evening. Geez, I never noticed how tanned I've become. I guess it's been a hot summer. How'd you escape the sun?" I asked.

Cassy looked down at her arms. "That last job was in thick bush. I guess I didn't see much sun. Not like this, on the train tracks. I don't care. I've never been a big tanner, though some summers I get quite dark. Can't always escape it. I always tanned a lot as a kid."

It seemed odd that we were taking a break from the heat and yet sitting shoulder to shoulder. I did not mind at all. Cassy wasn't complaining either. I was still holding that stone in my hand, tossing it up in the air to Cassy, and back to me. All of a sudden, she grabbed it out of the air and looked at it.

"Hey, look at this!" she bellowed.

Chapter 25. Sulphide

"What?" I asked and looked at it. Well damned if our hands weren't rusty and the rock a burnt brown. "Where did you pick this up?" I asked. "How did we not see this before?"

We stood up and looked around. "I just picked it up right here, on the ground where we were sitting," Cassy said.

I went to get my grub hoe and then returned to dig the ground up. There, beneath us was rubble; blocks of rusty rock. Cassy took a block and slammed it with her hammer. Inside was massive sulphide. It was a rich, orangey chalcopyrite. There was lots of it. We looked at each other. "Wow! This is awesome," I said. "Let's dig around and see the extent". We dug and whacked. The outcrop did not show any sign of sulphide. The extents looked to be confined. "What do you think?" I asked Cassy.

"It's impressive. Too impressive?" She replied.

"It's either a small plug of ore at the surface, or," I looked around, "more likely a train car spill, and this came from a mine in Flin Flon. Pretty suspicious to find a pile of high grade ore minerals at the side of the tracks." I stood there, sweating in the sun, looking at Cassy.

Cassy sighed. "Yes, you are right. But just in case, let's take some samples and mark this spot. We can come back and tear the ground up looking for any connection to the outcrop."

We gathered a few good samples. I took one just for me. I like to collect a few good samples here and there for my own collection. "Should we head back?" I asked.

"Yeah, nothing more we can do here and no point searching a new place this late. Let's go home and get some grub... and a cold beer," Cassy said.

"Fuckin' A." I added.

We threw our packs on and started heading back to the boat. It was a good hike, considering the weight we were carrying. Good thing was, we just needed to follow the rail line all the way back to the boat. I was so grateful to see it tied up at the shore.

We plunked our packs in. I put my shirt back on and we sailed back to camp in a jiffy. After dropping off our packs at the kitchen we both changed. I put on a pair of shorts, sandals, and a fresh T-shirt. Then I went down to the shore with a bucket and soap. I gave myself a bit of a wash. I also dumped my sweaty work clothes in a pail with some soapy water and let it sit for a while. I looked back up at camp and saw Cassy emerge from her tent wearing her cut-off jeans and a new T-shirt. She looked so good. I wandered back up the hill and went directly to the ice pit. Out came two beers. I held them behind my back and walked nonchalantly over to Cassy, circled behind her and stuck one can against her neck.

"Ah!" She cried out and twisted around. "What the..."

"Got ya a cold beer," I said, grinning.

"I owe you! Give it here." she snapped it out of my hand, plucked the tab open and took a big gulp. "Ahhhh, that's good."

"Cheers," I said, and tapped her can. "Good day today."

"Yeah, found some nice stuff," Cassy said.

"Uhuh, that too," I replied, looking at Cassy and smiling.

"What should we make for dinner?" I asked, taking a sip of my beer, enjoying the cold effervescence.

"Hows abouts tenderloins? We can have corn again and a salad. Whatcha think?" Cassy asked back.

"I like the sound of that. I can get the barbeque started," I told her. We parted. I got the charcoal and lighter fluid and started the fire. Cassy disappeared into the tent to start making the salad. Apart from a few moments bumping into each other, I cooked the pork and corn and Cassy made salad and set the table. We timed it well.

Chapter 26. Nicknames

As the corn roasted, David, Kyle and Laura drifted into camp looking like three banditos from the desert. They didn't change, just grabbed a cold beer and headed for the kitchen. David still looked cheery, exhausted and hot, but cheery. He slapped my back and said, "Titus, Cassy, you two have set the bar high. This looks fantastic."

"Thanks David," we both replied.

"Have a seat, everyone. Let's get this party started," said Cassy.

Everyone looked happy around the table, smiling, talking, eating and drinking. All the exhaustion and heat that plagued us through the day was forgotten, at least for now.

I asked Laura, "So what did you guys find today?"

"Shit all. Well, a bit of sulphide, but nothing much. How 'bout you two?"

"A bit of sulphide. I can show you." I went outside and pulled a rock from my pack and brought it into the tent. I put it on the table.

"Holy fuck!" David trumped up. "Are you kidding?" Everyone's eyes bulged at the sight of the shiny golden rock face. "Was it hard to find?"

"Uhhh...," I looked at Cassy, "actually, we sat on it for half an hour before realizing it was there." I said, smiling, "or maybe Cassy's ass just turns rock to ore. No proof either way, really." Everyone laughed. "But if I was Cassy, I would use that asset for the good of the mining company."

"You should have seen Titus. He was so hot out there he begged me for a break. That's why we had to sit down. I just picked the magical spot," Cassy teased. "Then I made Titus dig the whole area up."

"Uhuh," I responded, looking over at Cassy, "Sassy Dufferin, enjoys my sufferin'."

"Tight-ass Weatherby, always buggin' me," Cassy shot back to howls of laughter.

"Oh, burn ya!" Laura said, pointing at me.

"Not bad, Sassy. Not bad at all." I'm sure I looked sheepish, like an embarrassed kid. I was just caught off guard. I didn't expect such a great comeback. This may have been the beginning of our new family relationship. It was times like this that made a bush camp wonderful. For the moment, no one dwelled on where they lived, what they smelled like, or how hard they worked.

"So you all think that's funny, eh? I bet we could come up with good nicknames for the rest of you." I looked at Laura. "Hmm… I clearly remember you wailing on an outcrop like a jack hammer. You could be 'Thora, girl with a big hammer'." I got some snickers for that and Laura grinned. "David, David, you're a tough one. I thought about 'Red', but that's too simple. I'll come back to you. Kyle, you're pretty sneaky, chasing after the girls at the bar. You could be 'Wily Coyote'. What do you think of that?" Kyle grinned and nodded his head. "OK, David…"

Laura butt in and said, "How about 'dog fucker'?"

"Oh, harsh," I replied. "I was thinking more like, 'Navy Davy'. That sucks. You'll have to wait until you do something foolish and a name fits you," I said.

Laura continued her jabs, "That won't take long!" It was said in good humour though. Maybe I was missing something here. Maybe there was some sexual tension building between these two. This passive aggression may be a defensive mechanism from Laura, or simply her way of expressing a playful attraction. Then again, maybe she just got off on the wrong foot with David at the grocery store.

"OK, so now the truth. We don't actually know if this is a showing. It could easily be a pile of ore that just fell off the train as it choo-choo'ed down the track. After all these years, it might have sunk down, weathered and appears to be part of the ground rocks. Oh, by the way, brought some cool things back." I ran back out of the tent and collected a bunch of glass insulators. I brought them back in and placed them on the table. "Help yourself."

Kyle reached out and picked one up. "Cool. How'd you get these?"

Cassy answered, "There were a few telephone poles down and these were scattered around."

"Thanks," said David. "I'll take one." David reached out and helped himself. I was glad they liked them.

Laughter continued long after dinner in this tiny kitchen tent while the frogs rose to croak and all the night animals emerged from their hiding places to roam and chat in the evening stillness. After dishes, we moved to my tent. I strummed the guitar a little while we continued to talk. I wonder what the animals thought of my music. Maybe it's just as annoying to birds in the evening as their chatter is to me in the early morning.

"I think I'm going to bed," Cassy said. Laura agreed, and they got up to leave. "Night boys. Don't let the black flies bite."

"Hey, keep the farting down to a bare minimum, eh?" I asked.

"Ha ha ha, funny," Cassy answered. "Just watch it or I'll point at you."

I just smiled, strummed a little and sang "Smoke, on the water."

Tomorrow would be yet another day. Would I be out on the line with Cassy again? I liked being with her. I liked her a lot. I don't know where this is going. Is it going somewhere? I can't afford to lead this one way or another. I can only let things happen. There is a natural order to life. I put the guitar down, turned over and closed my eyes.

DAY FIVE - Rain

Chapter 27. Sleeping In

Day five arrived with a dismal monotonous tapping on the tent roof. It was dark inside the tent and the air was cool and damp. I rose, walked over to the front flap and peeked outside. We were socked in with a steady rainfall. Might have been raining all night for all I know, and could rain for days. What a dreary day. I really wanted to go out in the bush today, but this was a rain day. I stood there in my underwear for a few minutes, hiding behind the tent flap with just my head out, watching the rain drip off the balsam branches. You dream of days like this after a while, but not quite yet. I went back to bed, pulled the sleeping bag up around my shoulders and went back to sleep. No one else was up, and as soon as they realized it was raining would just stay in bed.

David rolled over and said, "How is it out there?"

"Pea soup and Niagara. We're not going anywhere today," I replied.

"Good," David said, and rolled over.

It was nice to feel some cool air. It had been so hot lately. I tried to recall my dream, but couldn't. Doesn't matter, my dreams seldom make much sense; just better to start a new one. I drifted off to sleep, imagining western mountains and chalets, pretty shops and green grass. I used to dream of being a hockey player, sailing around the ice past defenceman and slamming the puck past goalies. Other times I dreamt of being the goalie, just a stand in because the real goalie was injured, and I was impenetrable. Game after game, I had shutouts. I loved being the hero.

I slept till nearly eleven o'clock, as did others. I awoke to the sound of Kyle knocking around in the tent. David was reading in bed. Laura stuck her head in the tent to see what we were doing. "Geez, you guys are finally awake." She wore a yellow raincoat, water dripping off her hood. "Let's eat. We've been waiting for you."

"Alright," David replied. Laura left and we got dressed. None of us moved fast. Damp air has a way of seeping into the joints and slowing everything down. Putting on damp clothes is never pleasant, but there's no way to keep anything bone dry in this humidity. I dashed from my tent to the kitchen, hoping to avoid the drops of water falling off the branches above. I obviously did not dodge every drop as I could feel the water on my forehead.

In the kitchen tent, Laura and Cassy had made an eclectic mix of scrambled eggs, sandwiches, pasta salad and coffee. It all looked good to me.

"Wow, nice spread," I said. "You guys have lots of energy today. As soon as I saw the rain this morning, I went into comatose mode and resolved to abandon my devotion to consciousness."

They looked at each other and grinned like a couple kids. "Well, we didn't get up that early either. But didn't sleep as long as you bunch of layabouts," Laura answered. She was no longer wearing her raincoat, just her regular work clothes. Everyone assembled in the kitchen and took a seat. It felt like a Sunday back home, eating brunch on a lazy day.

"Did you guys sleep well last night?" I asked. All said yes, not surprisingly. The rhythmic tapping of rain on the roof, whether consciously heard or not, has a tendency to lull you through a sound sleep. I suppose the mind puts up a barrier to background noises which acts like a defence against wakening. I hear people actually buy gadgets and apps which play background noises, like rain, to replicate that sensation. Out here, with a thin veneer of canvas protection from the natural world, regular rhythmic sounds are alive and constant.

I, along with the others, ate a hearty amount. When we were done, I remembered my bucket of clothes down at the lake. I should have finished washing them last night, though with all this rain it didn't matter. I left the kitchen and headed for my tent. I put on my rain suit.

Cassy stuck her head inside and asked, "What are you up to?"

"I started a wash last night. Should finish it. You have any clothes you want washed?" I asked her.

"Sure, I'll get some," Cassy replied.

"I'll meet you down at the beach." I left my tent and walked down to the dock where my bucket sat nearly overflowing with soapy water. I picked up a strong stick and began drawing it around and around in the bucket like a washing machine does. Then I started the slow, repetitive cycle of draining the soapy water on land, squishing the dirty water out of the clothes and refilling with clean water. Squish the clothes, drain, and refill. I did that three times until I felt the soap was all out. By then Cassy had come down with a few clothes in hand. She sat them down on the ground. I pulled out some socks and twisted them hard to squeeze the water out. I realize the futility of this, given the steady rain, but just seemed the right thing to do. Then I pulled out a pair of pants.

"Hey, can you grab the ends?" I asked her, "and hold on tight." I began twisting. When she realized what I was doing, she twisted in the other direction and water drained off. After each item, I placed the clothing down on a nearby rock in a pile.

After my clothes were all done, I filled the pail with water, lathered my hands with soap and dowsed them in the pail. "OK, dump your clothes in here," I pointed to the pail. "Take this stick and swirl it about for a minute or two."

I stepped back and watched. When she was done I pushed my hands in and squeezed the clothes to work the dirt out and the soap in. I could feel a pair of very delicate panties with my hand. I admit it aroused me. I pulled them out, held them up high and raised my eyebrows.

"Pretty stuff, Duff," I said.

Cassy smiled back and said, "don't be naughty, Weatherby!"

I laughed. Before she could react, I made her delicate underwear dance and I sang, "Ah, ah, ah, ah, stayin' alive, stayin' alive. Ah, ah, ah, ah, stayin' alive." And then she snatched them right out of my hands. I just laughed and she grinned. We finished washing, rinsing and squeezing the water out of her clothes and then went over to the clothesline to hang them.

"It'll be quite a while before these get dry," I said. "At least we know they'll be well rinsed." There on the line hung my shirt, my socks, my pants, her shirt, and then side by side, my large boxer briefs and her petite lacy panties. It was quite a contrasting sight.

I wanted to get back into the warm, dry kitchen again. "I'm taking this rain suit off and going back to the kitchen. You?" I asked.

"Me too," she agreed. "What a shitty day."

Chapter 28. Administration Work

Moments later we were back in the kitchen tent. "What are you guys talking about?" I asked as I walked in.

"We were just about to start a religious conversation," Laura replied. "This should be interesting." There was a bottle of Forty Creek whisky on the table in front of Kyle. It was still unopened.

I have a better idea," said Cassy, who had come in to hear this announcement. "How about we get some sample prep and plotting done before that. It's a wee bit early to start draining a bottle of whisky. And if I know 'wily coyote' Kyle, that bottle will be empty before we finish the debate."

There was some good humoured laughter and agreement to catch up on work before having fun. And so the task of bagging samples, filling out assay tags, marking locations on the map, editing notes and basic mapping began. Some sat on the ground to work on samples. Some leaned over the table to draw outcrops, trees, rivers etc. on the map with pencil crayons. Some sat in chairs to clean up field notes, and there was general conversations about the rocks. All very dull and scientific. It was fun to pull the samples out and look at them closely with the magnifying glass. I loved searching the rocks for tiny crystals and veins and interesting minerals. It's like a mini world. Every rock is unique and beautiful at that level, like making a flyby of a new planet. I took notes on every sample.

A couple hours passed by. It was near three in the afternoon and all the office work was done. We had but two tasks left to do this day, make dinner and solve the mystery of the origin of life, while drinking.

"Let's have an early dinner, eh?" David suggested.

"David, are you hungry again?" Laura inquired. "Do you have a tapeworm or something?"

"Well, we had brunch like, four hours ago," he answered.

"Uhuh. What do you want?" Laura asked.

"I have a request." I chimed in. "How about spaghetti?" I looked around. No one objected. "Good, it's settled." I set to work digging out the sauce, pasta, meat, etc. Everyone helped out. Stove was lit, meat in the pan, sauce in the pot, peppers and mushrooms cut, and the pasta ready to drop in a pot as soon as the meat was added to the sauce. It was a good choice for a rainy day. The added heat from the stove felt good inside.

When all was said and done, it was a great meal. The rain outside started to abate and then the grey cast was broken with a burst of brightness inside the tent. I opened the flap to look outside. The clouds had moved off and the sky shone with radiant blue. We all stepped outside, went down to the dock and watched an incredible rainbow that had formed over the hills in the distance.

"It's a sign from God," Kyle said.

"What's he telling us, Kyle?" David responded sarcastically.

"We're here for a reason," he said.

"And that reason is?" David egged him on.

"We should stop looking for copper and start looking for a pot of gold. See, God's even showing us where to look." Kyle spoke, pointing off toward the rainbow.

"Are you shitting us, Kyle?" David wondered aloud.

"David, you're pretty gullible. Of course I'm shitting you!" Kyle said with a smile.

We all had a good laugh at David.

"Well done, Kyle. Well fucking done!" Laura said, smiling at Kyle, then smiling at David, enjoying this joke on him. David took it all in good humour and congratulated Kyle.

Chapter 29. Whisky

The sun hit us with a power we missed all day. It felt so warm. The air immediately rose in temperature. I suspect tomorrow will be hot again. We went back up to the tent and cleaned the dishes.

That's when the bottle of Forty Creek re-emerged. "Alright, let's hash this out," David belted out. Everyone grabbed their mug or cup and the pouring began.

"Cheers," I said, "to a fine day of… work. Now chug that first swig!" We all did and a second round was poured. This was no mickey, it was a forty pounder. No chance of running out any time soon.

"So you guys will have to enlighten me and Cassy. We don't know what started this debate or what it's all about," I said.

Laura entered the fray. "It's not a big deal. I don't know why these two are making it such an issue." Laura pointed to David and Kyle. "It started with David mentioning man a million years ago and Kyle disputing the date. Am I right, Kyle?"

"David obviously believes man came from monkeys. I disagree." Kyle reported. "I happen to believe God made us. Is that so hard to understand?"

"Uh… yes? Yes. Yes it is," David arrogantly responded. "Kyle, don't you think it's an incredible coincidence that we, humans, have such a similar anatomy to other mammals? Even to non-mammals. Things like legs, arms, stomachs, eyes, ears, and so on."

"No, it's just part of a design. Don't you think things like eyes and ears are rather advanced features in an advanced system? Did computers evolve? No, we created them. We created the parts, designed the systems and assembled them. They didn't just emerge. Technology is human-made system development. Life forms are God-made system development. Sure we have laptops and desktops and smart-phones, but they are designed on a basic platform. People and animals can be designed like that too."

"Well, what about dinosaurs? You dispute the age of humans. How old is the world?" David asked.

"The bible kind of estimates six thousand years, I think," Kyle suggested, without much confidence.

"So, how do you explain this progression of life in fossils? We can clearly see that life changed from simple bacteria in the oldest rocks through fish, plants, dinosaurs, and on to new animals. How long ago do you think dinosaurs lived?" David seemed impatient.

"Maybe they didn't. Maybe they are just impressions in the rock. Maybe all those old fossils are like artwork that went into creating the Earth."

"Really? That's not a very scientific argument, Kyle. When you look at a rock out here, do you not evaluate the folding, faults, rock types and how they formed?" David continued to press.

"Sure, but I dispute that the rocks are millions or billions of years old." Kyle was steadfast. "Why are you so sure all this couldn't have been designed and made by someone far superior than us?"

"It's not that I can't believe it, I just can't get past the logical and physical evidence. You can't tell me what or who this God is. You can't give me any answers beyond what a bunch of completely uneducated, superstitious, uncivilized backwards thinking people in a wedge of land on the other side of the world thought. They said God talked to them. They relayed their stories in books, letters and such. So today, we can't dispute their story because they aren't here to defend it. So we just accept it as is? That is crazy! Lots of books have been written, some became religions or philosophies. You don't believe them though, so why the bible?" David demanded.

"It makes sense to me." Kyle's answer was short and sweet.

"You know what else I don't get? God created man in his own likeness, right?" David asked, and Kyle nodded. "So if God existed before there was light, or anything, and God was alone, why did he need eyes, or ears? Why did God need a bowel, a bladder, and a penis? Seriously, when it rains, is God taking a leak? Not logical. Oh yeah, and if God created man to be his friend, then why was man lonely and then a woman created? And if God had this big plan where he knew everything that would happen, then why did he come up with woman as an afterthought? Obviously he had planned that or he wouldn't have given man the ability to procreate in his anatomy. That weird discontinuity in the bible should at least create doubt in anyone's mind."

"I haven't dwelled on it," Kyle said.

"Or how about Noah and his ark. So God flooded the whole world and Noah built a boat with two of every kind of animal on it. That's two lions, elephants, white rhinos, etc. What about Kangaroos? They only exist in Australia. How'd they get to Noah, and then back to Australia? How about food? How did Noah have food for polar bears and all the meat eaters? They were on that boat forty days. Then they landed and they all got off. So how come they all drifted away and magically found their niche, the place they were so adapted for? It isn't logical."

At this point, we were sucking back the liquid gold pretty hard as David's tone took on a rant. Cassy, Laura and I all sat back and watched with enjoyment as these two squared off

"I don't have all the answers, David. I'm just a man, not God. Maybe you should ask him. Maybe he'll answer you." Kyle smiled, which seemed to irritate David.

"I just don't get this blind faith stuff. If you told me the sky was actually green, and to just believe, I'd be pretty messed up to disbelieve my own eyes."

"Can you see ultraviolet or infrared? You believe they exist, right? Can you see an atom? You believe atoms make up matter though, right? Maybe your eyes are just incapable of giving you the whole story. Maybe you shouldn't just believe what your limited eyes can see." Kyle added.

That was pretty slick, I thought. I did not expect such deep insights from Kyle, and frankly, I had never thought of religion in those ways. Looked like David was caught off guard by that too. He sat thinking for a minute.

"OK, some good points there," David conceded. "I just have a hard time believing people who were incapable of understanding the world as we know it today. What if they knew the world was round back then? Or that the sun was a ball of fire and that fossils existed, and that disease was not based on evil? And then there is the cruelty of this world. Look around. This all loving God designed a world in which animals, and people, hunt down and kill other animals, causing pain and suffering. Viruses and bacteria destroy our insides. So we go through this odd mishmash of pleasure and pain for a brief moment and then retire to either a dismal land of pain or wonderful land of pleasure for eternity, eh? Sounds like a fantasy dreamed up by a society that knows nothing."

David turned to me for help. "Titus, surely you don't believe this stuff, do you?"

"I have my own ideas," I replied.

"Well enlighten us. I'm interested to know," said David.

Chapter 30. My Theory

"I have no evidence to back me up. I just have disconnected thoughts that have popped into my head over time as I try to reassemble the beginnings. I think there is some design," I stated, looking at David. "I believe not in the big bang theory, but in my own collision theory." I emphasized the word collision to distinguish my idea. "What caused the big bang? Why all of a sudden a mass of rock exploded? Where is this mass of rock from?"

"No, I believe there were two huge slabs, or rafts, drifting around in space," I went on. "Let's say it's like continental drift but within space instead of on the Earth's crust. And on these rafts there are advanced beings. And the design for life is there, like bacteria in a petri dish or spores in the air. When the slabs collided, a shattering of rock on the edge blew dust into space. Kind of like a puff of dust that must fly up when a meteor hits the moon. Maybe the slabs moved away again, drifting off in space. But we, the new universe, flew off like a dust cloud. Maybe those slabs are just out of sight. Maybe these slabs are way out there now. Who knows? But the energy of that collision was transferred to the dust cloud. You guys know what it's like when you ping a granite with your hammer; sparks fly."

All sat quietly, intent on hearing the whole story. I continued, "I believe that all energy is constant, equal and tied to life. The energy in a planet is related to the amount of life that can exist, and that life is reincarnated and spread. If a planet crashed into

Earth, the spores of life would be spread and become active when conditions are right. I think the Earth started to show life when it had a stable atmosphere."

"The spores of life started very simple and evolved over time. When one being died, it came back as the same or higher level. When I die, I will come back as another human, or maybe a slightly more superhuman, and this will continue until a new species is created. That's how we went from algae to human. The best algae came back with in an equal or more advanced state, depending on a past life. So I believe it's important to be the best you can be, so you advance the species, and yourself."

"Wow, that's different," Laura perked up. "So, no God?"

"No God, but definitely designers, ones that created a model for adaptive evolution. Maybe we are just an experiment. Maybe we got loose from the lab. Wouldn't it be amazing to see what life was like on those rafts?"

I think I captured everyone's imagination. My theory connected a designer with evolution. It wouldn't convince a religious person to give up their beliefs, but might make them think harder. My theory might make an atheist conceive of a higher power, just not one of good versus evil. Frankly, it was all airy-fairy bullshit. There was absolutely no basis for this 'new religion' of mine. It was complete science fiction, but it sounded good, as good as a big bang.

"That's not bad," David said. "I could believe in that.

"Maybe that is God, and people thousands of years ago couldn't articulate it," said Kyle.

Geez, my new religion already had two converts. Maybe the whisky was just on my side. I noticed David and Kyle had pounded back more than anyone. That's it, whisky shall now be an intricate part of my new religion. "Hey, hit me, Kyle. With the whisky I mean," I joked, holding out my hand to stop a punch.

He poured me a lot. "You aren't drinking enough. Catch up!" he said.

"I think I've had just the right amount. David though, he's sauced. Look at him," I nodded his way. "David stand up." He did, rather tentatively with an awkward smile. He was good and drunk. "David, watch my finger closely." I put my finger in his face, very close. I waved it about slowly and then pretended to smack his nose. He fell back into his chair and then toppled backwards onto a pile of food. Everyone burst out laughing.

"Very funny!" he said. "Look, I didn't spill my drink."

David lay there, holding his glass up. I reached across the table and helped him up.

"David, I think Kyle was praying you'd fall down, am I right Kyle?" I asked.

Kyle was giddy with laughter, barely able to say, "That's the power of prayer."

The one I hadn't been watching was Cassy. She obviously had drank a lot. She could not regain her composure, slipping into hysterical giggles over and over.

"Are you OK, Cassy?" I asked.

When she could speak again, she said, "Yes. I'm OK. So giant rafts and petri dishes, eh?" And then she fell into laughter again.

"Ain't no guff, Duff!" I said.

"Sounds heavenly, Weatherby," she replied.

Chapter 31. Dessert

I have never wanted to kiss anyone more than I wanted to kiss Cassy right now, right here. It was all I could do to hold back. I wonder if my face drew a serious expression, just for a moment, as I looked into her eyes. I didn't even noticed all the laughing at our silly comments. I just saw her and I heard my heart pound. Did I stare too long? Did I just tell her something hidden? I forced myself to look back at the table and down a gulp of... whisky! Oh man, that was whisky, not beer. Wow, that burned. I am a sipper. That was no sip. I nearly choked.
 "Are you OK, Titus?" Cassy asked, as I coughed.
 "Yeah," I squeaked out. "Totally forgot that was straight whisky. Yowza! OK, catching up, gimme a bit more." I asked Kyle. Not sure it was a good idea getting shit-faced, then again, not sure it was a good idea staying sober. Looking around, everyone was drunk, and everyone was having fun. This was a good day, despite the rain.
 "Any dessert?" Laura asked.
 "We got lots of pudding," David replied, looking behind him.
 "Can you throw me one?" Laura asked again.
 "Just bring a bunch up," Cassy suggested. "I'll grab some spoons."
 Quite a dessert, pudding cups and whisky. I chose chocolate. I love vanilla, but hate the vanilla puddings. I was wishing we had ice cream, vanilla ice cream. I can only imagine what it must be like to pick a pod of vanilla off the vanilla orchid and smell it. I recall the

incredible smells and tastes of fresh fruit in Mexico. It was nothing like the fruit at the grocery store in Canada. Bananas are creamy, coconut is aromatic, mangoes are juicy, and papaya is tender. I don't know how people who immigrate to Canada from tropical countries can stand it.

I slipped into a state of thought, probably the result of excess whisky. I remembered Cassy saying she had never been east of North Bay or west of Calgary. I had travelled from St. John's to Victoria and seen the barrens of Nunavut. I swam in the Atlantic Ocean, the Pacific Ocean and the Caribbean Sea. I've picked tropical fruit and seen barracuda while snorkelling. I feel like I have lived a lot in the past and she has not. Maybe she isn't adventurous. I felt an urge to want to share experiences with her. I wanted to see the excitement and joy on her face as she sees all these new things.

I glanced over and saw her sitting there, a silly smile on her face, listening to all the others chatter away. She is sweet. She is innocent. She is beautiful. I haven't met anyone in years that made me feel like this. Dammit, why now? I didn't want this. A three week job and then I leave. Well, a four month job would be just as bad because I wouldn't want to be here that long. I'm ready to make a change. There is no good situation here; I love and leave, or I refrain and regret. I don't know what to do. I'll figure it out. Now was when I wished there was a divine plan that had my life all set out for me.

David and Kyle excused themselves to go out and take a piss. Laura went to her tent to get a sweater.

Cassy and I sat on a short bench we made for the table. I turned and asked her, "When do you have to go back to the office?"

"Not until Monday. I still have a couple more days here. I'll only be out for a day or two and then back in camp. Why, you gonna miss me?" she said, smiling a silly grin.

I looked into her eyes as she spoke. I smiled at her too. "Who am I gonna wash my underwear with, Kyle?" I shuttered a bit. "Whose arse has the sulphide touch? We're a geological detective team, 'Dufferin and the Weatherby'."

For a moment we just sat there. Then I kissed her. Clarification, we kissed. She leaned into me and I leaned into her, and our lips touched in a warm and gentle way. Could it be she was thinking of this all night, just like I was? Or was this a momentary impulse? I didn't know. I just knew I wanted it. It only lasted a few seconds. I touched our noses and foreheads, then backed up and smiled at her. There was a look of both joy and apprehension in her face. We didn't speak of it. David and Kyle burst back in, followed by Laura. All three of them swayed and staggered into their seats.

"You guys are all piss drunk!" I said.

"Uh, look who's talking," Laura shot back. "How is it you don't have to pee?"

"I've been peeing under the table all night. Look..." I pointed at my feet. Laura glanced under the table. Actually everyone did. "HA! Made you look," I teased her.

"Really fucking mature," Laura replied.

David laughed out loud. "Fucking got me too. Geez, we are drunk."

"OK, I'll piss outside if it means that much to you, Laura. I'll aim at your tent," I told her, and jabbed my finger in her neck. She squealed and twisted her shoulders. I left the tent and went about 20 feet away to piss between a couple trees. I was drunk. I never drink whisky, so not used to its effects. But I was having a bit of trouble standing straight and not peeing on myself.

After I was done, I decided to walk down to the water for a moment of contemplation. It was still light, but with a lovely pink in the sky where the set sun found the remnant rain clouds passed off. The air was calm. I wandered out onto the dock and watched life in the aftermath of a rainstorm. The loons were calling each other out in the lake somewhere. Dragonflies buzzed the air, gorging on mosquitoes. We were all emerging from our shelters.

"Titus, what the fuck are you doing out there? Shaking that thing?" David called out.

"Yeah, yeah, I'll be back, you old arse fucker." I yelled to him.

I turned to walk back but must have lost my balance and one foot slipped off the dock. I slid into the lake and caught the boat with my arm. It did not make a big splash, but there I was, half in the bag and half in the lake. I had to go change. Thankfully I had one more pair of dry pants. I hauled myself up on the dock and dripped all the way back to my tent where I changed. It was not unnoticed when I came back to the kitchen.

"What the fuck happened to you?" Laura asked.

"What do you mean?" I answered.

"Um, you were out there a long time..." Laura paused, "and you changed your pants," she said, noticing the difference. How the hell did she notice? I bet she can barely see?

"That's suspicious. Jizz on yourself?" David jumped in.

"If you really must know, I went down to the dock and watched the sunset," I conceded, partially.

"And the pants?" asked David.

"Alright, I fell in." I had to tell them. There was no use in hiding it. "Just part way."

"How the fuck did you fall in?" Kyle asked, laughing at me.

Cassy had her hand over her face and was laughing so hard she couldn't talk.

"Go ahead, have a good laugh. If Kyle hadn't polluted me with this fucking rot-gut I'd have been able to walk a straight line. Who made that shitty dock, anyways?" I asked, flopping down on my seat.

"You did, tight-ass," Laura replied.

Cassy was nearly falling off the bench with laughter.

"I seem to recall you helping me with that, Thora. Must have been a log you put in," I chided her. She just smiled. "Well, I only went in with one leg. So, there's that."

"Then you aren't polluted enough," Kyle said and added more whisky to my cup. That was the last thing I needed now. I had had enough, but seems this party had not run its course quite yet.

"I better go to the washroom before I pee myself laughing," Cassy said, and disappeared out through the flap.

"Holy shit, Kyle, did we drink that much tonight?" I asked, looking at the near empty bottle.

"What do you mean 'we'? You aren't keeping up. Go on and drink some more. The rest of us are doing our part," he said. "And yes, we drank that much."

Kyle's speech was quite slurred and his eyes only half opened. He probably sucked back most of the whisky himself. From behind the tent came a distant voice. "Hey, there's no shitter paper! Laura, can you bring me some?"

"What the hell happened to the toilet paper?" I asked. "I saw a full roll up there last night. I even covered it with a bag." No one seemed to know. Laura dutifully grabbed a roll and took it up to Cassy. We all yelled back, "Use moss!" or something equally stupid.

Ten minutes later, Kyle was nearly passed out. David wasn't in much better shape. We decided to haul Kyle off to bed. We literally dragged him into our tent and tossed him on the bed. I don't know how he was going to get up in the morning. Laura wandered off to bed and David crashed. I took my wet pants to the kitchen to hang them up for the night. Cassy was passed out, slumped over the table.

"Cassy? You going to bed?" I asked, to no answer.

I picked her up in my arms. Her eyes half opened.

"That was quite a night. Let's call that team building," I said.

"It was fun, wasn't it? Not sure anyone's going to be useful tomorrow though," Cassy replied.

"Well, it's just prospecting. I doubt Kyle will do much rock banging. How you holding up? Did you have much?" I asked, knowing full well she had a lot.

"Way too much, that's for sure. Did you really fall in the lake?" she asked.

"I did." I nodded to the pants I hung up. "What was I thinking, walking that narrow dock, hopped up on whisky?"

"I don't know. What were you thinking tonight?" she questioned.

I assume this was one of those esoteric questions, intimating more than the dock event. Not sure how to answer because she might take my answer to mean the kiss. "I suppose my mind and legs were out of synch," I replied.

"Often have these synch errors, do you?" she probed.

"With my legs, apparently. They seem to take me places I don't expect to go. Sometimes they take me to great places, and other times land me in troubled waters." That was cryptic enough, I think. "We better get to bed or we won't be able to get up tomorrow."

"I know, eh? I'll see you in the morning. Coffee will never taste so good," Cassy said, closing her eyes in my arms. I'm not even sure she was aware that I was carrying her. I brought her to her tent. Laura was fast asleep. I dropped Cassy gently in her bed, opened her sleeping bag and pulled the cover over her. I couldn't help but stand there for a minute, staring at her sleep. She was adorable.

DAY SIX - Blueberry Island

Chapter 32. A Note

Day six arrived much too early on Schist Lake. Anything before noon would have been too early for the gang in this camp today. I have no idea what time I got up, but I was the first. The sun was pretty high already, so it wasn't early. I felt rough, to say the least, but no major hangover. I fumbled around getting my clothes on. I bet I was the only one to get undressed for bed last night. I moved slowly and quietly.

Once I stepped outside, the sun whacked me with a wave that made me dizzy. The air was still and hot, and the light blinding. I ducked into the kitchen tent and looked for the coffee. I couldn't find anything. Was I that fucked up? I lit the stove and then went back to digging around for the coffee. What is it with me and coffee, I can never find it and it usually ends up being right in front of me.

I finally found it, on the ground. I suppose all the knocking around we did in our drunken state last night sent it flying. I added the grounds and put the pot on the stove. I sat there, watching the pot like I was in a trance. I waited patiently for the bubbles to fill the small glass knob on the top of the pot. After a minute or two the smell started to fill the air and I began to wake up.

I made my lunch while I waited for the coffee to brew. A lot of people do not see the appeal of a banana sandwich, but I do. This time, I not only added banana, but a few scoops of peanut butter as well. That'll be good protein, though the smell is pretty offsetting at the moment. I tossed a few goodies into my lunch bag and a couple pop waters. Seems no one else is eager to get up. I filled a cup with coffee and blew the steam away. I couldn't drink it yet, it was way too hot and I can't seem to handle that. The only way I was going to shake this harsh and drowsy feeling was to get going. Fresh air can do wonders. Anyway, if I stick around I run the risk that cheery David will get up and want to chat. I don't think I could handle that this morning.

I pulled out the map and checked a place to go. Looks like I could go do an easy line on the east side, not far from shore. I grabbed a pencil and paper and left a note where I was going.

Dear Fuckups,
If you are reading this letter, then you've probably rubbed the shit out of your eyes and had a coffee already. Is it still morning? I doubt it. I, by this time, have traveled across the lake to grid three, east side, taking line 400S. There, you will find me mapping, sampling and shitting out whatever that rot gut was Kyle served us last night. You may even find a few chunks of spaghetti and my liver. Enjoy your hangover, bum fuckers!

Down at the lake I pulled one of the boats closer and tossed my stuff in. My coffee cup had a lid so I took it with me. A last look up at camp revealed no discernable life. All was quiet and still. They'd have coffee whenever they got up. The pot was still nearly full.

I untied the boat and shoved off from the dock. There is a little process you have to go through when you start up the engine. Firstly, you make sure there's gas. Who wants to get stranded out in the lake somewhere? Not me. Then you squeeze the primer a dozen times. Check the motor's in neutral, open the choke, and finally crank that rope. As small motors go, these are pretty good. They are quieter than many older ones I've used. One pull and the motor rumbled to life. I closed the choke and placed the handle to reverse, and slowly backed out. A quick twist to forward and I was off, swivelling around and pointing northeast away from camp.

There were sparkling ripples on the water and a slight breeze in my face as I tapped along the surface at medium speed. Not in any rush to get anywhere, I headed toward the end of the big point that juts down into the lake. There was an island beside it, but at this point the island really just looked like part of the mainland. As I got closer, I could tell there was a space separating the point and the island. I thought I'd check it out for fishing, see if it looked any good.

I neared the small inlet between the land and island and then rounded the point. Only about fifty feet of water separated the two. It was dark in here as the land on both sides rolled up into high hills. On the right was a small bay with a beach, completely hidden from all sides except right here in this tiny narrows. I slowly drove through, watching for rocks. When I emerged on the other end of the island, the lake opened up again and the waves pummelled the bow. As I accelerated, the boat bumped along, one wave at a time.

I had to backtrack a little, rounding the island and heading south east across the lake. Didn't take long to get to the shore. The landing was a bit tricky as the waves pushed the water down the long lake. The shore was rocky and scattered with bushes. I found a reasonable place to pull in and tie the boat. The train tracks were about fifty feet in front of me. I climbed the gravelly side and crossed the tracks. My grid was just ahead, in the bush, so I walked into the forest looking for a picket. It took about twenty minutes of wandering before I saw a cut line and then found a picket. I was in the right place, just not at the start of the line.

Chapter 33. West Grid

Cassy sat at the kitchen table. She smiled as she read the note Titus left. The coffee was still hot and steam rolled off her cup as she poured it. Cassy was trying to piece together in her mind what happened last night. She remembered things, but did she remember them correctly? Did she really kiss Titus, on the lips? Did he really carry her in his arms and put her to bed? She tried to recall any man treating her with such affection and respect before, but couldn't. Titus was on her mind, always. She adored him, and she knew how he felt about her. Dealing with that in a bush camp is a tricky thing, though. It's tricky enough for two grunts, but far more difficult for a manager and a grunt, especially when that grunt is older and more experienced. So many variables make this awkward, yet there was no denying this was real.

The tent flap opened and Laura came in. "You made it up. You're officially number three," Cassy said.

"Are you number one?" Laura asked, assuming the boss would be anxious to work.

"Nope. I'm number two. Titus the titan was up and is gone already. Here, he left this note," she handed the paper to Laura. A smile came across her face. Titus is a charming man. He can even dazzle with a short, offensive note, because it's always in good humour. "Have some coffee," Cassy suggested.

Laura poured a cup and sat down. "So what are you going to do today?" she said.

"I'm going to map a line west of here. I'll pick a close by one and make it an easy day. I have a feeling the boys are going to fuck the dog, so won't wait for them to get up. You want to come with me?" Cassy asked.

"Yeah, sure. Let me pack a lunch. What time is it, do you know?" Laura asked.

"It's about ten. I doubt we'll be too productive, no matter where we are. So might as well hang out together." Cassy added. "Some project lead I am, eh?" she said with a smirk.

"Last night was inevitable. We needed to drop our guard and have a laugh. We know each other better now. That'll make us a better team. I can't believe some of the things I learned about people last night!" Laura said.

"Yeah, me too," Cassy mumbled, not stating any detail.

The ladies packed a lunch. Laura added a few lines under Titus' note.

Boys,
Laura and Cassy are heading to the west grid, line 600N.
Hope you boys enjoy fucking the dog all day while us ladies are out doing the work!
Smooches xxoo

"That oughtta do it," Laura said and placed the paper on the open map. They gathered their packs and walked off into the bush behind camp.

Chapter 34. My Justice

I had walked along this cut line taking note of the rocks as I went. My will was not in geology this morning. I had no desire to explore. I quickly paced through the line, stopping briefly here and there until I reached the other end. The line terminated on the East Arm. It was rocky and I could tell there was a drop-off to the water, but hadn't gone all the way to the edge. I found a peaceful, soft spot under a magnificent pine tree. It was hot and the shade felt good. I checked my watch; two o'clock. I hadn't stopped for lunch. I just had no appetite until now. I pulled out my sandwich and slowly chewed it, glad to have some food in my gut but not appreciating the taste too much. My stomach was still a little tender.

I work hard, most days. Occasionally I trudge my way out through the bush in the morning and find a sweet outcrop under the warm sun where I can lay upon the lichen and sleep. I call it social fairness. I sacrifice everything for a paltry wage and dismal living conditions. There must be some professional justice I can exact, and this is all I have.

I was in a camp once that got socked in by fog and rain for eleven days past our usual food drop. That was eleven days we subsisted on berries, fish, and frankum. What compensation did we receive for such hardship? Didly fuckin' squat. That's just part of the job. You're expected to be tough, not like these namby pamby school teachers that threaten to walk off the job every other year because of class size or their obscenely generous benefits.

It would seem that as I age, my bitterness toward this profession grows. I have explored the forests from Deer Lake to Dawson. I have tasted glaciers, rivers and lakes from North Bay to Nunavut. I have encountered muskox, moose, and marten from Timmins to Tuktoyaktuk. There isn't a rock type I haven't touched, tasted and tapped. So why am I still here, in another mining town, on another contract job out in the bush? What else am I going to do? That has been the burning question and rhetorical answer for some time now. It hasn't changed. I suppose at some point it will change, when I have a better answer, or more courage. I feel I'm on the cusp.

I may spend my day of justice lying in one place for hours, humming a song, listening to birds, snacking, snoozing and day-dreaming. There is a lot you can learn from lying still on the forest floor. Evolution has weaved the fabric of life into a blanket of many colours. This tiny microcosm of our planet is a momentary snapshot of a time and place on Earth. Geologically speaking, this moment is brief and unique.

In case you wanted to know, I stand about five feet eleven, though I prefer to tell people I'm an inch below six feet. All they hear is the six feet. I suppose it's like an advertised price of $5.99; people hear the five and don't consider the extra ninety-nine cents. I have medium short, unkempt hair. It was cut for me in the last camp by the cook. I wear brown work pants and a brown work shirt, or T-shirt on these hot days. Occasionally I top my head with a dull green work cap. I am very fit.

I pushed my pack behind my back and rested my head against it, gazing up through the tall pine and balsam at the the rich blue sky. Puffy white clouds drifted by, strands breaking away and evaporating into thin air. It's easy to imagine this place as the pinnacle of serenity, but that would not be quite true. The lions do not lay down with the lambs. Mosquitoes and deer flies would gladly cut my skin to taste my blood. Red ants and wasps would not hesitate to sting me. Even many adorable and cuddly looking animals possess claws and teeth that would shred the skin. Only a few animals out here would treat me with apparent kindness, like the toad who sits in my hand peacefully, or the dragonfly who lands on my shoulder for a rest.

It usually takes a couple of weeks of living in the bush to become tough enough that minor irritations don't bother you anymore, and then you can really appreciate where you are. My hands are like tough leather from constantly handling rocks. My legs and stomach are tight from walking the rugged land, bending and lifting. My arms are strong from wielding a hammer and axe. I am in peak physical shape and health.

All true, yet we are always just a slip away from injury. This is a dangerous job. We face burns, breaks, cuts, drowning, illness, animals, and much more without any help. This particular job is better than most. Often times a camp is built far away from roads where no communications exist. If there was an accident, there'd be no way to get help. Yet, somehow most of us survive. Why is that? It's not from caution.

There is no time to pussy-foot around. With experience comes an ability to read the bush, walk adeptly, adapt to surroundings and handle tools with skill. I'm sure this is true of all occupations; experience crafts ability.

My blank mind, watching the clouds drift by, turned to thoughts of Cassy. I was taken away to another place and time, a world far from the bush. I pictured her face and imagined kissing those lips again. I still can't believe we kissed last night. I wonder if she remembers it. Yes, I'm sure she does. She kissed me as much as I kissed her. One thing's for certain, she likes me, and she's comfortable with me.

Chapter 35. Caribbean Swim

I decided to get up and go to the shore and see what the lake was like. This was the East Arm, the place everyone raves about. I stopped at the rock and looked down. It was the most beautiful shade of turquoise, just like I remembered the Caribbean. The rocks were jagged, but one rock was flat on top right down by the edge. The water looked pretty deep, I'd say six to ten feet off that rock and crystal clear. It was hot out. I really wished I had brought my soap. I could have cleaned myself up. Maybe later. But for now, I wanted to take a swim.

I peeled off my sweaty T-shirt, undid my pants and dragged them down to my ankles. I slipped my boots off, then my pants. I carefully placed all my clothes on a high rock and stopped to look around. I was completely naked, standing up high on the shore, gazing out to see if there was anyone. I was all alone. I climbed down to the flat rock and without much thought took a big jump into the lake. I sank down but never touched bottom. It was deep, despite the clarity. I swam out about fifty feet, enjoying the cool water on my skin. I dowsed my head a few times and stroked my hair back. A few minutes later, I emerged from the lake and stood on the rocks, dripping with water and letting the sun warm me.

This was one of the greatest benefits of exploration. I could indulge in this kind of freedom without worry. The caveats however are numerous. I was alone. Summer is short. Some days the bugs would devour you. All in all, today I would nourish this pleasure and enjoy the titillation of my natural state. I am not a puritan. I am not embarrassed. I know I am attractive and I feel pleasure being naked. Of course, there's no pleasure when it's unappreciated or scorned.

I shook the worst of the water off me, dressed and then headed back to the boat. I was feeling fine now, refreshed, though still not clean. I walked fast through the forest until I reached the boat. I took another tour on the way back, stopping once again to see that small island. This time, I landed on the beach to have a look. It was great. The sand was nicely packed and clean. This would be a great place to have a real bath. It was close to camp, calm water, a solid beach that went back about thirty feet, and it was completely private. I looked around and then checked just inside the woods. The hill started almost immediately and rose up with rounded granite outcrops filled with blueberries. I picked a few and ate them.

I will come back tonight and get a real bath. Now, I've been on jobs where I took no bath or shower for months, but that's because it was cold outside, or we camped on a shitty lake. But when I get an opportunity like this, why not clean up. OK, perhaps the real reason is because I don't want to smell bad around Cassy. Let's be honest.

I untied the boat and headed back to camp. I was getting hungry, despite having my lunch not that long ago. And I wanted to take a dump, preferably in the shitter where I could sit down and relax instead of squatting out here. I'm becoming a man of leisure, it would seem.

I pulled the boat up to the dock and tied it off. The other boat was still there. Maybe no one got up today. I walked up to the tents and dropped my gear off, then went into the kitchen. "Well well well," I said. "You're all alive."

"If it isn't the keener," Laura replied. "How was your day?"

Not bad. I discovered an emerald today," I announced.

"Emerald?" Cassy questioned. "What are you talking about?"

"The East arm. That lake is like an emerald. We should have camped there," I replied. "So, get my note?"

"Uh-huh, very funny. I added a part for the boys here," Laura said, picking up the paper and handing it to me.

Kyle chimed in, "and we appended a note at the bottom of that."

I read what the girls wrote. Below it, Kyle had scribbled, 'Go fuck yourselves!'

"Ah, such beautiful prose," I noted. "So, what did you all do today?"

"The boys got up late, I mean later than us, and met us out on the west grid. Laura and I took a line and Kyle and David took a line. We all felt like shit the whole day. That's it," Cassy reported.

"Don't worry, I felt like shit too," I said. I just needed to get out in the fresh air, that's all. So, what's for dinner, or have you all been sitting around the table here feeling sorry for your weak stomachs?"

"We've got that covered. Kyle was going to start the barbeque as soon as you got home and we plan on making ribs. RIBS! All smothered in barbeque sauce," Laura answered.

I could see David's face pale at the mention of ribs and sauce. I can only assume he has the weakest stomach in camp. "Great! I love ribs. I'm hungry, let's get the show on the road, eh?" And with that the wheels were in motion. In no time this hive of activity began preparing a great meal. The last of the corn was used. The ribs smelled like a smokehouse in heaven, and not surprisingly everyone wanted pop, not beer. After dinner, we all cleaned up the dishes. David and Kyle retired to their beds for a nap. Laura had a book and stayed in the kitchen to read.

Chapter 36. Bath Time

I went to my tent and grabbed a bag, a towel, a bar of soap, my toothbrush and paste. I grabbed a pail in front of the kitchen and then I went down to the beach to collect my freshly dried laundry off the line. I stuffed that into the bag. Cassy came down to see what I was up to.

"I'm going to take the boat out and take a bath." I told her. Not sure she knew what I was referring to.

"Oh, can I come?" she asked.

"Sure. Get your stuff," I replied. Maybe she thought I was just going for a swim, or just dip my head in the lake. We'll see how this plays out.

She came running down to the dock wearing sandals, a bikini and holding a bag. We jumped in the boat. "I found a great beach just over there on that island. Let's go there." I said, and she nodded.

I drove the boat across the bay and entered the small narrows, slipping the bow up onto the hidden beach. Cassy was up front and she jumped out to tie up the boat. I waddled up to the bow and then stepped out, pulling the boat up the beach a little higher. Cassy was walking along the beach, toes barely touching the water, screwing up her courage to swim.

I filled my pail with water and then walked way up the beach to the trees. I waited a moment and watched as Cassy finally walked out into the narrows and swam. This was a bit of a risk, though I did tell her what I was going to do. I thought it was assumed I was taking a bath. If Cassy was mature, there'd be no issue. Otherwise, she might react badly. Would she get upset, scared, or act silly? My gut feeling was that she's not childish, and everything will be fine.

I removed my shirt and boots. Then I turned toward the trees and slid my pants down and off. I can't lie, I enjoyed this. I took the water and splashed it on me, saving most in the bucket. Then I rubbed the soap on me, lathering everywhere, front and back. I was covered in suds. I took the pail and drained it over my soapy head. Yeesh, that was cold! Now I had to go to the shore and get more water. I held the pale in front of me, turned and saw Cassy watching me. She looked away as I walked down to the lake. I knelt down, filled my pail and dowsed myself twice more. Then I ran into the lake and swam over to her.

"I left the soap up there in the pail if you want it," I told her.

"OK, I'll use it," she said and swam to shore. I swam closer to shore and sat on the sandy bottom. I'm not a good enough swimmer to stay out there that long. I could see from my peripheral vision that she soaped herself up, even under the bathing suit. She was as thorough as I was. After a quick rinse she jumped back in and swam around, freeing any remaining soap on her. Then she came closer and sat on the sandy bottom near me.

"See any soap left on me?" she asked.

"Nope, you look clean. Hows abouts me?" I asked her.

"No suds," she said.

"Good. Now think how great it will feel to slip our clean bodies into those dirty fart sacks tonight. I'd kill for a nice bed with clean sheets and a pillow, a plump feather pillow." I said. "I don't even need a mint on it, like the fancy hotels do. Though that's not a bad policy, even at home. Imagine that, a mint on your pillow every night when you go to bed."

Cassy giggled. Her perky little smile lit up her face. "If I had a mint, I'd put it on your pillow tonight," she said.

"That's a lovely thought, but I don't even have a pillow," I said, sadly.

"Awww...," Cassy teased and splashed water at me.

"Oh oh, that was dangerous. You want a water fight?" I teased back.

"No, no, no," she replied and jumped up. Then, out of the blue kicked water at me.

I jumped up and chased her. I grabbed her and picked her up in my arms. I carried her a few steps out and tossed her into the water. It was still pretty shallow and she floated for a moment, laughing. I stood there in the waist deep water, pointing my finger at her. I took several steps back toward shore, then turned to watch her swim.

I was no doubt partially engorged from being with her. The swollen member lay there like a log. I looked down and realized just how large, and exposed I was, floating near the surface of the water. I wanted to turn and walk up the beach, but I loved this game. So I stood longer. Cassy waved at me and I waved back.

"You had enough?" she yelled.

I nodded. "I'm just going to do my teeth, shave and get dressed."

"OK, I'll come in," she yelled back.

I went up to the trees and pulled my razor, toothbrush and paste out from the bag and went back down to the water's edge, this time without a bucket to hide me. Cassy wasn't showing any disturbance with my nudity, so I was in no rush to get dressed.

I bent down on one knee and began brushing my teeth at the water's edge. Cassy came out of the lake and went over to the boat. She had left her clothes in a bag inside the boat. I looked over now and then. I saw her take her bikini top off. I saw her breasts. They were gorgeous. She gave herself a quick towel dry and then slipped a loose yellow tank top over her head, which draped down to cover her from top to her bottom. Then she slid her bikini bottoms off. I wonder if she knew I was looking at her. I couldn't see anything because the tank top covered her, but then she bent over the boat to reach something and the tank top rose above her waist. I had a full view of her beautiful bottom. Again, it was stunning; round and creamy.

There was no way I could stop my erection from growing. Thank God I was crouched so she couldn't see. I had to look out over the water and imagine elephants and crocodiles. I thought of mean, vicious, ugly animals chasing me. That allowed the erection to subside and all I was left with was an engorged limb hanging below me like a big Bratwurst sausage.

I stood up, turned, proud of the size my member displayed, and walked up the beach to my clothes where I promptly changed. I was clean and my clothes were clean. My mind on the other hand was absolutely filthy with thoughts of Cassy.

I bagged up my dirty clothes and walked over to the boat. "I haven't felt this clean in days. Thanks for coming with me. I had fun," I told her.

"Should we head back?" Cassy asked.

"No, it's still early. Let's do a little exploring. Come on," I suggested.

Chapter 37. Embrace

I led her up the beach to a hill and we began to climb. We ate blueberries along the way. We could have spent hours in one spot eating blueberries, there were so many. We continued to climb until we reached the island summit, a round, bald hill. At the top we had a great view of the lake and even our bay, though the camp was nestled too far in.

Cassy sat down on the soft moss atop the rounded rocks. She twisted her head back and forth.

"You OK?" I asked. "Sore neck?"

"Yeah. I guess hauling those rocks out yesterday put a strain on me," she replied.

I sat down behind her and splayed my legs out beside hers. "Here, I'll give you a massage," I said. I put my hands on her neck, one on each side and began massaging the muscles. "Let me know if it's too rough or too weak."

We were silent for a moment, then I asked her, "Cassy, do you like your job?"

"Yeah, I guess so. Why?"

"I just wondered. You like living out in the bush, crashing on office chesterfields, breaking rocks?" I asked.

"Well, I don't hate it. I like the outdoors, and I like rocks. Maybe the job isn't the best, but I've never had any other job. What about you? You must like it, you've been doing it a long time."

"There are things I like and things I don't like. I just find it harder every year. I get the feeling I'm missing out on so much," I said.

"What do you want, then?" Cassy asked.

"I want a home, you know, a house somewhere. I want a car and furniture and a dog, a black lab named Dolly or Heck." I moved up closer behind Cassy and wrapped my arms around her stomach and rested my chin on her shoulder. "I always imagined I'd have a nice home with a grass yard and I'd have weekends off to go biking or play softball. I'm tired of moving from one place to another. Seems like it's never going to end." I pushed my lips into her neck, not so much a kiss, just a touch. "Tell me, what do you want? Where would you like to be, if you could be anywhere?"

Cassy was slow to start. Perhaps she was in a state of shock, or just flustered. "I don't know. I never expected to have much, so never thought about it. I assumed I'd end up in a small house in a small town, like Flin Flon."

I kissed her neck. I kissed her cheek and put my cheek to hers. I raised my hands up her arms to her shoulders and for a moment played with the straps on her tank top. "My dream is to go out west, to Vancouver Island. The weather is nice. The mountains are beautiful. The houses are pretty and they sit in cute, neat neighborhoods in small towns. I want my family there. I want my kids to grow up in a place like that," I continued.

I pushed the straps of her tank top over her shoulders and they fell down over her arms. I waited a moment and then took the straps in my fingers and drew them down further along her arms. Her loose tank top drooped down over her breasts and fell. I gently reached up with my hands and cupped her breasts, slowly caressing the soft undersides. I kissed her shoulder and neck and then her ear. She gasped and trembled. I raised my hands to feel her small nipples. I touched them between my fingers and thumbs, feeling every small bump and groove, teasing each nipple as they grew firm and long. I rested my lips on her shoulder, tasting the soft skin, and then gently caressed her breasts. I peered down over her shoulder. It brought me great pleasure to see her beautiful breasts.

"You're very good at this," she said, quietly.

"At what?" I asked.

"At seducing me," she replied.

I stopped caressing her, though continued to hold her breasts, and said, "Cassy, I'm not seducing you. I'm loving you."

Cassy turned her face toward mine. I brought a hand to her cheek and kissed her lips, passionately. We stayed locked together this way for minutes. I tasted her lips and probed with my tongue to feel every soft, wet curve of her lovely mouth. Then she lay back against me and I held her in a tight embrace.

In the distance I heard the train whistle blow. I lifted Cassy's straps back up to cover her breasts and we stood up to watch the train slowly wind its way along the shore of the Northwest Arm. I put my arm around Cassy as the train disappeared into the forest. In the other direction, the sky slashed the tops of the trees with orange strokes.

"We have to give this place a name. It's special," I said. "This is where we had our first kiss."

"Uh, no it isn't. We kissed last night, in the kitchen," Cassy said.

"Ah, so you remember that," I smirked. I wrapped my arms around her and kissed her on the forehead. "That was the best first kiss I've ever had."

"Really? It only lasted a couple seconds," Cassy remarked.

"Not for me. I remembered it all night." I looked at her as I held her in my arms atop this rocky mound.

"Maybe we should go back. I'm sure everyone will wonder where we are," Cassy suggested.

"Yeah, it's going to be dark soon anyway," I agreed.

We walked back down over the bulky outcrops into the trees and out onto the beach. I had to gather up my clothes and other things and take them to the boat. We cruised back along the lake through the small orange ripples that stretched toward camp. As we came to the dock, we could hear Kyle playing the banjo from somewhere in a tent. I spent a few minutes dumping my dirty clothes in the pail with some water and soap before leaving the shore.

Chapter 38. A Mystery

"Hey!" I belted out, bursting into my tent where the music was coming from.

"Where the fuck were you?" David asked.

"Cassy and I went out to take a dip and explore Blueberry Island." I don't know where that came from. It just popped out. Made sense though. The island is covered in blueberries.

"What did you find?" asked Laura.

"Blueberries. What did you think we'd find, a secret civilization of advanced apes?" I joked with her, sarcastically.

I picked up my guitar and started strumming along with Kyle, hoping that would block any further discussion. It didn't. I excused myself. "Gotta take a shit. Back in a bit," I said, and left the tent. I walked up to the outhouse and comfortably nestled my bum on the log seat. This was my place of contemplation. I suppose when you are able to relax enough to move the bowels, you are relaxed enough to free the mind.

I drifted away in thoughts to a highway, long and straight, plowing through the wheat fields of Saskatchewan toward a glowing sunset. The car type didn't matter. The features not important. It was my car, with a seat that conformed to my ass from many hours of travel. Where was I going on this journey? Who cares? It was west, and it was far. It would take me days and nights, and end when the salty sea tickled my toes. A quiet plop eased some tension and I smiled like Mona Lisa at the triumph. I reached for the... aww, not again! No paper on the makeshift hanger. I looked around to see if it fell.

"Hey, there's no shitter paper! A little help please!" I yelled down to the tents. A moment later David brought me a new roll. "Thanks," I said, feeling a bit foolish, yet again.

I walked down to the lake to wash my hands and then back to my tent. "Guys, whoever finishes the paper, can you please replace the roll?"

Everyone looked at each other, puzzled. No one admitted to using up the toilet paper.

"Well if no one's using it, where the Hell's it going?" I asked. No one knew. It was a mystery. My father would have said, 'well it didn't just get up and walk away'. I'll avoid being like that. "OK, I'm going to put it in a bag and nail it to the wall."

I sat down on my bed. "I was surprised you were all up when we got back. You know, when we left, David and Kyle were passed out and Laura was slumped in a seat, reading. I figured you'd all be asleep when we came home."

"Just needed a catnap," David said. "I feel fine now. Got another bottle Kyle? I'm ready to drink again."

Kyle smirked. "I think there's a drop left in the old bottle, if you want to suck it dry."

Cassy sat on the end of David's bed digging at something in her foot. I asked her, "What's going on over there, Cass? Digging for treasure?"

"Ha ha, I've got a sliver. I can't seem to get it out," she replied.

"Hang on, I've got a needle," I said, rummaging through my little sewing kit. I pulled the needle out, grabbed a flashlight and walked over to her. "Here, shine this flashlight on it." She did without a fight. I started picking at the skin, opening the area up so I could reach the sliver. When I was able, I pulled at it with the pin until it was sticking out and then plucked it with my fingers. I held it up for her to see. It was not insignificant.

"Ain't you tough, Duff." I said.

"You know me, Weatherby," she shot back, smiling.

"Better get a band aid on that," I suggested.

"I'll get one," said Laura and she went to the kitchen.

I went back to my bed, picked up my guitar and began playing again. "Jump in, Kyle. How 'bout a bit of Neil Young. Old Man?" I suggested.

No reply needed. Kyle took up the tune right where I was, then picked away on his strings to add a melody. Everyone sat back and enjoyed. We played for a while till the night was dark. Everyone turned in and fell asleep quickly.

About an hour later there was a large bang out behind camp. Everyone sat up. "You hear that?" I whispered to the other guys.

"Yeah," Said Kyle. "What was it?"

"I don't know," I answered. I grabbed a flashlight I kept under my bed and brought it up. "I'll go check."

"Wait for me," David replied.

We all got up and slipped on our boots. We left the tent, tentatively, so to speak, and looked behind camp where the noise came from. Three flashlights scoured the forest. "Look," I said, "a bear, in that tree." There was a small bear clinging to a tree just beside the barbeque. I guess he was getting a taste of the grill and dropped the lid down, which made a thunderous bang.

"What's going on?" Cassy asked. I turned and both Cassy and Laura were standing behind us with their flashlights beaming at us.

"A bear, up in the tree over there," I pointed to a jack pine with my flashlight and the reflective eyes shone back at me. "He was checking out the barbeque," I answered.

We three boys started yelling at the bear and throwing sticks or stones. "Hey! Haw! Get outta there. Go on!" The bear shot down out of the tree and ran back into the darkness of the forest. I can only imagine what the ladies were thinking. Three grown men in their underwear yelling like imbeciles at the forest. I'm sure if a spy satellite was drifting by right now, there would be some very amused secret service agents scratching their heads over this one.

As bear encounters go, this was rather mild and uneventful. It looked like a young bear, probably far more scared of us than we were of him. We all adjourned to bed once more in hopes the bear had tasted enough and wouldn't come back.

DAY SEVEN - The Rock Ledge

Chapter 39. Laundry

Day seven came with a return to normal life. It was a bright morning and we were all rested. I still smelled good from my evening scrub. I was excited to see what today would bring. My clothes went on quickly and I was out of the tent in a flash. Laura and Cassy were already in the kitchen brewing coffee and making their lunches.

"Hello ladies, that coffee smells fucking awesome! Who's responsible for that?" I asked.

"We both did it," said Laura.

"Then you are both fucking awesome!" I replied.

"What happy bug flew up your ass this morning?" Laura asked, smiling.

"It was a deer fly, as in 'dear Titus, you is one fly boy!'" I quipped.

Laura and Cassy looked at each other, puzzled. Cassy asked Laura, "What the hell was that?"

"Don't ask me. I don't understand half of what he, or any of the boys are talking about," Laura replied.

I rummaged through the food to make my lunch. I wanted two sandwiches, a chocolate bar, a pudding, two pops and a few cookies. I filled my cup with coffee and snorted a whiff of steam to get the smell inside me. "What am I doing today?"

"What do you want to do?" Cassy asked.

"Go back to bed, obviously," I joked. A look of indignation was cast my way. "Alright," I started to talk, and looked at the map on the table. "I want to go back to the same place as yesterday, the grid by my emerald lake." I pointed to a line. "I can take this and the next line. You want to take the next two lines?" I said to Cassy, hoping she'd be near me.

"Yeah, that would be fine," Cassy answered. "You want to go to the south east, Laura?" Cassy pointed to the next grid down, about one kilometre south. "We can send David and Kyle there as well. You three can fill in those lines, so we're all in the same belt."

"OK," replied Laura.

"I'll get ready. You and I can take one boat and Laura can take the guys in the other boat. Sound OK?" I asked. They all nodded in agreement.

I took my lunch over to my tent and got my pack ready. Then I went down to the beach, brushed my teeth, rinsed out my laundry and hung the wet clothes on the line. By the time I was done, Cassy had come down to the dock. We pushed off and headed across the lake to the east grid. This was a familiar ride for me, though I avoided the detour past our private beach on Blueberry Island.

I tied up the boat and we crossed the tracks. I knew where my last line was and led us along the side of the tracks to our middle lines. "OK, the two middle lines are here and just down there." I pointed along the tracks northward. "So we have to do these two lines and the next two. You want to take this one, I'll take the next and we can meet at the end for lunch, then backtrack on the outer two lines, that one," I pointed back south, "and my outside line down there. What do you think?"

"Yeah, that's good," Cassy replied.

"There's good outcrop in here, so should take the whole morning to finish a line. We'll have a good appetite by noon. I'll see you on the other shore," I said. I started to walk away, then turned and called back, "Don't get lost, eh?"

Cassy grinned and waved. She disappeared into the woods and I walked on down the tracks.

Chapter 40. Paddle

"Would you guys hurry up?" Laura yelled up at the tents. She stood by the boat down on the dock. David and Kyle walked down to the boat with their packs in hand. "What took you so long?"

David looked at Laura and said, "I had to comb my hair." Clearly a joke, by the look of his messy hair. Laura frowned and they all got in the boat. They sped off across the lake, but before they got too far, the motor sputtered and died.

"What happened," Kyle asked David, who was driving the boat.

"I don't know." David squeezed the primer bulb and then ripped the cord. Over and over he tried, but no rumble.

"Check the gas," Laura suggested.

David opened the top and looked in. He lifted the tank and shook it. "Dry," he reported.

"Shit!" said Laura. "What a waste of time. Why didn't you check the tank?"

"You were in such a rush to get going, I didn't think about it," David replied.

"Grab a paddle," she said, to no one in particular. Kyle picked up a paddle and Laura took a paddle and they started making their way back to camp. It was a tough slog against the breeze. David sat there feeling bad that he didn't check the gas before leaving, but grateful that Laura calmed down so quickly. Laura has a short fuse in the morning. A few minutes later, Kyle announced, "I gotta pee."

"Seriously?" said Laura. You can't wait till we land?" Her level of aggravation was rising.

"No. You kept yelling at us to hurry up. I thought I'd go when we landed across the lake," said Kyle.

Laura sighed. David took the paddle from Kyle and Kyle headed to the front of the boat.

"What are you doing?" Laura asked, impatiently.

"I'm taking a piss!" Kyle replied.

"Well go to the back. I don't want to watch you piss into the wind off the front." Laura said, shaking her head.

Kyle looked at David who just shrugged. Kyle made his way to the back, unzipped his pants to begin a stream out into the lake. Laura filled her lungs with air and yelled, "FUCK! Sorry, just blowin' off some steam. David, Paddle!" Poor Kyle was so shocked he nearly fell over the side. Again, they inched their way toward camp.

"Go on Kyle, you can piss if you want," Laura said.

Kyle sat for a few moments, no doubt easing his bladder before resuming his stance at the back of the boat.

Chapter 41. The Rescue

I had barely walked twenty steps along my line when I found an outcrop. This is going to be a long day. I tapped at the rocks to get a clean face and see what it was. A mafic volcanic with stringers of quartz. I pulled out the compass and took several readings of strike and dip, made some notes about the rock type and then drew a few pictures of the folding and veins. It was a pretty ordinary rock, but definitely the correct host for mineralization. I sat down, licked a fresh rock sample and examined a bit of the veining with my magnifying glass. I heard what sounded like a loud scream.

What the hell was that? I put the rock down and walked back along the line to the tracks. With my hand over my eyes, I looked out onto the lake. I could see a boat out there. It wasn't moving, as far as I could tell. Maybe someone's in trouble. I waited a minute, but the boat stayed put. So I walked down the tracks to where I left my boat and jumped in.

A few minutes later I was bubbling through the water to find out what was going on. Looked like someone was standing at the back. What the fuck was he doing? As I got closer, it became apparent two people were paddling and a third was pissing off the back. I slowed down, so not to make waves, and gave Kyle a chance to finish draining the hose. David was waving both arms like he was lost at sea.

I pulled up beside the boat. "What's going on?" I asked. "Engine trouble?"

"No gas," David answered, sheepishly.

"OK, I'll tow you in," I told them. "Now I've got a name for you," I said to David, "Wavy Davey." David smiled.

I pulled my boat ahead by hand, snatched their rope and tied it off to my stern. Then I engaged the motor and slowly hauled them to the dock. I let them drift to one side of the dock and I went on the other side. "I'll wait to make sure you get going again."

Laura jumped out and went up the shore to get gas. David picked the gas tank up and placed it on the log dock. They filled it up, completely draining the jerry can and then Laura tossed the empty plastic can up on shore with the might of Thor.

"Shall we try this again?" said David, smiling. Laura didn't smile, she just shook her head a little. David squeezed the primer and then pulled the motor to life. It was a solid rumble. We all backed out and headed off in our assigned directions. I couldn't help feel sorry for David, but also wonder what other predicament that trio would get into.

I landed again, same place, and tread that familiar ground to my outcrop. I lost a lot of time. I'd have to hustle down this line. I picked up my gear that I'd left behind and plodded off to the next occurrence. There were several outcrops along the line, but they were all the same. I saw no sign of shearing or gossan, so made some simple notes and kept going. I made decent time. When I reached halfway, I stopped for a quick bite. Out came sandwich number one, mortadella, tomato and mayo. I rested against a big rock that was flat enough to be comfortable.

The forest here was thick which kept the temperature moderate. There is a time for sun and a time for shade. The thick bush cuts the breeze, though and that helps the bugs find you. I swatted at a few mosquitoes and deer flies as I ate. Cassy was going back to town tomorrow. I wished I could go with her. I'd kill to sit in a restaurant and eat Italian. I thought back to that first day, when Cassy and I climbed the hill and sat by the water tower. Didn't think much of the town then. I'd love to see all those lights now. Maybe I wasn't being reasonable with myself. Would I be happy anywhere, with anything? Or was I just a complainer? If I was at a diner, would I wish I could be at a bistro? If I was in a Ford, would I wish it was a Lexus? Maybe the more I have the less content I am. Hard to tell. I have been without anything, nice or otherwise, for so long.

A Canada Jay hopped from limb to limb in front of me. He kept his distance, but seemed to want to let me know he was there. It's not unusual for Jays to get fed by loggers and miners out in the bush. These birds have a tendency to become accustomed to humans. I tossed a few bread crumbs on the ground in front of me. He saw and moved closer, careful to retreat if I moved. He dashed to the ground and grabbed the bit of crust, and hopped back up into the tree. I have fed these birds by hand in some camps.

I checked my time. It was getting late. I packed up and continued down the line. The rest of the way had ample outcrop and fewer trees. The sun beat down on me as I sampled the rocks and hiked over boulders and deadfall. I had to hustle as I was late.

When I got to the end of my line, Cassy was sitting on the ground waiting for me. "What took you so long? I was done half an hour ago."

"You wouldn't believe me if I told you," I said, and dumped my pack on the ground.

"Oh, a story, eh? I love a good story. Let's hear it." Cassy replied.

Chapter 42. Connecting

"I was on my first outcrop when I heard a yell," I began. I was a little out of breath.

"I heard that. What was it?" Cassy asked.

"Well, I went back to the shore and saw a boat drifting out in the middle. I couldn't tell who it was. So I took our boat and went out there. It was the three stooges, two of them paddling against the wind and one peeing with the wind. Apparently they ran out of gas. So I towed them ashore, waited to see they were mobile again and then came back."

"I bet Laura was pissed," Cassy added.

"I assume that was her screaming. She looked mad, but was happy that I showed up. It would have taken them forever to get back to camp," I said.

I stood there in the sun, the sweat dripping off my face and my shirt clinging to me. "Wanna go for a swim? I'm dying here."

Cassy turned and looked out over the lake. I assume she was looking if anyone was out there. She gave me a goofy smile and said, "OK."

I went to the edge and looked down. There was a big flat rock right at the waterline. It was a perfect entry board and the water looked deep. I dragged my shirt up and over my head. Then stripped off my boots, pants and underwear. I tenderly made my way down to the flat rock.

I turned my head to look up at Cassy and smiled at her.

"I'm in the buff, Duff," I said.

"I can see, Weatherby," she replied and smiled back at me.

I stood there a moment, admiring the lake, then jumped in with a big splash.

"Ahhh, that feels good," I called out.

I swam about fifty feet, dunking my head in and out. I turned to see Cassy up top. She was turned away toward the forest, and naked. What a lovely figure. Her button ass was as round as a ball.

She turned her head toward the lake and yelled, "Hey, turn around!"

I did so while she climbed down on the rock and jumped in. She swam out to me and practically did circles around me. I'm more of a treader. When she finally stopped in front of me, I moved forward and kissed her. It was a quick kiss. My stability in the water is dreadful. I'm like a duck in air, flapping madly to keep from plummeting.

Cassy paddled off and I plowed my way back to the big rock. I hauled myself up and sat there, my legs dangling down in the water. Cassy looked like a free spirit, a mermaid playing games with the fish. I wonder if she has any worries or does she just take life day by day. She would have made a great hippie, if she had been born fifty years ago. Maybe hippies are timeless at heart. I bet if you gave her the simplest hand-made present, she would be overwhelmed with emotion. She doesn't seem preoccupied with material things.

Cassy swam closer and clung to a rock nearby.

"You know what?" she said. "I've never seen a man naked before."

"You must have," I replied. "How is that possible?"

"I was an only child. I never saw my father naked. I never had a boyfriend until I was twenty. He wasn't even my boyfriend, really. We went out a few times. Then, one night we were at a party and he took me up to a bedroom. He turned off the lights, we got into bed and five minutes later it was all over. All I remember was him on top of me, pushing it in and humping. It was awful. It actually hurt. I don't think he even kissed me that night. When he was done, he got dressed and said he was going back to the party. That was the first and only time I ever had sex, and I didn't even see him naked."

"He missed all the good parts," I said

Cassy swam out into the lake a ways and then back over to me. She placed her hands on my thighs and raised her legs up to the surface behind her, floating. Her perfect bottom crested the water and small waves splashed against her legs. I could not believe how gorgeous she was. Her skin was smooth as silk and fresh with youth. I sat there, tanned all over except for that slice of body normally protected by shorts. There, in that area, I was white with winter shelter.

Cassy tickled my legs with her fingers. Seeing her body made me fill with excitement. I had no control. All I could do was sit and watch this spectacle unfold before her eyes. I wasn't embarrassed though. I enjoyed it.

Cassy moved further in. She reached over and touched me, feeling me, holding me in her hand, examining me with her fingers and eyes. The more she touched me with her gentle fingers, the stronger I grew. I could feel my heart pound with excitement and anticipation. She said nothing, she just continued exploring. She drew her fingers over me, tickling me with wide eyed curiosity and looking to see my expression.

Then Cassy did something that totally surprised me, she kissed it. She peered up with those darling eyes and smiled. I smiled back. I don't know what was more exciting, feeling those beautiful, soft, wet lips against me or seeing that sweet face give me pleasure. The combination was overwhelming. I heaved as air filled my lungs. My heart thumped as I watched. She gave me a small, slow lick as if to taste me, then I watched myself disappear, inch by inch. She drew her tongue along my sensitive skin, feeling all the contours.

I reached under her arms and lifted her up to sit on my legs. I kissed her, passionately, running my fingers up and down her back. I kissed her some more and then, holding her back with my arms, arched her away from me just enough that I could nestle my face in her soft, round breasts. They were such a pleasure to feel against my face. I kissed her and tasted her skin with my tongue, reaching upward to her nipple. I wanted it in my mouth. I wanted to suck on it like I was a hungry baby searching for sustenance. I felt every fold and feature of that nipple with my tongue, stroking it gently, listening to her for sounds of pleasure. I engulfed her other breast, teasing her nipple until she breathed hard, heaving her chest.

Once again, I lifted her up, this time to a standing position. There she stood, in front of me, totally naked. Everywhere in front of me was unadorned skin; the creamiest soft skin a man could want. I put my hand around behind her and gently slid my finger down the crease between her legs. I touched her like a small breeze. That gentleness made her gasp.

I reached forward and let my lips brush against her. It was a small, simple kiss. A second kiss and I let my tongue come out and touch her softly. With every stroke I let my tongue probe deeper inside with heightened pleasure. I tasted her over and over, teasing and stroking. My lips dug deeper until my front teeth pressed against her. I let my fingers roam, finding openings to tease. I ran my tongue all the way from the top down to the end and back again, playing with the edges of every fold. Each time she moaned with pleasure.

I reached up for her waist and led her down, this time on top of me, surrounding me with a little tightness before I slipped inside. My arms embraced her and I kissed her lips. This simple act was beyond anything I had ever felt with a woman before. This was not sex, this was love, in its most beautiful, intimate measure. I was in no hurry. This was where I wanted to be, and what I wanted to feel. The sensation of her soft membrane against my erection eased me into a kind of hypnotic state.

Cassy slowly moved her body around, feeling me inside her. I lay back, resting my head against the earth. I looked up at those beautiful breasts hanging in front of me like a gift of pleasure. I massaged them, playing with her nipples while I slowly heaved my groin against hers.

She lay down on me and kissed my mouth, feeling my lips and teeth with her tongue. We moved together until I couldn't take it anymore. "Cassy, kiss me," I begged her. We kissed, passionately and I heaved harder. "Cassy, I want to come. I'm coming!" I gasped. Cassy moaned and gasped with me. I felt the muscles inside her gripping me in rhythmic throbs, tightening around my erection. Was she coming too? It felt like her pussy was squeezing every drop out of me.

We relaxed. Cassy lay her head on my shoulder. Then I kissed her lips.

"So Duff, did you enjoy it this time?" I asked her.

"It was volcanic. You rocked my world, Weatherby," she replied with a smile.

"You mean with my igneous intrusion?" I joked. I got a good laugh from her.

"Hows abouts you, Weatherby? Did you enjoy that?"

"I think I shot my wad clean out your ear," I said, tugging on her earlobe and examining it closely. She whacked my shoulder. I kissed her and we sat up together, she still on me, still connected to me. I had not dissolved to soft yet, a testament to the incredible pleasure I felt being inside her. As I kissed her again, I leaned forward and we both tumbled into the lake, laughing. I slid out of her. The cool water soothed my hot, sweaty body, but I was sad that I was no longer inside her. We swam for a few minutes before landing on our flat rock and ascending the shore.

"Geez, we haven't even eaten lunch yet," I said.

We dressed together, feeling completely free to be naked with each other. "Did you stop for a snack on your line?" Cassy asked.

"Yeah, you?"

"No, I have all of it left." she replied.

"I could help you out with that. I seemed to have worked up quite an appetite," I said.

"Back off! Get your own sandwich!" Cassy said. "I believe I worked up an appetite too."

"Yes you did. That was a good workout. That should be part of a daily routine, along with bran, coffee, and a healthy crap."

"Whoa, don't forget about cold beer," she added.

"You... complete me," I joked, pointing at her.

Chapter 43. Raftology

We sat on the ground under a big tree and opened our lunches. Good God, she did bring a lot. Her bag was literally full. How does she eat that much? Of course, she does bop around like a firecracker, burning up calories all the time.

"You wouldn't happen to have a pizza over there, would ya? I'd kill for a combo, extra cheese, chewy crust," I said.

"Cheese!" Cassy replied. "I should have put that on the shopping list. No, sorry. I got no pizza. You like the combo, eh? I like Hawaiian. By the way, I want to go to Hawaii. I've seen pictures. Must be like paradise there."

"I'll bet it's like a whole different world. Can you imagine being some explorer, setting out from England in the sixteenth century and landing on a tropical island? I bet it would be like a caveman blindfolded and whisked off to Bay Street in front of the Exchange," I said. "Well, that might be a bit extreme. But you know what I mean."

"Yeah. Wouldn't time travel be cool?" Cassy replied.

"Oh, I'd love to see what the world would be like in a thousand years from now. Of course, who knows what might happen. Maybe we'd be the next dinosaur, or maybe, according to my religious beliefs, the giant space rafts would collide again and wipe the whole universe out. After all, we are just an experiment."

Cassy laughed. "Don't take yourself too seriously, though that is definitely an intriguing theology. If anyone could spin that into a religion, you could, Mr. Smooth."

"The last thing the world needs is a new religion. Let's just call it a hypothesis. What I really need is a philosophy to go with it. What should we include?" I asked.

"All the aforementioned... cold beer, rough bran, strong coffee, and good sex," Cassy concluded.

"Yes, agreed. Those shall be the four pillars of... uh oh, what is this religion called?" I asked.

"Bbcs? The first letters of the four pillars," Cassy suggested.

"That's the best you can do? No, unacceptable. How about Raftology? Titus and Cassy, first apostles of Raftology. Do you think people will build idols to me? Will they bow down to me in the future?" I joked with her.

"Yes, wooden idols. They shall call them 'woodies'," Cassy said, quite irreverently, considering she was talking to the leader.

I laughed. "I can live with that. They shall be large idols, called giant woodies, in honour of me." I looked over and Cassy was laughing now, her face buried in her hands. "Have I amused you? Be careful, my powers are great. Now, go in peace, and may my woody be with you."

Cassy threw her head back and laughed out loud. "OK, stop! I have to catch my breath."

"I'm sorry, did my woody choke you up?" I asked, trying not to smile.

"Good God!" Cassy replied.

"Are you talking to me?" I said. "I don't mind you calling me Titus. God is not part of raftology and I'm not all stuffy about being a deity."

Cassy grabbed a cookie and threw it at me. I laughed. I suppose that was enough. All joking aside, I do like my concept. It is believable, considering the possible extents of space and that huge rafts might drift around and collide. But that theory, or more aptly a hypothesis, is like any other about the origin of the universe. It's complete conjecture based on absolutely no empirical evidence. So, yeah, that would make it a regular religion. Kind of hard to call that a scientific fact. Doesn't matter one way or the other, we will probably never know the truth, unless we see a raft and meet the inhabitants. I doubt anyone will ever know how we got here or where we came from. I can live with the idea of heaven, but not too comfortable with the idea of hell.

"You do think about these things, don't you?" Cassy asked.

"How could I not? We're sitting in a forest with no entertainment, just our own thoughts. We're like cavemen and cavewomen ourselves with lots of time to ponder life. I think about things all the time, like why the hell am I sleeping on a piece of plywood, in a tent, in the twenty first century? Is life a gift? If so, what am I doing with this gift? I am not a religious guy, but I am philosophical. I like to dig deep down and try to solve mysteries. It's the human experience," I rambled on. "I never heard your religious beliefs in our conversation. Where do you stand on this?"

"Nowhere, I guess. I didn't grow up religious, so I don't think much about it. I think whatever happens, happens. No reason for anything. Too much suffering out there for life to have a reason. Everything suffers; plants, animals and us. Everything is born, so to speak, and everything dies, even the rocks. Lava flows, mountains grow, glaciers break it down, waves crumble the stones to make grains that accumulate and sink till they melt and it starts all over. And what are we made of? All the minerals in the rocks. We're just animated rocks. Someday the universe will die, and a new one will be reborn. What's bigger than that I can't answer, so don't try."

"Fair enough," I answered. A deer fly buzzed around my head several times and landed on my knee. Deer flies, the fighter jets of the natural world, evolved to be keen aviators with highly developed eyesight and smell and a sixth sense that tells them exactly where to land. What to do? He will definitely attempt to find a weakness and dig his hungry jaws into me, lapping up my blood. But if I hit him, I will cause suffering and end his life. Is this part of 'whatever happens, happens'? Because if it is, then I have the choice to save him or kill him. I left him alone. My charity will be short lived. I'm sure this brief reprieve from self defense will end soon with a knee jerk reaction, so to speak.

I've often thought how wonderful it would be to go through life not harming anything; not cutting trees, killing animals, picking carrots and potatoes, just existing with nature. But nature is all about coexistence through survival, and everything in nature depends on the rest of nature. Plants compete for sunlight and water with each other. Mushrooms exist on the death of other plants. Herbivores ravage plants, carnivores ravage animals and omnivores ravage everything. To be one with nature is to survive on nature. It's a cold, harsh reality that can only come from the symbiotic relationships nature nurtures. Nowhere is this more apparent than out here in the forest where the relationships are critical. We are more buffered from it, because our food is shipped in. But that food comes from somewhere on Earth.

"I could just lay back and sleep here all afternoon," Cassy mumbled through her lunch.

"You'd make a nice pillow for me," I said.

"Are you going on about pillows again? You sure like your comforts. I bet if we had a lazy boy chair in camp, you'd spend the whole evening in it," Cassy replied.

"I'd call it my captain's chair. I hope it reclines." I put my head back and closed my eyes, pretending to dream about it. I held out my hand and said, "Can you pass me the newspaper, and a beer?" I couldn't help but smirk.

Cassy reached over and slapped my hand.

"Ouch! That was a rude interruption of a very nice dream," I said.

"Good," Cassy answered. "Go do some work, you lazy bastard. Next time you have a nice dream, dream about me. At least give me a chance in that lazy boy."

"Did you finally finish that monster lunch," I asked.

"Yup. I needed it. I wore myself out... swimming," Cassy said.

I laughed. "That was a hell of a swim." I gathered up my gear and threw my pack on. Cassy did the same. I put my arms around her neck and said, "Catch you on the other side."

"You've never let me fall yet," Cassy said, smiling.

I kissed her. "You taste like nuts."

"You taste like bologna," she replied with a smile. "That seems fitting."

I just laughed and we both disappeared into the woods, in opposite directions.

Chapter 44. Really?

The three amigos were travelling back along their lines toward the boat. They all had a reasonably dull day mapping rocks. None met up for lunch, they just stopped wherever they were and ate. Now they were converging on the boat. First came David, then Laura and finally Kyle who was furthest away to the north. All were in good spirits and seemed to have forgotten the morning disaster. Laura drove the boat back to camp, guiding it gently up to the dock. David hopped out of the middle and tied the back to the dock. Kyle tied off the front and the three walked up to the tents with their heavy packs.

There were a number of tasks that had to be done around camp. The axe was loose at the decaying handle, so Kyle built a fire and placed the axe head in the flames. That would expand the metal and burn the wood. Kyle began banging away at the axe head to knock it off the handle.

David started the barbeque. He rooted through the food to find something to cook. Looks like the rations are running low. He pulled out some pork chops and sauce and placed them on the table, then took a chair back to the barbeque to watch the coals.

Laura washed her clothes in a bucket. Maybe she had seen Titus and Cassy wash clothes and decided to do the same. Clothes don't often get washed in a camp. Everyone usually stinks equally. It all cancels out in the end. She rinsed them and then hung them on the line.

"How's it coming, Kyle?" Laura asked. Looked like the head was nearly off.

"It's coming. Want to fetch me the new handle up by the tent?" he asked.

Laura walked over to the tent and grabbed the bare handle lying on the ground and brought it to Kyle. Several more whacks and the head fell off. Kyle threw the old handle in the fire along with the axe head to heat it up again. Laura went into the kitchen and brought out a couple chairs.

Sitting by the fire, though back a ways as it was hot and smoky, Laura asked, "So how was it out there, today? See anything interesting?"

"Dull rocks. Nothing worth looking at. Took a few samples. I saw Cassy and Titus."

"How? They were a kilometre away?" Laura asked.

"I stopped for lunch by the shore. I could hear splashing up the lake. I saw them swimming. It could have been someone else, but I doubt it."

"Holy fuck. Are you serious?" Laura belted out. Kyle nodded like he didn't care. She didn't say anything more to Kyle. He was not her confidante. That was a shocker. Laura couldn't help but think something was going on, a little hanky panky. She also felt a tinge of jealousy.

David came down to see them. "Hey, what are you two up to?"

"Just sitting by the fire," Laura replied, still digesting the news that Laura was having a good time with Titus while she was hanging around with Kyle and David.

"You realize it's nearly twenty-five degrees out here?" David stated.

"Where were you?" Laura asked.

"Up at the barbeque." he answered. Laura raised her eyebrows, then he realized the irony of his statement.

"Kyle was fixing the axe," Laura added.

"Oh shit," Kyle said. "The axe head. It'll be red hot now." He fished it out with the new handle and worked the top end into the axe hole. "Come on, baby. Get in there," He said coaxing the handle in. The reference was not lost on Laura as she still thought about what Cassy and Titus might be doing out in the woods. Then she thought she must be just imagining things. Did Kyle really see what he thought he saw? He wasn't clear about it and they were a long ways away. Maybe they were just throwing rocks in the lake. Maybe it wasn't even them. Well what's it matter. We'll all be gone in another week or two.

"What are you cooking," Laura asked.

"Pork chops. The coals are still burning down. I just came back to get the pork chops. I left them on the table," David replied. "I haven't planned anything else."

"OK, I'll make some vegetable and rice," she said, and got up out of her chair. Kyle was pounding the axe head still, forcing the handle all the way in. When he was done he took it to the lake to soak.

Chapter 45. Relax

Our boat coasted up to the dock. Cassy jumped out and tied it to a post. Packs over our shoulders, Cassy and I traipsed up to the camp. "Howdy," I said as I held the kitchen tent flap back.

"Hey," Laura answered. "How was your day?"

"Not bad. Boring rocks. You?" I returned the question.

"Same. Good weather today, eh? A bit hot, maybe," Laura replied.

"Whatcha making?" I asked.

"Beans and rice. David's up at the barbeque making pork. Do you like pork?" she replied. All her comments hinted at the possibilities of hanky panky.

"You weren't too tough on him today, were you?" I asked, hoping to cultivate a little patience and consideration for the slightly more feeble minded. "You know he always means well."

"I dropped it right away. We haven't mentioned it," Laura replied. "We did lose half a morning though."

"Good. How about tomorrow you and I go do a couple lines together. We'll send Kyle out with David," I suggested.

"Alright. That sounds good." Laura was all smiles.

"I'll go dump my stuff off and come back to help," I said and disappeared.

Actually I just wanted to go crash on my bed. That was a full, though exhilarating day. God, if only every day could be that good. Imagine every single day of your life, out in the beautiful wilderness of Manitoba, warm and sunny, swimming in clear, turquoise water, making love and then coming home to a cold beer and barbeque. I just need a nice cabin instead of this tent and I'd be all set.

Despite the urge to lay down and daydream, I wanted to help Laura, or whoever needed help. My guess is, Laura needed the company today. I don't think there is much companionship between her and Kyle and it's obvious that she loses her temper with David over his mindless and childish antics. Just the same, I wanted to talk to her about him. Maybe she wouldn't admit it, but I was curious if she had a thing for him. I wondered if anyone was curious about Cassy and me. We do spend a lot of time together. I hope no one asks. I don't know what I'd say.

"I'm back," I said, popping into the kitchen. What do you need?"

"Can you stir the rice? It's almost at a boil," she answered.

"Sure." I put my hand on her shoulder to move her aside slightly, just so I could get at the rice. I felt a slight tremble or twitch. I know that feeling, a weakness. That's the sensation you get when someone you are attracted to touches you. It's a completely innocent touch. But you feel a little weak, like a tickle of pleasure. It doesn't mean you have feelings, just that you are touched by someone attractive. I was a bit surprised by this, given Laura's seemingly brisk attitude. I just figured her to be less sensitive.

"Titus!" Kyle called out.

"I'm in the kitchen," I called back.

Kyle came into the kitchen holding a bag. I looked at it. "What's that?" I asked.

He showed me the side. It was all chewed up, leaving a big hole. "That was the shitter paper," Kyle replied.

"Fuck me!" I said. "Now we know where the paper keeps going. Something is stealing it. I wonder what it was. Any ideas?" I looked at Kyle and Laura. They both shook their heads.

"Maybe a squirrel or mouse?" suggested Laura.

I just shrugged. "Maybe we have to hide it in a tin can. Fucking animals! Don't they understand the importance of this stuff to a human's arsehole?"

Kyle laughed. This was not a common occurrence. I looked at Laura and said, "Kyle thinks this is funny. Look at my ass... do you see it smiling?" I turned around, then looked over my shoulder. Now I had Laura laughing.

"Let's eat meat!" came a yell from outside as David approached the tent. He brought with him a plate heaped with steaming pork chops.

"Cassy!" I yelled. "Din din time! Get your ass over here!"

The food was all ready. I tossed some plates on the table, then cutlery. Kyle had retrieved beer from the cold pit. Cassy dragged herself into the tent looking quite tired. Ahh, the luxury of being the project lead. Let the lackies do the chores. Actually, she was very good at doing her part. She was just tired, partly my fault. I shouldn't bust her proverbial balls. She is a good soul.

We sat at the table and ate well. It was a full day for all of us. It was a good day for some of us. It was perhaps less than a good day for others. But we all survived. Tomorrow the roles will be reversed. Cassy will be going to town. I will miss her. I already know how much, though the fullness of it has not hit me yet. The anticipation brings a sad anxiety.

"Cassy, when you go to town, can you get more beer? And a bottle of rye. I'll pay for it," Kyle asked.

"How about we all pitch in," I added. "The beer has been one of the best features of this camp. And ice, of course. Gotta have cold beer."

"OK, but I'll ask if the company will pay for the beer, not the rye though. I think they owe us that much," Cassy replied. "Anyone want some liquor, just tell me before I leave and I'll get it."

We cleaned up the dishes, plotted on the map and tagged samples so Cassy could take them into the office with her. We all worked together, taking turns at different chores and helping each other out. I was feeling a little stressed and opened a bag of chips. I get anxious the night before any big event. I used to fret terribly the night before an exam. I wouldn't sleep well, thinking about all the names, dates, equations or whatever the subject was. I wasn't a stressed eater but always had the munchies. Ever notice stressed backwards is desserts? Maybe there's something to that, though I'm more into Cheesies, chips and honeycombs.

"I'll stoke the fire outside. Why don't we go out and have some more beer with the chips," David suggested.

"I'll get the guitar," I said, and Kyle silently went to get his banjo. We brought all the chairs outside and found a place to sit. The fire, completely unnecessary in the summer heat, was a symbol of life. Can you imagine, fire, the destructive chemical reaction between carbon and oxygen is life to us. It's what keeps us warm in the winter, our own private mini sun.

I dropped my chair and adjusted the legs on the uneven ground. People don't realize the enormous comfort a chair provides to the human design. Sitting on the ground is a tremendous reprieve from walking and working. But sitting in a chair is the ultimate in relaxation. It lets the knees, buttocks and back rest. In some ways, we are all like old men in a new civilization.

We relaxed in this easy, light mood. Cassy sat on one side of me and Laura on the other, the boys across from us. There was conversation, but I spoke little. Cassy seemed in a happy mood, as did the others. I strummed the guitar and occasionally drifted into fingerpicking a little riff.

Cassy looked over at me. "You're pretty quiet tonight.

"I'm deep in thought, with deep thoughts," I replied.

"Introspective or retrospective?" she asked.

"Never look back. You'll only find regrets," I said. "You seem bubbly. Glad to be going into town?"

"Are you kidding? I'm gonna eat at five star restaurants, catch a movie, maybe ride the roller coaster at the fairgrounds. Did I miss anything?" she replied.

I laughed. "Maybe you'll be so enchanted, you'll never want to come back. I know it ain't fancy here, no Gucci and Cordon bleu, but we got a nice view of the sunset, and a pretty OK shitter," I said.

"Yeah, a shitter with no paper," she frowned.

"That's right. We have to solve that mystery. We'll spend some time hunting down the shitter paper while you're prancing around town doing all that big city stuff. Sure you want to leave now? You're gonna miss out, big time," I said to Cassy, a grin on my face.

"I want to hear all about it when I get back, every fascinating detail of the lost shitter paper. Sounds like quite a caper," Cassy said, acting interested in toilet paper.

"I already narrowed it down."

"Oh, really, Columbo. And who did it?" Cassy asked.

"I don't know yet, but I've ruled out the butler. We don't have one. God, I wish we did. My boots need a good shining and I'm ready for another beer. Not that I'm too lazy to get up or nothin' but I'd really just rather yell 'Geeves!' and have it served to me on a silver platter. Is that asking too much?" I joked.

"Maybe out here it is. Even In the big city of Flin Flon. OK, All of Manitoba. Just sit there, fancy pants. I'll beer ya," Cassy said and got up to fetch me a beer. I smiled and watched her leave.

DAY EIGHT- The Sad Poet

Chapter 46. Goodbye

Day eight would be, to all in the Schist Valley, a nice summer day. To me though, it would be a long and lonely day. In fact, the loneliness would last for two days. Cassy would be gone until tomorrow night. I can live without the sex, it's the presence I miss; yes, her presence. I can't say I ever really missed someone before. Funny how I prided myself on being able to go off into the bush for several months, and now I was worried about two days apart from one person.

I sat up and ran my hands through my stiff hair. It felt thick. That silky, clean feel had vanished. I wiped my face and rubbed my eyes, but remained sleepy. It was finally a cool morning. I dressed and shoved my feet into my boots. Where was David and Kyle? They weren't in bed. I must be the last one up. I went next door to the kitchen and everyone was there.

"Hey, look who's up?" Laura said.

Geez, I can't believe I slept in. I cast a small grin toward her and proceeded directly to the coffee. I plunked myself down into a seat and closed my eyes for a minute, hoping to wake up more slowly. David ranted about a mosquito that annoyed him last night. Apparently you can draw out a conversation about how annoying something is longer than the annoyance was. Kyle entered the kitchen and informed us that the shitter paper was gone again. I reached down into a box and tossed him a roll. "Kyle, bring the roll back when you're done. No point in leaving it out there," I said.

"Uh-huh," he replied, "But I want to know where it's going."

"How 'bout we do a little reconnaissance tonight and see if we can track down the culprit," I suggested. Everyone seemed to agree. This could be a fun little game. As for now I still had a few things to take care of. I quickly assembled lunch, prepared my pack, and brushed my teeth. Then I went to the dock and waited by the boat for Cassy. There was a great breeze coming down the lake. If I had flowing hair, this would be a good scene for some kind of shampoo ad, apart from the dingy work clothes. The boat was already filled with bags of rocks. I don't know when Cassy loaded them in.

Cassy hopped on down to the boat like a teenager with way too much energy. She had a map tube in her hand. "All set?" I asked.

"Yup, I'm ready to go," Cassy replied.

We both got into the boat and set off toward the dock. This route led us head on into the wind and the boat slapped over the waves. Cassy rested her chin and arms on the bow of the boat as she watched the distant views become passing points. The dock rolled into sight and we approached slowly. It's always nice coming and going without that need to load and unload a ton of gear.

Cassy hopped out and tied up the boat. I took my time. When I stood up on the dock, I raised my arms over my head and stretched. Cassy said, "Come on slow poke." She waited till I reached her and then she wrapped her hand around mine, leading me over to the truck.

"Why'd you have to park so close?" I asked. Cassy just grinned.

"I was a little worried back at the camp. You were waiting for me down at the dock. Looked like you were eager to get rid of me," Cassy said.

"No," I answered, "Sometimes the anxiety of waiting for something to happen is worse than just getting it over with, like worrying about ripping a bandage off or getting a needle. If I was the boss, I'd keep you a prisoner of Schist Lake and tell Barry to figure things out on his own. I'm sure he's capable of that."

"I'll be back in two days. I'll bring you something from town, OK?" Cassy reassured me.

We reached the truck. I put my arms around her and kissed her. "I know you'll be back, but I'll miss you anyway." We kissed for a few minutes more.

"I'll miss you too," Cassy replied. She buried her face in my chest and squeezed me tight.

"Must be love, Duff," I told her and smiled.

"I agree, Weatherby," Cassy countered.

That was something I wanted to say, and hear, especially now. I would be banging around the bush and camp for the next two days wondering how she felt. I suppose I already knew, but sometimes you just need those reinforcing words. I gave Cassy one last hug, a warm embrace, cheek to cheek. Then I took a step back. "Alright, get the fuck outta here, would ya?" I smiled.

"I knew you couldn't wait to get rid of me!" Cassy shot back, pointing a finger. Then she smiled and jumped up into the truck. She fired up the motor, rolled down her window and motioned me over. When I approached, she put her hand on my face and kissed me. "Take care of the camp, eh? You're a born leader. They all respect you. I can see it. And find that damned thief that keeps stealing the toilet paper."

"You can count on me, captain. If there's one thing I can't stand, it's a dirty arse. Drive safe. When do you want a pickup?" I asked.

"Pick me up in two days at four. I'll have dinner in camp. Can't eat out at these classy restaurants every night, you know," Cassy quipped.

"Alright, see you in a couple days." I kissed her one last time. "Take care, eh?"

I backed away and Cassy pulled out. I just remembered all the samples. "Hey!" I yelled to her.

She stuck her head out the window. "What?"

"Forgetting anything?" I asked.

Cassy waved me to the window. "OK, one last kiss."

I did kiss her, of course, and then said, quietly, "the samples?"

"Oh God! How could I forget? And the map!" Cassy laughed out loud. She backed the truck down to the boat, jumped out and we both loaded samples and the map tube into the bed of the truck. A final wave and she drove off down the dirt road. I watched until she was out of sight and the dust settled. I felt as though she was an active, multidimensional figure, and I, a simple thin leaf, attached to the forest, hanging onto a branch until fall comes.

I really wanted to stay a while and just fuck the dog, but I knew Laura was waiting for me back at camp. I told her we'd work together today. So, I headed back to camp. Hopefully it wasn't too late so Laura wouldn't ask any embarrassing questions and yet late enough that her mood was more pleasant than her usual early morning attitude.

The boat ride back gave me some time to reflect on my job. It was definitely a young person's job. This was a good place to be for an adventure and to save some money, enjoy the land, make friends, and be productive. I wasn't just out here camping. I had an important role to fill. I was living in the bush, but with a mission, not just some back-to-nature notion. My day was filled with useful work. I mapped the land, analyzed the rocks, cut lines, measured geophysical properties, and took soil samples and much more. I could be responsible for the next copper mine.

Some may think what I do just helps an international conglomerate make money, but I don't see it that way. I look around and see people, all people, relying on the results of my work. No one could drive a car without steel, which is made with iron. We all depend on copper pipes and wires. We go through life completely oblivious to the elements that come from mining, whether it's aluminum for cans or silica for glass, plaster for construction, or diamonds for saw blades. This, right here in the bush was where it all started, with someone like me.

I must have been in auto drive mode because I landed at the camp and didn't even remember the ride down the lake. Laura came out of the kitchen tent with pack in hand. I went up to my tent and collected my pack. "So, where are we going?" I asked.

"I don't know. You didn't plan this?" Laura asked in a grumpy, critical way.

She can be such a bitch sometimes. What the fuck was she doing while I was taking Cassy to the truck? She's not a child, can't she take a bit of initiative and do more than her basic duties? So much for letting her have any sense of responsibility. If she needs to be managed, so be it. I sighed and said, "We'll do lines 1200 and 1300 in the east grid." I then grabbed my pack, went to the boat and tossed it in. I took the driver seat and waited as she followed and got in the boat.

It was a quick ride to the east block where I landed the boat. Laura was quiet. Perhaps she felt bad about her abrupt attitude. "You take 1200 and I'll take 1300. I'll be at the 500 picket by lunch," I said. I wasn't in any mood to be chatty. I slung my pack over my shoulder.

"Sorry," she said. "I shouldn't have snapped at you."

I nodded. "See you at lunch." And with that I was off to my line.

Chapter 47. The Bombshell News

Cassy sat at the kitchen table eating toast. Barry wasn't even up when she arrived at the office. Her coffee was half done and the crispy toast had left a shatter of crumbs on the plate in front of her. All the samples she brought back were still in the truck. Barry rounded the corner from the bedroom and entered the kitchen rubbing his eyes. He was wearing nothing but his slightly tight-waisted white underwear.

"Oh, you're here already," Barry said, acting surprised. He just stood there for several seconds.

"Yeah, I got in about fifteen minutes ago," Cassy said, trying not to look down.

"Oh, sorry," Barry replied. Then he took a cup down from the shelf, poured his coffee slowly and said, "I'll be back in a few minutes and we can talk."

It was plainly obvious Barry was advertising his goods, or getting a cheap thrill. Really, she thought? He was not well honed. His six pack was more like a keg. And when did anyone think tidy-whities were sexy? There's no way he couldn't have smelled the toast and coffee. Cassy thought he must have known she was there. But in her naive way, she thought maybe he was just half asleep. She didn't really care one way or the other, as long as he didn't annoy her.

About five minutes later Barry returned, clothed. "So how are things at the camp?" he asked.

"Good. We're on schedule. Should have all the mapping done in about twelve days. I have a load of samples in the truck."

"Can you take those over to the lab right after breakfast? The sooner they get in, the sooner we'll get results. Did you bring a map back?" Barry asked.

"Yup. I put it on the office table," Cassy answered.

"So tell me what you've seen so far," Barry asked, not really looking especially interested.

"We found a few spots with mineralization, and one great gossan; massive sulphide. But, we don't really know if it was in situ or just a pile of ore that fell off the train. We will have to do more work to see if it's connected to an outcrop. I have a sample to show you. It looks like chalcopyrite," Cassy said.

"Yeah, tear that spot apart. Would be good to know if it's the same as the ore in the mine here. Is it beside the tracks?"

"Yeah, makes it suspicious, eh?" Cassy said.

"Well, you'll have lots of time. I found out from head office that we have funding for three months. I'm sending in the line cutters next week to see the property. I want to keep you guys in that camp till early October. You can map for now. When we have some drill targets, I'll send in a drill rig and you'll have plenty to log. If anything comes out of it, we'll have enough work until December. So when you get back to camp, let them know, OK?" Barry informed her.

This was a bombshell. Cassy immediately worried about Titus. She knew he didn't want to be stuck out there for several more months. But, then again, maybe he'd be happy knowing he'd be with Cassy for a while. Could go either way. Barry rambled on about provisions, camp stoves and such, but Cassy only heard her own thoughts as she stared at her coffee cup.

"And I need you to organize all this. Build a schedule for the crew. You'll be in charge of the whole operation. It'll be a multi-million dollar project. Can I count on you?" Barry asked.

Cassy heard this. She considered it an important responsibility. This was good for her. Maybe she could even get her own place in town. Well, maybe not yet, if she'll be out in the camp most of the time.

"Yes," Cassy replied and nodded her head.

"Great. I knew I could count on you," Barry cleverly replied. "What do you think of the crew?"

"They're good. They work hard and they're smart. We've had a lot of hot days, but no one's complained. Everyone's pitching in. We have a bit of an issue with the shitter. Seems some animal keeps taking the toilet paper. Can't leave it up there. Weather's been good, just had one crappy day." Cassy reported like a project manager.

"What's the fishing like?" Barry asked.

"I don't know." Cassy laughed. "Can you believe no one has gone out yet? I didn't even think about it. Weird, eh? People always want to go fishing."

"So what are they doing in the evening?" Barry asked.

"Playing the guitar and banjo, washing clothes, playing cards," she replied.

Cassy conveniently left out the sex on Blueberry Island and the rock ledge. Oh yeah, and the drunken evening. No need to recount every event. Cassy was pretty sure hanky-panky would be met with a swift rebuke. In all likelihood, Titus would be fired. Cassy had no intention of bringing harm to anyone at the camp. She would protect them, unless they did something Cassy felt was unacceptable. To her, the camp was a microcosm of society. People live there, they do not belong to the company like property. They have every right to live, not just work.

"I'll take a look at that map now. Can you get me a sample of that gossan?" Barry asked.

"Sure." Cassy jumped up and bounded out to the truck to retrieve the sample she saved to show Barry. Back in the office, Barry was leaning over the table looking at the map. "Here," she said, "this is for you." Cassy handed him the rock. I nice, clean, shiny face of golden metal shone.

"That's impressive. Looks like ore. Too good to ignore or pass off as spill though. We will get an assay and report it. But we'll have to rip that area apart to verify one way or another." Barry put it down on the table. "So show me where you found it."

Cassy pointed to an x on the map with a tag number next to it. "Here," she said.

"Well, there's nothing impressive about the rock type or features. And looks like you didn't see much in nearby outcrops. It's a longshot. If it had been further from the tracks I'd take everyone off mapping to search for more." Barry sighed.

"We found a little sulphide here, and over here," Cassy pointed it out. "But minor amounts."

"See if you guys can dig around more. Look deeper, not just at the obvious outcrops. We need some drill targets. OK, get those samples over to the assay lab," Barry said.

"OK," Cassy nodded and left.

Chapter 48. Moose Crossing

I reached the five hundred picket and tossed my pack down. I was fricken starving. I didn't know if Laura would come over for lunch or not. I didn't really care. I would have been happy to eat my lunch in peace today. I sat down by a pine tree and opened my pack. After a minute of rummaging around, I pulled out the sample bag and unwrapped a sandwich. What did I make? I can't remember. I think I just grabbed some meat and pickles and stuck it between bread. Now I'd pay the price of my cranky morning. I started to eat when I heard a noise behind me. That was odd, Laura should be coming from the other direction. I turned and looked. Nothing. Probably a squirrel. They can sound like an elephant in the bush. A minute later, I heard it again. That didn't sound like a squirrel. Maybe Laura was playing a trick on me, though considering her surly morning, it was doubtful. I turned again to see a bull moose standing about fifteen metres behind me. He saw me and froze.

"Hey, I ain't yo bitch! Keep on moving!" I said quietly.

He stepped forward but made a wide berth around me, watching closely as he approached. I was surprised to see him continue on his path. Normally a moose will run when he knows he's spotted. A simple word can terrify the beast. As he passed he just kept an eye on me, and I kept an eye on him. Too early in the year to fear a moose, but anything that big deserves lots of respect. Once passed, he kept walking, in no rush. I carried on eating. I finished my sandwich and cracked open a pop when Laura came plodding down my line.

"Hey. What were you doing down there?" I asked.

"I totally didn't pay attention to the pickets till I hit six hundred, then cut across and back tracked," Laura answered.

"Well, you just missed a neighbourly visit," I said.

"What do you mean?" Laura asked.

"A moose. He just passed me. Not a care in the world."

"Really? Maybe he was sweet on you. Did he wink at you?" she asked, smirking.

"I think he was a little more worried that he might have some competition out here. He gave me the stink eye, a little warning to leave his harem alone," I teased her.

"Oh geez! Aren't you full of bull shit! And what's this? You're eating before me?" Laura said.

"Well I didn't know if you were coming over or not," I replied.

"Shit head," Laura said and kicked my boot.

"Sit down and eat." I pointed to the ground in front of me. "You got some catching up to do. I already finished one sandwich. I didn't have anything this morning for breakfast," I said.

Laura dumped her pack on the ground. "I gotta take a pee," she said.

"There's a good spot, right there at that tree," I told her, pointing right in front of me.

Laura grinned, embarrassed. "Yeah, sure. You'd like that, wouldn't you?"

"Fine, you don't want my help... go find a tree of your own," I said, holding my hands up in surrender.

"Um, girls don't need trees," she said.

"Guys don't need a tree either, it's just more fun with a target," I replied.

"Don't worry, I'll find a spot," Laura said and wandered off behind me.

"Alright," I yelled out, "But watch out, there's a horny moose on the loose." I laughed to myself. I heard no reply. Minutes later, Laura returned.

"Everything work out OK?" I asked.

Laura just smiled. She pulled out a sandwich and took a big bite. "You play a sport?" she asked.

"I used to; hockey. I was good at it too. Not good enough for pro, but good. I was a winger, right wing. You? Play anything?"

"Yup," Laura replied. "I played volleyball. I was OK. Actually I played lots of sports till I was about sixteen, then just volleyball. I hated giving it up when I finished school."

"I think we all gave up a lot when we left school," I said.

"You sound like you have regrets," Laura added.

"Don't you?"

"No, not really. I like it out here," Laura said. "Where do you wish you were?"

I didn't answer right away. Then I spoke. "Vancouver."

"You just went serious," Laura said. She stared at me. She went serious too. "Maybe there's something brewing, or stewing in you."

I looked down at the ground for a moment. I think she was right. I think I was coming to a critical point. My relationship with Cassy had really created a dilemma. A week away from heading south, lots of reflection and possibly changing my whole life, and I fall in love. And I can't tell anyone. I think I had a lot of stress pent up inside me. Normally, I can joke my way through any crisis. Not this one.

"Yeah, maybe I'll do something when we're done here. I don't know what. What do you do when you know nothing else?" I posed a question and looked up at her.

"Titus, of all people, I'm sure you'll figure it out," Laura said. "Why Vancouver?"

"It's far away. It's completely different. It's beautiful and mild, and on the ocean. It's a big city. It's the opposite of... here."

"I didn't know you hated it out here. You fit in so well. I thought you liked the bush," Laura continued.

"I do. But think of everything we're missing. Things like cars, and cell phones, and laptops, and TV, and... stuff." I couldn't bring myself to say love, family or marriage. Maybe I thought it would make me look weak. Maybe I would give away too much.

"Maybe, someday you'll be sitting at a desk, behind a computer, in a little cubicle looking out at the trees, and wish you could hear the birds, smell the spruce, and taste the water. It'll be hard to come back to this if you leave for a while," Laura said.

"Maybe I stayed in it too long, or should never have begun. Why can't I have both? I just need to win the lottery." There it is. I just drifted into humour to mask a serious talk. But Laura dragged me back in.

"I suppose we all hit out limits. I'm not there yet. I enjoy this," Laura said.

"All of it? Ever spent a winter on a drill job?" I asked.

"Yes."

"How'd you like that?"

"I could live without it," she admitted.

Chapter 49. Poetry

"I've spent lots of winters logging core and running geophysics in Northern Ontario. Last winter I spent five months in a tent on the edge of Big Trout Lake. I was never warm. The whole winter, I wore a big wool sweater inside the tent. A stove can't warm up a tent when it's forty below. Me and two other geologists and six drillers. It was the first time I ever felt depressed. I even wrote a poem about it. Who the hell writes poems?" I said.

"Well, let's hear this epic poem," Laura said.

"Hmm, I'll have to think for a second. It was a dark poem, as you can imagine."

I looked up, rubbed my chin and tried to remember the lines I wrote.

Black as black can be
The mountain top, the towering tree
The sun is gone, the winter's here
The sky is dark, the air is clear
Good night my friend, good night to thee
It's time to sleep and time to dream
For spring will come and we'll be free
With joys of life and warmth to breathe
But as for now, it's black as black can be.

"Tada," I said, holding my hands up and smiling.

"Pretty good," Laura said. "You were depressed. I'd be worried if the poem didn't find spring again."

"I thought that fricken winter would never end. You know, the drill captain nearly died. I had to go out on the skidoo at two in the morning to check the core. Half way there I found the drill captain walking back to camp. His skidoo broke down and he had a seven kilometre walk in fresh snow at forty below. He was kind of a heavy guy. He would have frozen out there that night. April came and they sent some asshole up to manage the camp, but not give us a break. Wow, I remember that April. It was the first whiff of mild air. It was like seeing a wedge of land in the distance after being lost at sea. Finally, we got out. I never went back to work there. I can tell you one thing, I'll never do a winter drill job again."

"My job was easy," Laura said. "I stayed at a motel last winter near Kirkland Lake. You got ripped off!"

"No kidding. So what did you and the boys chat about the other day out on the line?"

"I don't know. I don't pay much attention to them."

"Really? So, of the two, which would you go on a date with?" I asked, smiling.

"Seriously? That's like choosing between dumb and dumber," Laura said.

"So you'd pick dumb, because dumber is, you know, obviously dumber. I had this feeling there was an intimate tension between you and David." Laura didn't answer, but I think it was clear I was wrong.

"What would you prefer, a fancy pickup or a Cadillac?" Laura asked.

"Cadillac. If you had asked me two years ago I would have said a pickup. Today, a caddy. Someday I'll have a fancy car," I said. "Strange you mention cars. I had a dream about cars last night. I was driving an old Volkswagen beetle and a wheel fell off.

Next thing I know I'm riding a big horse," I vaguely recounted my dream for her.

"I'm sure it signifies something," she said. "Maybe your plans to escape keep falling apart. The wheels come off and you're dragged back into the old life."

That did sound plausible. Maybe I have, subconsciously, tried and failed to move on. "That's very...," I farted out loud, "... ass toot of you."

"You fucking idiot!" Laura replied, laughing out loud. She covered her nose and made a scrunched up face.

Chapter 50. Luncheon

Cassy had been running around town all morning, dropping off samples, collecting results and checking on some geophysical equipment. It was nearly twelve thirty and time for lunch. She was near Mickey's Cafe and decided to grab something to eat. She stood at the entrance and waited for the waitress to seat her. On the way in, Ron, who was sitting alone holding a menu, saw her and shouted, "Hey, Cassy."

"Hi Ron. Catching a late lunch?" Cassy asked.

"Yeah. You know all those pesky geologists in town, keeping me busy," he joked. "You alone?"

"Yup."

"Join me. I just sat down a few minutes ago," he demanded.

"Sure. You're the best lunch date in town." Cassy sat down with him and the waitress handed her a menu.

"Can I get you something to drink?" Asked the waitress.

Cassy looked at Ron for guidance, and raised her eyebrows. "What are you going to have, Ron?"

"Well, since this is a special lunch, I will have a Pilsner, but only if you're having one too," Ron said to Cassy.

"Well, since you're forcing me to have one, I guess I better." Cassy looked to the waitress. "Pilsners it is." Cassy looked back to Ron. "I'm so glad I ran into you. I was just going to grab a sandwich and go. Now I can enjoy lunch."

"Fuckin' rights," Ron added. They both smiled. "How have things been? Busy in that camp of yours?"

"You know what you want for lunch?" The waitress interrupted.

Cassy ordered a western sandwich and Ron ordered the chilli.

"Yes. Things are going well. We've mapped almost half of the current grids."

Ron raised an eyebrow. "Are you implying there'll be more grids?"

Cassy looked around, then said, "Off the record?" Ron nodded. "I was just told this morning we plan to continue several more months with mapping and geophysics."

"I already knew. I mean I had a good hunch. Barry hinted at it. You guys need the credits to keep that land. But I won't breathe a word. I heard nothing from you. I've really meant to come out and visit the camp. Anyway, I'm happy for you. I'm glad you have lots of work going forward." Ron said.

Cassy looked down, the smile vanished from her face. She'd be lousy at poker.

"Something wrong, Cassy?" he asked.

Cassy looked up right away, realizing she had telegraphed her thoughts. "No. A little complication, maybe. I don't know Ron." Cassy stopped. Ron just sat and waited. "Secret?"

"Of course," Ron agreed. "What's going on?"

"Remember your buddy Titus, the guy you drove to the office a week ago?"

"Yeah, nice guy," Ron said. The beers and lunch plates arrived.

"We're kinda... dating. No one knows. It's a camp, eh? You know how that can be," Cassy nearly whispered.

"OK, but how is this a problem?" Ron asked. "This should be good. You've got him captive in camp."

"The thing is, he doesn't want to be captive. He's feeling burned out. He talks about life beyond the bush. And I'm falling for it all. I'm totally torn. I want to follow him to... I don't know where, and do... I don't know what, but I have this job here, and it's a good job. As soon as I tell him the job is extended, he's going to crumble. I know he will."

"He's had a lot of company. So many geologists face this. You come from the city and have a blast for a few years and then face this career crisis. Where's the payoff? Where's the life? I bet eighty percent of geologists find another job by the time they're thirty, and a few just can't break free, though they want to get out. They become bitter and end up drunks. If you ever feel this way, just get out while you have the guts. Worry about the future later," Ron lectured her.

"I'm just confused about everything right now. If he wants to run, I should let him. If he only stays because of me, he'll be bitter." Cassy muttered under her breath, "Fuck! Why can't it just be simple?"

"If life was always simple, where would the progress be? We'd all just lay around and never change. Unfortunately, we are at the head of the evolutionary ladder. It's in our bones. If it means anything, Titus seemed like a really good guy. He's worth saving. One way or another. You know that old saying, if you love something, let it go. If it comes back to you, it's yours. Maybe that's true." Ron was full of wisdom, or at least relevant platitudes.

"I've been whining about me this whole time. What's going on with you these days?" Cassy asked.

"Well, since I know all about you, I might as well tell you a wee secret." Ron hesitated a second. "I'm going under the knife next month. A knee replacement. I banged it up long ago carrying heavy packs up and down boulder hills in the Territories. You know when you come down, hopping from one jagged boulder to another? Well sooner or later your knees will give out. I was laid up for six weeks after that job. Now I'm paying the price for my carelessness. It's not a dangerous operation. First one I ever had though. All my years out in the bush and I never broke anything."

"Sorry to hear that. I know what you mean though. The older I get, the better I understand mortality. I still take dumb risks. If you need anything, I'll make sure I'm in town and I'll help out anyway I can," Cassy offered.

"Thanks. All I can think of is, I may need someone to stock the fridge with beer. It's a great responsibility though," Ron said with a smile.

"I'll bet you're out dancing in no time," Cassy joked. Ron clicked his fingers and shook his shoulders like some sleazy seventies gigolo. They both laughed. Cassy felt good having someone to confide in. She certainly would never talk to Barry about anything personal. Ron gave her a lot to think about.

Chapter 51. Willows

It was the end of the day. I had found a small swamp with some old diamond willows somewhere along my line, so I cut five nice trees about six feet long. I strapped them to my pack lengthwise so I wouldn't be banging into trees and bush on the way. I lumbered down the line, staggering with these poles wobbling about. Laura and I met back at the boat.

"What did you do?" Laura asked looking at me.

"I started a logging company. I can probably get a plugged nickel for each one of these sticks. Naw, these are willows. I'm going to carve one, for a decorative walking stick, seeing how old I am now. I got enough for everyone, unless you're too much of a snob to whittle with me. Come on, whittle with me," I begged her.

"Not sure I like the sound of that. I don't know, I have a pretty busy schedule. And I tend to like whittling alone," Laura joked back.

"Fine. But I'm gonna whittle right in front of you. I also want to form a knob right on the end of my stick." I teased her. She rolled her eyes and got in the boat.

I threw my pack in, then handed her a stick. She reached for it. "Hey, watch it. You're touching my knob!" I said.

"I thought you were more mature than dumb and dumber. Boy, was I wrong!" Laura said, and yanked the stick clean out of my hand. I actually fell forward a bit and she laughed. I tossed the other sticks in and off we went, across the lake to home. Once there, we dragged all our gear up to the tents and retrieved a cool beer each. No ice was left, but the ground was cold at depth where we dug out under a fallen tree root. Time to sit out front, drink a beer and relax. Wasn't long till dumb and dumber showed up. OK, I shouldn't call them that. Coyote and Wavy showed up. They were all smiles, glad to be back home.

"Hello boys. Go grab a beer and join us."

"Yeeeeeeeeehaw!" David yelled out.

"I'm fuckin' starving," said Kyle. "I'm getting the barbeque started."

"Kyle, let's bring it over here. No need to go back there." I put my beer down and we carried the charcoal and barbeque out front where the chairs were. We started it together. A good spray of lighter fluid and the flames were sky high.

"Wooooooooooo! Let's scorch that motha fucka!" yelled David.

"You OK, David? Find a lost world of sex starved alien women on your line today? You seem more hyper than usual," I said.

"Just happy to be alive, Titus. Just a goddamn fucking great day to be alive!" David yelled out.

I wonder if it had anything to do with a lack of stress from Laura out in his neck of the woods today. I won't bring that up. Let's just let him feel good.

"What are these sticks for?" Kyle asked.

"These are diamond willows. I found them in a swamp. They're good for carving into walking sticks. They just look nice," I replied.

None of us would ever use a walking stick. For one thing we are all experienced at walking through the bush. But also we have a ton of other weight, from hammers and grub hoes to axes and packs.

I reached down and picked one up. I carry a good knife strapped to my side. I slid the knife out of its sheath and began slicing bark off. Underneath were diamond shaped patterns of wood, some in dark brown and some in pale beige. Everyone picked out a stick and began carving.

"So how was your day, fellas?" I asked.

"Not bad," David and Kyle both answered. They had begun whittling too.

"Did you miss Laura?" I asked. David just grinned. "I know she missed you. She even made up pet names for you." I goaded them.

"Uh-huh, like what?" asked David, suspiciously.

"I don't remember. Something adorable. By the way, I saw a moose today. He was like fifteen metres away. Didn't run or anything." I recounted my story.

"Really? What did he do?" David asked.

"Nothing. But he asked me where you were. He said you were a great bum-fuck and he missed you. I told him that you didn't want him anymore and you were seeing an elk now. He said you were full of bull! I had to correct him... because you're full elk now, you know, elk dong."

Kyle laughed hysterically. I looked over at David and pointed at Kyle, and furrowed my brow in surprise at his laughter. I've never seen him laugh like that before. Even David and Laura laughed out loud.

"Seriously though, I did see a bull moose, that close too," I said. "It was the highlight of my day. No, I take that back. Lunch with your esteemed colleague was the highlight of my day." I looked over at Laura and smiled. "Very entertaining." I didn't get much reaction from the boys.

The coals were turning white and Kyle retrieved the last of the meat we had; T-bone steaks. He tossed them on the grill and then generously coated them with salt and pepper. The smell was intoxicating. Someone pulled out a tub of macaroni salad and sliced a couple tomatoes to go along with the steaks. It was another good camp dinner, though that was the last of the meat and beer.

After dinner, we all continued whittling our walking sticks. It did help take my mind off of Cassy, but only if I concentrated on it. Otherwise, thoughts of Cassy crept into my head. I hated the thought of her at the office with Barry. Not that I didn't trust her, I did, completely. I just didn't trust that weasel. I had this sense of protection in me, call it an instinct if you will, but it was undeniable.

Sure, lots of women want men to be some kind of new age being devoid of all the evolutionary traits that got us here, and some men love to play along with that, but life is not an artificial social experiment. In my way, I can be Cassy's hero, and in her way, she can be my hero. But I cannot be something I am not. A man who is weak cannot just feel strong and a man who is scared cannot ignore fear and just feel courageous. We are who we are, no matter what someone else wants us to be. That's my opinion. I'll make that part of my Raftology, though in my religion, nothing is written in stone.

Chapter 52. Up a Tree

"Hey, we still have a task tonight," said Kyle.

Everyone looked at each other. I said, "What?"

"The shitter paper. Let's find out where the shitter paper's going?" he replied.

"You're right," said David. "Let's go hunting!"

"OK, we can fan out behind the shitter. We'll all go in a different direction and look for traces of paper. There's got to be a ton of it out there somewhere, unless something's eating it," I stood up and waved everyone on. "Come on."

We went to the outhouse. I directed each one to take a path outward. "If you find anything, shout out, as loud as you can."

"We need a code word," David said.

"A code word? OK, what do you want it to be, David?" I asked, knowing he'd get into the spirit of things if I went along with it. Of course I knew he'd choose something tasteless, too.

"Ass wipe," he said. "Get it? Ass swipe." He accentuated the word swipe. "As in steal?"

"Fine, when you see something, yell ass wipe," I said and smiled.

Off we went, radiating away from the outhouse. I saw nothing, not even a trace. I must have walked two hundred feet when I heard "Found something!" A second later I heard David yell, "Use the code word!" Then I heard Laura yell, "I'm not yelling ass wipe!" another moment passed and I heard David childishly yell, "You said ass wipe!"

I wandered over to where Laura was. She, David and Kyle stood there, staring up at a tree. I looked up too and there, hanging from the branches, was a week's worth of toilet paper. We walked around the tree, searching for any sign of life when Kyle yelled out, "There, look, I think it's a marten."

Sure enough, it was a marten. That cute but devilish face peered down at us in contempt. It must have used the paper to make a nest, or just a comfortable bed. Who could blame him? I'm a man of leisure, I understand. We had a good laugh at this odd looking pine with toilet paper hanging off it like some kind of misguided Christmas tree of the holy commode. We yelled and yelled, but he stayed put. I wouldn't leave that bed either. It looked more comfortable than mine.

"Well, we're not going to move him," I said. There was both a sense of excitement that we solved the mystery, and a sense of disappointment that we wouldn't get rid of the problem. But mostly it was just a good laugh.

"Alright guys, I'm gonna read for a while and then go to bed," I said

"Yeah, me too. Whittled enough for one night," David agreed. Kyle concurred.

"Laura, why don't you hang out with us for a while? It's too early to go to sleep," David suggested. Yes, David suggested it.

"Alright. I'll bring a chair and a book," Laura replied. Maybe she liked the boys more than she let on. I often saw her laughing along with them around camp. She was as silly as they were at times, in a more reserved way, and after ten in the morning.

We all settled down and did our own thing, occasionally chatting until the light dimmed and Kyle got into his sleeping bag. Then it was time to turn in for the night.

DAY NINE - The Confession

Chapter 53. Recliner

Day nine arrived. Shit, a day without beer, or meat, or Cassy. I got up and peeked outside. It was cloudy and cool. A day without sun too. I just want to get out on the line and look at rocks. Nothing much to do hanging around camp. Better not rain. That would be the worst; get out into the bush and then it starts raining. My use of expletives would surpass the number of articles. I may even invent some new words.

I got dressed, organized my backpack and went to the kitchen tent to make coffee. I sat there and watched as the coffee perked. The camp was silent, not a sound to be heard. I must have been up earlier than I thought. I grabbed a pudding cup and slowly peeled the top off. I had no energy to get up and get a spoon, so I just licked it out of the package. I could hear the mosquitoes tapping against the tent outside.

I was still wearing the same clothes I wore for the last three days. Not unusual out in a camp, but after cleaning up recently I was well aware of the sweaty smell. I still had a set of clean clothes. I'll keep them for tomorrow when Cassy comes back. I know she'll smell like roses. Can you imagine, a hot shower every day? That hasn't happened for me in years.

I looked down at my fingernails. They were cut short, or more aptly worn down from rocks, and dirt was packed up under the nail edges. That will have to be rectified. I turned my hands over. The skin was rough and tough, hardened from work and dulled of senses. The lines were accentuated in some areas, and worn shiny in other places. The silver ring wrapped around my right pinky pinched the skin at the base of my finger. I could barely see the small rock hammer imprinted on it. My geology ring once meant so much to me, and now seemed a symbol of control. How did I, a strong confident man, become such a dependent? I shouldn't need anything or anyone. I navigated my own way through school and into the professional world. I should be able to follow my gut the way I can follow a compass through an alder swamp.

    I filled my cup with strong, black coffee. I'm not a fast drinker. I need my coffee to cool down a bit. Sometimes I put it down, waiting for it to cool a little, and then forget till it's cold. I don't think that'll happen this morning. Coffee, at this point, is the only thing I can focus on. A camp that runs out of coffee is like a pirate ship without rum; a perfect recipe for mutiny. I'd be the first one to slice the captain's head off and throw his mercenary body overboard. It's a good thing new supplies were coming tomorrow. We're low on everything.

    I took a sip of coffee. Dammit! Still too hot. Time is ticking by far too slowly. I'm full of reflection this morning. I suppose that happens when you're all alone and too lazy to get up and do something. I don't know why they make these tents out of white cotton. I could use some dark drapes or just dye the damned thing black.

I heard shuffling in another tent. A few minutes later, David came into the kitchen. "Hey, you're early. Couldn't sleep?" he asked.

"Guess I just miscalculated this morning. Coffee's ready if you want some," I said.

"Sounds good," David answered. He filled a cup and sat down. David was surprisingly subdued. Maybe he recognized my state of mind and kept his sparkling attitude in check. "Whataya say we go fishing after dinner?"

"Sure. Good idea. I haven't thrown a line in yet. Usually it's the first thing I do at a camp. Let's troll up the Northwest Arm and check out the bays along the way," I suggested. This seemed a great distraction. Just what I needed.

"OK. What do you think's in here?" David asked.

"I'm sure there's pike, pickerel and lake trout. Might be bass. I bet it's a pretty deep lake, at least up the Northwest Arm. You got some good tackle?" I asked.

"Yup. I got enough to cover all fish types. I have lots of line too if you need it," David answered.

I nodded. Maybe this day would be better than expected. I could occupy my time bashing rocks, making dinner and then fishing, rather than sitting on the dock pining away like a loser. Why didn't I think of this, or some other activity before? It's really not my style to sulk. Perhaps the problem is deeper than longing. Maybe I was really worried about what would happen when the job ended. Where would that leave me and Cassy? Would she come with me? Was I ready to commit enough to drag her away from her job? A decision would come in a matter of days.

Kyle came in, followed by Laura a few minutes later. They both went straight for the coffee, then grabbed something to eat. I took the opportunity to make lunch. The bananas were developing brown, age spots. I hate ripe bananas. I like a banana when it's just far enough past the green stage that you can easily peel it. From here, the taste gets stronger and texture softer, neither of which I appreciate. I grabbed an orange and an apple, plus chocolate bars and pudding. I like a big lunch.

"You know what I like about camp?" I asked.

"What do you like about Camp?" David asked, smiling a little grin as though he expected an amusing answer.

"No phone. No one can call us. I hate talking on the phone. I'm sure Barry would be asking 'How are things going?', 'Tell me your status', 'Find a mine yet?'. And then there'd be other people pestering us with inane conversations about the weather and bugs and crap. Wouldn't mind a TV though, and a leather, reclining chair," I babbled a bit.

"What are you, an old man? You'd turn into a grandpa real soon if you sat in a comfy chair and watched TV every night. You should be glad we don't have that here." Laura lectured me.

"Yeah, I suppose you're right," I agreed.

I picked up my coffee and took a sip. Dammit! It's cold. There was a perfect window of opportunity to drink it at just the right temperature, and I missed it. Coffee tends to go from hot to cold very quickly in the great outdoors. Must be the air circulation. Little drafts draw the heat out quickly. I sighed and drank it anyway, lamenting the warmth I missed out on. I suppose I could have poured another cup, but chances are I'd screw that one up too. Seems like one of those days.

"I'm going down the west grid, line 2200," I said. "I could use the walk. I don't even think I've seen the west grid yet."

"I'll come down there too," Said Laura. "I know the way."

"I want to see the East Arm. I'm taking the boat over there. Wanna come, Kyle?" David asked. Kyle nodded. Kyle would go anywhere. I don't think he cared where he was working. The bush is the bush to him.

Laura and I wandered off behind the camp toward the west grid. It would be a healthy walk, but at this point, a long walk was what I needed.

Chapter 54. The Mine Geologist

A plume of dark smoke drifted high into the sky above the giant smoke stack on the copper smelter. Cassy drove through the gates and parked the big old Ford pickup truck near the Hudbay office. She dropped down out of the truck and carried a small sack with her up to, and through the front door.

"Hi," Cassy bellowed to a man behind a desk. "I was hoping to chat with Mike, the geologist for the A27 Mine. He said he'd be by here at eleven thirty."

"Oh, no one mentioned it to me, but it's quite possible. He drops by here several times a week. My name's Hugo. I'm the smelter manager." Hugo stood up and stuck his gigantic hand toward her.

"Nice to meet you, Hugo. I'm Cassy. I work for Cliff Mines. We're doing some exploration in the area." They shook hands. It was quite a contrast. Hugo's hand almost swallowed up Cassy's petite hand like a catcher's glove. "How are things with the smelter?"

"It mostly runs itself," Hugo said, humbly. "I hope the price of copper stays high. We'd be a lot busier if the economy was better though. I'm worried the price might drop. Seems we aren't processing as much this year as last."

"Yeah, I know, eh? I think we're lucky to have some money for exploration. We'd get more properties and people working them if we could raise more capital though." Cassy tried to sound like a corporate executive. She really didn't know what she was talking about.

"You want a coffee?" Hugo asked and motioned to a pot on a desk by the wall. It was a typical blue collar office; dusty, drab and full of old office furniture and stacks of papers. The fluorescent lighting bleached the colours in the room.

"Sure," Cassy answered, feeling at home in this room. She slipped a paper cup off a stack and filled it from the pot. "How long have you worked here?"

"Going on twenty two years," Hugo answered. Behind Cassy, the door swung open and Cassy turned to see a thirty-something man enter the room. He was average height with short, dark brown hair and pale skin, probably from spending his time underground at the mine.

"Hello," he exclaimed. "I'm Mike. You must be Cassy."

"Yes, nice to meet you," she said and shook Mike's hand.

"I hope you haven't been waiting long," Mike said.

"No, just a few minutes, and Hugo's been keeping me entertained."

"Good. Do you want to go to another office and talk?" Mike asked.

"Here is fine with me," Cassy replied.

"OK. What would you like to know?" Mike continued.

Cassy pulled a chunk of massive sulphide from her sack and handed it to Mike. "We came across this. There is a chance though that it's not an outcrop, just a spill from the train. I wanted to get your impression of it."

Mike took the sample and turned it over in his hands, examining all angles.

"Wow. That's a beaut!" he said. He pulled out a small magnifying glass from his pocket and looked at it closely. "I can see it's hosted in a felsic volcanic. Look closely at this band along the edge." Mike pointed it out. "The sulphide is typical of Flin Flon ore, but I would suspect nearby deposits would be similar. There are no distinct characteristics that would prove it came from Flin Flon, though it is very characteristic of the ore here. My suggestion is look for any trace of sulphide in situ. I suspect that's difficult or you would have tried that first.

Mike continued examining the rock while Cassy sipped her coffee. "Have you found any other less concentrated showings nearby?" he asked.

"Not really," Cassy answered. "We found minor pyrite and chalcopyrite in veins and blebs, but no more than usual."

Mike passed the sample to Hugo and then walked to the wall where a large map was pinned up. It outlined the geology for the entire area. "This is where the mine is," Mike pointed to a dark green area with streaks of beige. "Where was this sulphide showing?" he asked. Cassy was a little tentative, but pointed to the bottom of Schist Lake. Likewise, it was dark green with nearby patches of beige. Of course, half the map was like that.

"I'll give you a clue for mapping these ore bodies. Look for wide sweeping 'M' curves in the folding," Mike said, dragging his finger to form a large 'M' where the mine was. He did that in a few places where mines were located. "And look for a mix of mafic and felsic."

"OK," Cassy said, soaking this experience in.

"Listen, I don't have time today, but if you ever want to take a tour underground, I can show you around," Mike said. He passed her his business card. "You can call me anytime."

"I'd like that. Thanks a lot Mike," Cassy replied, though sensing he may be trying to lure her into a date. She collected her sample from Hugo and put it back in the sack. "Nice meeting you Mike, Hugo," Cassy said.

"You too," replied Mike. Hugo gave her a wave, and she left the smelter office.

Well, it was not definitive, but it did look like Flin Flon ore. That was both positive and negative. It could have been spill, but If it wasn't, then it might be another rich ore body like the one at Flin Flon. Cassy had not told Barry she was dropping by the smelter. This would be a little initiative of her own. The guys at the smelter would have nothing to gain from a little insider knowledge of Cliff Mines.

Cassy drove over to the grocery store where she wandered the aisles picking out a week's worth of food. She paid particular attention to meat. A full geologist is a happy geologist, all things considered. She could have just given a list to the store and they'd fill the order, but she did not relish hanging out at the office, which is where she'd be otherwise. She filled one cart, parked it to the side and then began filling a second cart. If she missed something, it wouldn't be the end of the world. She could always whip into town and pick it up one evening. But who wants to waste time doing that. Maybe everyone else in camp would, at least once in a while.

A bag boy helped her load the truck. His name tag said Henry. He was a red haired, freckled lad, about nineteen, tall and lean. He, along with a lot of other kids, probably dreamed of doing something exciting and important, but lived in a town with few jobs. Cassy thanked him and drove off, thinking of more places to go and more things to do before returning to the office.

Cassy made a run to the liquor store to get a bottle of rye for Kyle, then the post office to pick up a parcel for the company, and finally the drugstore to get some vitamins. Cassy lacked iron, and liked to get supplements. She couldn't think what more to do, so she just drove. She passed the home furnishings store and a thought struck her. She slammed on the brakes and made a U-turn. This was it, her last stop before going back to the office.

Chapter 55. My Confession

Laura and I had finished half our lines and met up for lunch again. "Hey, just like old times, eh?" I said as we settled down to eat.

"Old times? It was just yesterday," Laura replied.

"Really? Seems more like twenty four hours ago. Don't you feel like time is going by way too slowly?" I asked.

"Time seems perfectly normal to me. Anyways, at your age you should be glad time's going by slowly. Before you know it, you'll be grey and deaf."

"I'll be deaf in no time if you keep rambling on about how old I am. Three years and you'll be caught up to me," I said.

"I will never be caught up to you. You'll always be an old man to me," Laura said with a grin. "What did you bring for lunch?" Laura asked.

"Same old crap; couple sandwiches, chocolate bar, granola mix, orange, apple, pudding, pop-water," I replied.

"How can you drink that club soda? Don't you want some taste?" Laura frowned.

"I like taste, but prefer not to drink a big scoop of sugar and fake flavour. How can you stand that pop?" I asked, looking at her brightly coloured canned drink.

"Guess I'm used to it," she replied.

"Look at this apple. It's awful." I held it up for her to see the bruises.

"You're in a sour mood today. What bug crawled up your nose?" Laura said.

"I could use a cold beer, or fresh bread, or meat, or something worth eating." I took a bite of the apple and then tossed it into the ferns behind me. "You'd think they could let us come into town for a night, or dinner or something. It's not that far."

"I thought you were Titus the Titan, the guy they could dump way back in the bush for five months and forget about. You're coming undone after just one week." Laura made a good point.

"It's been nine days. Nine days, two hours, sixteen minutes and forty three seconds, but who's counting," I stated, looking at my wrist as if I had a watch on. I didn't.

"You're like a different guy," Laura said, surprised by my attitude. "You've been moping around for the last couple days like a lost dog. Ever since... ever since Cassy left, you've been moody." Laura stopped talking. I didn't say anything. I noticed she was staring at me. "You miss Cassy! You, and Cassy. Of course! I'm right, aren't I?"

I didn't know what to say. "Me and Cassy, what? BFF's?"

"Have you and Cassy been, doing it?" Laura said with the widest, dumbest smile I have ever seen.

"Doing what, bowling?" I said, sarcastically. "Uh-huh, we sneak out at night and go bowling."

"You like Cassy. No, you're in love with Cassy! And she...?" Laura waited for an answer.

"Yes. Are you satisfied? I confess. I'm in love with Cassy. Yes, she's in love with me, or so she says. And yes, we grind like mortar and pestle. I miss her. Don't tell the dumb brothers, OK?"

"Holy fuck! I have never heard of this happening in a camp before. What do you plan to do?" Laura asked.

"I have no idea. I want to ask her to leave with me, but I'm worried that she'll want to stay here, with her job. We haven't talked about anything like that though. I had it all planned out when I got here; finish this job, then head south and hopefully break free of this god forsaken bush life. Now I don't know which way to turn. I didn't expect this to happen. Can't decide if this was good luck or bad luck. Just fate I suppose."

"Why don't you just ask her to go with you?" Laura suggested.

"I'm afraid of what her answer will be. And why would she go with me? I don't even know where I'm going. I don't know what I'll end up doing or where I'll end up living. She's settled in here with big man Barry. I'm like a lost soldier, trying to find my way through a minefield back to safety. I only took this job because it was a short one. In and out, and make a few bucks."

"Well, you got the in and out," Laura quipped.

"Uh-huh, I got more than I bargained for. I should've just kept my distance. That would've been the smart thing to do. But I just couldn't. The titanium man is now talc man, weakened by the affections of a girl. Why are women always the downfall of men, huh?" I goaded Laura.

"Because, Talc man, you guys are never as strong as you think you are. You're just stubborn. Cassy brought the real Titus out. If you're smart, you'll stick with her. Are you gonna eat that orange?" Laura lectured me. She's right about one thing, I can be stubborn. I get an idea in my head and I can't see anything else.

"Here, I'm not that hungry," I tossed her the orange.

Laura peeled the rind off the orange. "See, this here is you. Sour on the outside, but sweet on the inside." She took a bite of one slice. "And pitiful. Ha ha ha ha! Get it? Full of…"

"Yeah, I get it," I interrupted her. "Very funny." She tossed half the orange back to me and I ate it. Geez, this thing was full of pits. I spit one of them out, up into the air, and it fell near her feet. She spit a seed at me too and we started a mini seed war.

"Just think, you could have the same kind of love affair with David. Well, maybe not the same. More like he'd do something stupid, you'd call him a fucking idiot, he'd cry a little and then you'd have pity sex with him," I teased her.

"Shut up!" Laura said, and laughed. "That bone head's not boning me, ever!"

"Such denial," I muttered.

Chapter 56. Camp Visitor

Ron backed his old truck up to a trailer that held a silver aluminum boat. He got out and checked the location of his hitch. He was only a few inches away from the ball mount, so grabbed the coupler and pulled it up and over the ball, seating it well and clamping the lock down. He wrapped the chain through the hitch for added protection and then slipped a carabiner through the coupler tab. Ron plugged in the electrical connection for the brake lights and tested the coupler to make sure it was well seated.

Inside the boat were a couple oars, the gas tank, a safety kit, and plug. Ron kept a floatation device up front in the cab with him. With everything secure, Ron started up the truck and slowly drove down the road from his house. He knew every lake, backroad, and mine within five hundred kilometres, on the Manitoba side that is. He had a map sketched in his mind with secret sights and places not found on any printed map.

He followed a gravel road several kilometres into the bush till he reached a large dock. Backing the boat down the ramp with great precision, he stopped the truck, exited and released the tie that held the bow to the trailer. The boat floated and Ron led a rope over to the dock where he secured it to a cleat. The truck then pulled the trailer out and he parked over by the forest edge. The whole process was done in a matter of minutes, as had been done on countless lakes many times before.

Ron drove the boat with his nine point nine outboard motor down the lake to a bay where he spotted a few tents. He killed the motor and let the boat drift to a sandy beach where he got out and pulled the bow up high and dry. It was nearing four fifteen, though no one was around to greet him. He knew people would be back soon enough and he wandered around, checking out the camp. He grabbed a chair, went back down near the dock and sat where the breeze flowed off the water.

Ron often dropped by camps in the area to chat with people and get a sense of what was being accomplished. This was not a necessary part of his job, but helped him understand what was going on in his territory. Some companies were a bit underhanded, claiming work they never did. Ron often knew which companies were trustworthy and which were not. He didn't check on every camp, just ones he had a suspicion of or particular interest in.

Off in the distance, Ron saw a boat coming toward the camp. It was a small aluminum red and silver boat not much different from his own. As it reached the dock, two fellows climbed out looking curious about their visitor. Ron got up and walked over to the dock.

"Hello," David announced.

"Hello, boys. How's it goin', eh?" Ron greeted them.

"Not too bad. Glad to get back for dinner, though not sure we have much to eat," Kyle replied.

"Running out, eh? I can remember being down to beans before. It sucks, but then makes a fresh shipment all the better. "I'm Ron, the regional geologist for Flin Flon." Ron held his hand out.

"Hi Ron, I'm David. This is Kyle." They all shook hands. "What brings you out to our humble camp?"

"No reason. Saw Cassy in town and she told me where you were. Thought I'd drop by and say hello," Ron replied.

"Come on up and I'll show you around," David said.

They all trudged up to the camp and the boys dropped their packs at the kitchen. "This is the kitchen tent. Looking a bit bare, eh?" David said.

Ron smirked. Then David led Ron to the other two tents to have a peek inside.

"You guys did a great job. Comfortable little camp you've got here. I bet you get a nice breeze coming down the lake, eh?" Ron praised them.

"Yup, and we can walk out to the western part of the property or boat out to the eastern parts. Nothing missing, except town is too far away," David said with a chuckle. "How about a drink. Want a coffee or pop?"

"Sure, whatever you have is fine with me," Ron accepted. They went to the kitchen and David started the stove for coffee. "Sorry, I should have brought some stuff in for ya. I didn't realize you were so low."

"No problem. Cassy will be back tomorrow with a boat load of grub," Kyle added.

Inside, the coffee began to make that old, familiar sound perking in the pot.

※※※※※

Laura and I were trodding along through the bush back to camp. I'm sure our thumping footsteps could be heard pounding the ground far ahead of us. We dumped our packs down outside the kitchen. I smelled that fresh brew and yelled out, "I smell coffee! Whoever made that, I'm gonna give you a big, wet..." I swept the tent flap open and stopped short. "Oh, didn't know we had company."

"Never mind that, where's my big, wet something?" David said and laughed. Kyle grinned, enjoying my embarrassment.

Laura pushed me all the way in so she could see who was there. She didn't recognize him. I looked at David and said, "A big wet piss in the face, smart ass." I turned to Ron, "How are you? Didn't know you'd be out to visit us. Good to see you again. Ron, right?"

"That's right," he said. I reached out and we shook hands like old friends.

"This is Laura," I pointed to her and she shook his hand. "Ron's my friend from town. He gave me a ride to the office when I was wandering aimlessly like a farm kid who fell off the pumpkin wagon riding through town. You came at the worst possible time. We are nearly out of grub and all the beer's gone. And of course the project geologist is out of camp, too. Glad you're here just the same."

"I know Cassy's not here. I ran into her in town. We had lunch together and she told me about the camp. Thought I'd pay a visit and see how things are going," he said.

"Have you had the tour yet?" I asked.

"I have," Ron replied. "A fine job you've done here too. That dock is good and stable, and your beds look almost comfortable. I'll have to inspect the outhouse before I go though." Ron laughed.

"Well, you'll have to take a roll of paper with you. Seems a marten has taken a shine to the paper we leave up there and has built himself a bed far more comfortable than what we have."

"Ha ha ha," Ron laughed again. "Is that right? Never underestimate the ingenuity and tenacity of a wild animal."

"I'm going to start dinner," Laura stated. "You gonna stay Ron?"

"I don't think you have enough grub left. Don't worry about me," he replied.

"Oh I'm sure we have enough for one more. Let me see what we can whip up," Laura said. Ron smiled and nodded. "Why don't you and Titus go sit outside? We'll get working on dinner."

Chapter 57. Advice

Ron and I took a couple chairs down to the beach with our coffees. That was nice of Laura. Not sure why she let me go. I mean I barely know Ron. But maybe she thought I could use a chat with an outsider, considering my moody state today.

We dug the chairs into the sand and settled down. "How is Cassy doing? I suppose she's pretty busy with office stuff," I asked.

"She seems to be OK. I think she misses the camp. She told me as much. How are you doing, Titus?"

"I'm OK." I left it there with a slightly awkward silence. "Where are you from, Ron?"

"Thunder Bay, born and raised. Went to school there, too. And you?" he asked.

"Kitchener. Went to Waterloo. I guess Flin Flon's not a whole lot different from Thunder Bay, eh?" I asked.

"No, suppose not. What's your plan for the future?" Ron asked.

"Wow, I wish I knew. Not this," I said, and shot him a smile.

"When I worked in the bush, I had a motto... 'don't miss an opportunity'. I banged on every door and took every job I could. I always looked for a better one than the last, or a better company. I spent about six years in bush camps. I got an underground job at the mine here in Flin Flon. One day I ran into the regional geologist and he told me they were looking for a junior geologist. He asked me if I wanted to apply. I told him I'd follow him to the office and fill out the application right away. He laughed and said, 'that's the kind of answer I want to hear'."

"I got that job. I got married a year later, bought a house, had three kids and moved up to resident and finally regional geologist. You know, he told me that few geologists wanted to take the risk. They all thought it would be a dead end. Not me. I saw an opportunity. If you see something you like, don't be afraid to take the risk. Fate has a way of taking care of the details. You've been out in the bush for years, what's your motto?" Ron asked.

"Keep the peace." I said, and laughed.

"Yup, that's a lesson best learned early and always remembered," Ron agreed. "Squabbling in a bush camp can make life pretty miserable. Do you like the bush?"

"I do, but I expected more from this profession. I thought if I put in my dues, I'd get a real job in a mining company, with benefits and regular hours. A job with responsibility and decent pay. I hoped to be in Toronto or Vancouver. Doesn't seem to be working out that way. I just keep going from one contract to another, working seven days a week and living in bush camps. Actually, this camp is better that most. I have been stuck in some real bad ones, summer and winter. When I think about friends back home that get paid good money and only work 37 hours a week, I really wonder. I was OK with it for a few years, but feel duped now." I told him.

"They've got you pigeon holed. You don't complain. I've seen some geologists get hired and then become delicate. They end up with the cushy jobs. Companies know they can work you hard and get the grunt job done. You have to remember, from a corporate point of view, you're a resource. Your specialty is grunt work, in their eyes. Not everyone has your knowledge and can live out in a rough, isolated camp. The ones with good jobs in Toronto are the salespeople, unfortunately." Ron sounded sympathetic.

I had to think about what he was saying. He's much older and wiser than me. He's been through it already. Expecting someone to work for free is unreasonable. Demanding it is a form of abuse. When there's no alternative and it's forced for no return, it becomes slavery. When an entire system expects free labour, then there's no escape. This is obvious in third world countries where people work for unscrupulous companies, feel trapped to the point of exhaustion, fall into depression and turn to suicide.

In the first world, this can happen to those whose minds are trapped by a sense of hopelessness. There is, of course, always hope, but not to a mind that's blind. We all see the world through a lens, whether it be sharp and clear, or fuzzy and warped. That's the weakness of the human mind. I feel trapped in this occupational world, but I also feel there's still some hope for me. This is my window of opportunity, albeit with a foggy view. My choice should be clear though: escape now. My dilemma is Cassy. I want to escape, but not without her. I want both worlds.

"I wish I could tell you what to do. But I think you already know what you have to do. How you do it is a matter of choice. How that works out is a matter of fate. Just be a man of action. Not sure that was much help," Ron lamented.

"Yes, it was. It's perhaps a bit more complicated than you think, but I get it," I replied.

Laura stuck her head out of the tent and yelled, "Dinner!"

"This should be interesting. I have no idea what they could have scrounged up," I said. We carried our chairs back up to the kitchen. Plates were set and David was dishing out canned cream of corn, pork and beans, and fried corned beef. An eclectic dinner of canned goods.

"Hey, this looks good!" Ron trumped up. "If this is what you make when you've got no food, I'm coming back when you've got a new order." Everyone laughed. Dinner served us well. Our plan to go fishing tonight probably would have been better scheduled a day sooner. But the corned beef was fine.

"All I can say is, thank God Cassy's not here," Kyle said.

We all looked at each other. "What do you mean?" I asked.

"Have you forgotten her most embarrassing moment? This dinner would have made her fart all night." Kyle replied. We all laughed at this, except Ron.

"I'm missing something," Ron said.

"Cassy told us a story about a night she farted so much, she cleared out the camp. If you happen to see her, tell her this story is one of infamy now," David interjected.

We had a few laughs over dinner and then Ron bid us goodbye. We all stood down at the dock and gave him a wave as he drove his boat up the West Arm back home.

Chapter 58. Fishing Trip

"Are you ready to go fishing?" David asked.

"Yup," I replied. "Anyone else want to come?"

Laura and Kyle shook their heads. So I collected my rod and tackle and boarded the boat. David came bounding down to the dock full of exuberance. He jumped in the front and we putt-putted our way out of the small bay and toward the Northwest Arm. We rounded Blueberry Island and continued a short distance up the shoreline to a rocky face.

"Wanna try along here? We can drift and cast a bit. Looks like a solid drop-off. If we get nothing, we can troll along till we hit a bay," I suggested.

"That sounds good," David replied. So I killed the motor. There we sat, very slowly moving along the shore. "What are you going to use?"

"I'll try a red devil. Looks good for pike here. Too early for pickerel," I answered.

"OK, I'll put on a silver spoon," David said.

We cast against the rocky face of this shoreline. Fifteen minutes passed by with no bites. Then David yelled, "Got one!" He reefed hard on the rod, the tip bending way over. He dragged it up to the boat. I looked down and it was a small, a very small, pike. I reached in and lifted him up.

"Nice going, David! First fish of the trip. Maybe we should let this one go, eh?"

"Yeah. We'll get bigger," he acknowledged. "At least we know they're in here, eh?"

"For sure!" I said. "Let's troll a ways." I put the motor in neutral, yanked the cord and then twisted the handle to troll. The engine sputtered along and we tossed our lines out a good distance. We travelled on up the lake without so much as a nibble. I suspect the lake is deeper than we know.

We reached a spit of land jutting out into the lake way up. A road came down this peninsula to the lake with beautiful houses on either side, each with waterfront lots. We rode on by and into a big bay. I guided the boat around the edge, off shore maybe thirty metres. About halfway round, my rod bent over. My first thought was weeds. I held my rod and it felt like dead weight.

"Dammit, I must be snagged on something." I said. I killed the motor and started pulling the line in, which really just pulled the boat backwards.

"Shit!" said David. "Looks like me too. Must be a solid weed bed or sunken logs down there." We both pulled at the lines, dragging ourselves backwards.

My line was almost straight down now. "Well, might just lose this fricken lure. I can't budge it," I said. I pulled the rod up and reeled in, then pulled up and reeled in a bit more. "Oh, maybe it's coming." All of a sudden, my line ran out, buzzing with the drag. "What the fuck?" I yelled. "David, I got something! It must be huge!"

"I know," said David. "I think something's pulling at mine too."

We both battled the fish for twenty minutes or so. Well, I have no idea how long, but it seemed an eternity. Finally, I got mine to the surface long enough to see it. This was a huge pike. I mean, the head was like an alligator. "David, how the hell are we gonna get these things in the boat?" I asked, knowing full well we probably weren't.

"Fucked if I know. I'm not reaching down there," David replied, his voice shaky.

I got his head up by the boat. He made a wild shake and tossed the lure clean out. "Mine's gone, thank God. That was scary."

"Well, what am I gonna do with this... ah, the line snapped!" David said. He looked a bit glum for a second, then looked at me and said, "Holy fuck, man! Can you believe that? We gotta come back here after we get a giant net or dagger. Those were trophy fish!"

"Those were bigger than anything I've ever seen. I mean, that's the stuff you see in old promo photos for fishing camps. I wish we had gotten at least one in though. No one will believe what we just caught," I said.

We were not far from that peninsula with the fancy houses. We cruised on past them slowly. I heard a train whistle blow and I killed the engine. I was looking straight down that dirt road. The train crossed it very slowly. I suppose it had just left town. It was a freighter hauling ore, lumber and fuel tanks. I bet it was destined for The Pas and then Winnipeg.

I moved the boat further down the lake and watched as the train skirted the shore, heading toward the grid I had mapped earlier in the week. It was still slow, but picking up speed. From here, it most likely wound its way through thick forests for a long way, maybe all the way to The Pas before slowing down.

DAY TEN - The Last Sunset

Chapter 59. Food Fantasy

Day Ten. Yes, I've been here ten days. In some ways I feel like it's been a hundred days. I guess I'm just weary, and missing Cassy. As you can imagine, no one in camp even believed we caught a fish, let alone a giant pike. Make that two giant pike. I didn't really care, but David did. He detailed every second of the event, arguing the size and strength of the mighty beasts, as he called them. It's hard to say he embellished the story, given that I saw these fish and they were impressive. Even now, the morning after, David is still talking about it. I, on the other hand, just want some coffee.

My day was set; pretend to be interested in work for several hours, eat a can of stew and pick up Cassy. I had a lot to tell her, from the marten that loves toilet paper to our visit from Ron and fish the size of blue whales. I better clean up while I'm on the line so she doesn't think I'm a caveman at the boat dock.

I went through my morning routine; coffee, prepare my pack, a pudding cup and bread for breakfast. There was only vanilla left. I'd have to suffer through it and look forward to a new supply of chocolate. I assembled my lunch. I found a can of stew, a pudding, a chocolate bar and an orange. I refused to take another apple. It would be a lean day.

If I had got that monster pike in, I could have cooked it up last night and taken some today. Was this the kind of thing Ron was telling me? Was I afraid to take risks, like grabbing that fish? I didn't used to worry about anything. I remember my first field job. I was on the bus bound for Timmins and thought of nothing but adventure. Where did that fearlessness go? Now I balk at dragging a stupid fish in the boat.

Everyone scrounged through the remaining supplies for lunch food. We still had a number of canned goods, but no one liked that. I carried a pocket knife with a can opener in it. I reckon most others did too. These Swiss army knives are indispensable. I decided to go to the east grid alone. I'd have to go get Cassy early. Of course if anyone wanted to come to the east grid I could just make it a short day.

"I can take a boat to the east grid too," said David, "if someone wants to come with me."

"Yeah, I'll come," said Kyle.

"I can go to the west grid," said Laura.

"Well, why don't we all stick together," I suggested. "You can do what you want, Laura, but makes sense if we're all close by rather than one stuck out in the west grid. If you come with me, I'll just bring you back early. If you go with these guys, you can come back with them. Up to you."

"Alright. I'll go with these guys. Doesn't matter to me." Laura shrugged. She knew I would want to pick up Cassy alone. She was not going to suggest tagging along. She made it easy for me.

I was putting off thoughts of an afterlife with, or without Cassy. I wanted to revel in this time I had with her, yet still dream of life far away. At the moment, my thoughts all surrounded food; pizza straight from a stone oven, linguine with a white clam sauce, sushi with a side of tempura, and an ice cold dark ale. All of these things would have to wait a couple more weeks, as would the start of my new life. Should I start planning now? Should I start hinting about going south, or west together? My gut was full of butterflies. It's like riding a new rollercoaster; there is great excitement and mass anxiety all at once. Best to shut this out for now and play it cool. This is where I usually blow it with a girl. Falling in love is a fog that muddles the mind.

Sun and cloud patterned the early sky. I prepared my backpack and headed down to the boats as I do every morning. All the others came down to the boats too. They hopped in one and I hopped in another and we all rode off to the east grid in tandem. I eased my boat over, slowly butting against theirs and gave a gentle nudge. They pushed back. With their added weight, they easily nudged me over to the right and won the battle of boats. We smiled at each other as we continued on, playfully. I waved and veered off my way and they veered off their way to our respective lines. In a way, I was glad to have a day alone on the line. I enjoy company, but once in a while it's nice to contemplate life quietly, alone for a day.

I could see the contours of the shore where my line was located and set the boat to land. This looked like good bush. In a matter of minutes I was wandering through the trees, half thinking about rocks and half thinking about steak, the kind with juice running out as it sizzles on the grill. Ever walk by a good steakhouse? The smell is like a drug for the senses. I saw an outcrop just off to the right and meandered that way.

Chapter 60. Management Skills

Cassy had been up for an hour, plotting symbols on a master map in the office. She was transferring all the data from field notes and maps onto what would become the report map. Sample data was perhaps the most difficult to add and the most important. If a sample registered a great value but was in the wrong place, a lot of hard work and time would have been wasted. That might be like winning the lottery and misplacing the ticket. Cassy got up early enough that she could get work done in peace and then go run errands when stores and offices were open.

Cassy heard Barry in the kitchen helping himself to the coffee. A few minutes later he wandered into the office and greeted Cassy. "Morning," he said. "How's the map coming?"

"Good," Cassy replied. "Looks like they took a lot of samples and covered the ground well. It's a shame it's taking so long to get assay results."

Barry grunted an affirmation. "Don't forget to contact Standard Geophysics and arrange for some equipment. We need to have it ready by September. And go see the line cutters and show them the new grids we want cut," Barry droned on. He pulled out a small map with the grids outlined on it and handed it to her.

"OK," Cassy said. She put the map in a small tube and placed it on the table nearby.

Barry looked over the map Cassy was plotting on. "How come there's not much data down here," he pointed to a part of one grid. "And over here, there's not much. You're letting them get away with shitty work."

"I haven't seen these areas, but could be less outcrop," Cassy answered.

"Ah, bullshit! Make them dig around. Looks like they just got lazy." Barry bellowed out. Cassy thought he was just being an asshole. There were clearly soil samples there; an indication that they couldn't find rocks to sample. But Cassy just nodded. Barry turned and left the room. It's possible Barry was just asserting his status as the boss. Nobody said he was a good boss. Some bosses use management styles that are self-conceived, for better or for worse. In the mining business, most managers are just geologists thrown into the position without any training of any kind.

Cassy finished up adding symbols and sample I.D.s to the map. She didn't refill her cup with coffee, just left the office. She was thankful to be on her own for the day now. There was a lot to do. She drove across town to the engineering company that rents geophysical equipment.

Chapter 61. Chores

Like most parts of town, you can easily park on the road in front of any building. She jerked the truck to a stop and hopped down from the cab. She looked up at the sky of blue with puffy white patches and thought what a good day to be going back out to camp.

Once inside the building, she stood at a counter where people often buy maps and such and waited for someone to greet her. A stout man in a tweed suit came out from an office room and said hello. "Hi," replied Cassy, "I work for Cliff Mines. We want to do some geophysics in the fall and want to book handheld electromagnetic and gravity meters."

The stout man pulled out a form from under the counter and started filling the fields in. "What is your name?" he asked. He was all business. There was no hint of pleasantry.

"Cassy Duff… " She hesitated for a moment, recalling the silly name Titus had called her. "Cassy Dufferin."

"And you're with Cliff Mines, eh?" he continued.

"Yes, that's right." Cassy smiled.

"OK, no problem. I can have them ready for you on September fifth. When you pick them up I'll need a credit card. We need a deposit in case of damage. You ever used these before?" he asked, and then cut Cassy off. "Doesn't matter. They're easy. I'll add in a user guide for you." He disappeared into the back for a moment. When he returned he had a magnetometer in his hand. "This is for EM." Basically, it was a box on a pipe. The man came around the counter and showed Cassy how to carry and take a reading.

Next he brought out a gravimeter, which was a box on a tripod. The man pointed out a few buttons and described how to use the machine. "It's all in the user guide," he said. He had become decidedly more helpful and pleasant, though continued to be all business. Cassy thanked him for all the advice and left the building.

Cassy then drove to a small warehouse type building outside of town. A sign above the door read 'A1 Line cutting'. Inside, Cassy met with a large native man named Abraham and showed him the map of the property where grids must be cut. Abraham looked the map over. "Oh yeah. I talked to someone on the phone about this. We're going in soon to have a look at the property. How many kilometres?" he asked.

"I don't know," she answered, taken back by the unexpected question.

"I can schedule the work, but gotta know how far. Can't tell you how much or how long to do it if I don't know how far."

"I can estimate," Cassy said, a little flustered. She looked at the map, adding up the distances in her head. "Looks like about seventy-two kilometres."

"Is this a bush job? I don't see any roads in here," the man asked.

"Yeah, we have a camp in there now, down here," Cassy pointed to the bay on the map. "The only road is up by the old mine shaft at the head of Schist lake. There's lots of room at our camp if you want to build there."

"We'll probably pick a different spot. I'll see. So when did you want this done?"

"Can you start in a couple weeks? The sooner it gets started, the sooner we can map the lines. We have to get it done this fall," Cassy said.

"No," he said bluntly. "Got a lot going on."

"Hmm, that's too bad," Cassy replied, and paused a moment.

"We could pull in some line cutters from other jobs and their break time, but would have to pay 'em double. That's gonna cost ya," he said.

"I see," Cassy said, knowing he was trying to gouge her. "We got geologists on site. I'll talk to my boss. Maybe we can do the line cutting ourselves. Otherwise might have to shelve this project till next year." Cassy looked down as she spoke, attempting to call his bluff.

"OK, let me see who we can get to start cutting. I'll let you know. Give me your number, eh?" Abraham said.

Cassy scribbled the number down along with her name and Cliff Mines. She thanked him, smiled and exited the building. She felt good about her role in managing the project, as she should. Too many others new at managing might have caved in to a little intimidation.

There wasn't that much left to do. She had all the shopping done, plotted the map, dropped off samples and arranged the fall work. All she had left to do was load the truck, get more ice and get some gas for the boats. Cassy grabbed a sandwich at Tim Hortons and then headed back to the office. Barry was sitting at the table reading a newspaper and eating potato chips. He looked up as she walked in.

"Hey, how'd it go?" Barry asked.

"Fine. I arranged the geophysics and line cutters," she said.

"Good. I'm going to get you guys to do some of the line cutting too. You're cheaper than the line cutters. I'll have them direct everything and show you what has to be done. Don't tell the crew till it's time," Barry said. This blew Cassy's line cutting bargaining away.

Barry's condescension was apparent. Cassy was a little incensed by the use of the crew to do line cutting, but not surprised that geologists were cheaper than line cutters. Geologists are not paid well. She felt awkward holding back on this until lines were to be cut. It was a trick; 'oh, by the way, we want you to do this shit work 'cause you're cheap'.

Barry had one more illusion. "And don't tell them we have three months work ahead, just that the job is extended indefinitely."

Cassy understood this deception. The crew would be kept around as long as the work was funded. As soon as funding was cut, they'd be cut. As long as funding poured in, he could string them along without a break. Cassy didn't respect this management technique, but suspected it was common.

Cassy sat down and ate her sandwich while Barry continued to read the paper. "I'd like to spend as much time in the camp as possible. I can do more good there than here," she said.

"Well, that's OK for now, as long as you come into town a couple times a week and take care of business.

We'll see how things go. I may need you to do some office work on another project I have planned in the fall up at Wabishkok. This will be a busy year, clear through to next fall. I'm going to count on you a lot," Barry said. "Next month the V.P. of exploration will be here for a visit. I'll talk to him about you."

"Thanks," Cassy replied.

She perked up on this news. Perhaps things might work out OK. The project was going well, she was getting responsibility, and Titus would be here in camp for some time. What more could she want?

Cassy finished up her lunch. "Alright, I'm going to pack the truck. I have to stop by and get ice and beer and some jerry-cans of gas for camp, then I'll head out."

"Alright. How about coming back into town in four days. I want to keep an eye on how things are going," Barry said.

Cassy nodded and began dragging food out of the freezer and fridge. She had several boxes to load the food into. Barry continued reading the paper. Once filled, Cassy took the boxes out to the truck, along with some gear and items she had put in the living room.

She sped off toward the gas station to get gas and ice, and then to the liquor store to stock up on beer. From there, she drove out to the lake. She arrived about an hour early. After parking the truck in the shade and covering the groceries with a blanket, she walked down to the dock, laid back in the sun and fell asleep.

Chapter 62. Sneak up

I dragged myself out of the water and up onto a less-than-ideal rock for standing. There were no flat table rocks here to lounge on. My naked body dripped water and I shook the excess off. It was a nice, hot day to dry off in the sun. I had soaped every inch of me and rinsed off. Now I could shave, brush my teeth and relax before lunch. I know what you're thinking, that's a lot of downtime for a work day. Well, I guess it is. And the world can stuff it.

My razor and soap sat on the rock and I began to lather my face. The hair was spiky to the touch, even on my rough hands. With no mirror and ripples in the water I simply shaved and felt as I went. Once satisfied, I cleaned the rest of the soap off and then brushed my teeth. I'd probably have to do that again after lunch. I climbed a few rocks to find one that was acceptably flat, and there I sat, enjoying the hot sun and gentle breeze. The lake and shorelines lay before me. I never tire of seeing sights like this. It may look beautiful in winter too, but it's hard to relax and enjoy the scenery like you can in summer.

I didn't stay long, just long enough to daydream about Cassy and dry off. I gathered my stuff and rose higher on the rocks to where I left my clothes and backpack. I got dressed in the clean clothes I brought.

I opened my lunch to find the can of stew. There was an abundance of sticks and bark around, so I gathered a pile and made a fire. I added more wood until I had some good coals. My knife has an attachment to open cans and I punctured the lid, sawing up and down around the edge until it was three quarters open. That was good enough.

I placed the can into the fire amongst the coals. I forgot a fork, so I looked around for a piece of wood I could flatten with my knife to make a quasi-spoon. I could use it to stir the stew and then eat with it. You always need to be resourceful in the bush.

Once the stew had bubbled, I pulled the can out and let it sit for a few minutes in the dirt to cool down. It actually made a nice change from sandwiches. I ate a pudding too, and then my orange. Having devoured the whole mess in short order, I doused the fire and sat back to digest the grub. I would have to go soon. I had to walk back to the boat and then go to camp, and then go get Cassy.

I decided to just get going now. No point in waiting. I gathered my gear and hustled back through the bush to the boat. Didn't take long to get back to camp. I dumped my gear up by the tent and then took the boat on that familiar ride to the old head frame. I was quite early, but anxious to see Cassy.

I rounded a point and up ahead saw the dock. Surprisingly, a truck was there. It looked like the company truck. As I got closer I could make out the slim profile of a person lying on the dock. I slowed the engine to a crawl, then killed the motor. I used the oars to row the rest of the way. Without a sound, I slipped the boat up to the dock and tied it off. I carefully stepped onto the dock and slowly walked over to Cassy where I knelt down at her head, bent over and kissed her. She didn't open her eyes, but she smiled. "Is that you Titus, or some other guy whose kisses taste sweet?"

"I didn't surprise you?" I asked.

"I heard you coming a mile away. Nice try, sneaking up on me in work boots," she said. Cassy reached up and grabbed my shirt and pulled me down. I kissed her again. We lay together on the dock. I felt her fingers next to mine and put my hand on hers.

"I missed you," I said.

"I missed you too, my titan of Schist Lake," Cassy replied. "How are things in the camp?"

"Boring. We're pretty much out of food and all out of beer." I nuzzled her cheek.

"You smell pretty good; too good for a prospector," Cassy noted.

"Oh, do I?" I answered, nonchalantly. "Oh yeah, I had a bath and changed into my Sunday clothes at lunch. And you smell like a garden of roses."

"That's just my natural aroma. I never stink like you," Cassy said.

"Uh-huh, and you never fart either, right Princess Cassandra?" I joked.

"Hey," Cassy said, poking me, "who told you that was my real name? Only special people are allowed to call me Princess." Cassy laughed. "Well I guess no one is more special than you. Oh, geez, we should probably get to camp. The truck is full of groceries and ice."

"Alright, but just for the record, I'd be more than happy to lie here on the dock with you for another couple hours," I said.

"I know. Me too," Cassy agreed.

We got up and walked slowly to the truck, hand in hand. I looked in the back and flipped the blanket off to see all the boxes of food. It was a lovely sight. "Oh good God, all that food is giving me a woody!"

Cassy reached into the case of beer and pulled out a couple. She handed one to me and said, "Cheers!"

We bumped cans and I downed mine in a matter of seconds. "Wow! That was worth waiting for. You're the giver of great gifts," I said.

"That reminds me, got you something else." Cassy spotted a bag and handed it to me.

I was surprised. "What's this?" I asked.

"Well open it up," she demanded.

I opened it and pulled out a pillow. "You didn't. You are the most thoughtful person in the world," I said, and I kissed her. "Thanks Cass." Once again, I was touched by her kind heart.

"Well stop hugging the pillow and let's get this grub loaded in the boat," Cassy said.

She hopped in the truck, started it up and backed it down to the boat. I followed her on foot, still hugging my new pillow like a little boy and his teddy bear.

I went around back and flipped the tailgate down. We both began sliding boxes out and placing them in the boat. Once it was all loaded, I drove the truck back to the trees and parked it. The boat looked rather precarious with the stacked load in it. My pillow, in its bag, sat atop the load like a dollop of whipped cream on a sundae. Once in the boat, I pulled my cherished prize down to a more secure position. Cassy cast off and I gently drove the boat down the lake to our camp.

We nearly drifted down the lake we went so slowly. I brought us up along our small dock and moved the boat closer to shore than normal. After tying up, we hauled all the groceries, ice, gas and gear up to camp, and then put it all away. Finally, the work was over. It was about three o'clock in the afternoon.

"Hey, you want a snack?" I asked Cassy.

"Yeah. What do you have in mind?" she said.

"I can make us a sandwich. I had lunch, you?" I asked her.

"Let's split one," Cassy suggested. "I'm just gonna change. Gimme a minute, OK?"

"Alright," I called back as she disappeared into her tent. I looked at all the food. I opened up a loaf of bread and began making the mother of all sandwiches. A little mayo and mustard, a couple slices of turkey, tomato, lettuce, and a slice of cheese. I took a long knife and began slicing it in half.

Cassy called out, "Hey!"

Chapter 63. Camp Love

I looked out of the kitchen and over toward Cassy's tent. She stuck her head out. "Can you come here?" she said.

I stepped out and went over to her tent and opened the flap. There, in the middle of her tent she stood wearing a tiny blue teddy. I walked over to her and gazed up and down. I placed my hands on her face and kissed her.

"Titus, take my nightie off," she whispered.

I slid the straps off her arms and it fell to the ground. There she stood, stark naked in the pale, diffuse light. I pulled my T-shirt up over my head. She helped me. I undid my pants button. Cassy unzipped my fly and opened my pants up. I pulled them down to the ground.

"Cassy, take my underwear off," I asked.

Cassy reached into the waistband and pulled downward. My boxer briefs were stubborn, held tight by my body. As I became exposed, I could feel Cassy's warm breath against me. Cassy pulled my underwear all the way to the ground and I stepped out.

I wrapped my arms around Cassy and kissed her, enjoying the feel of her body against mine. I lifted her in my arms and laid her on the bed, then joined her. I kissed her from head to toe, not missing an inch of skin. My fingers explored every part of her, lingering wherever I felt her body react with pleasure. Her breasts were soft against my face. Her labia like basashi on my lips.

I finally entered her and gently submerged until I was fully inside. I lay heavily against her, gently rocking and rolling, sliding and nudging until we both felt the heat and excitement bring us closer and closer to an intense limit we couldn't control. I placed my lips against hers as we finished together.

I stayed upon her a while, gently kissing her, letting my heart slow, until finally sliding out and lying beside her in that tiny makeshift bed. She sat up, wanting to look at me. She touched me, looking and teasing, feeling the contours of my body as I relaxed. I enjoyed her interest in my body. I loved that she was attracted to me. She was both innocent and curious.

Cassy lay back down, facing me. She ran her hand over my stomach and chest. "I think you really care about me," she said.

I turned to her and answered, "Of course I do. Never doubt that."

Chapter 64. Dear Thora

The buzz of a motor grew louder until it suddenly died. The sound of people chatting and laughing thundered up to the doorstep. The flap of the tent swung open and Laura's face beamed in under the sunlight.

"Hey stranger," Laura bellowed, "how ya doing?"

Cassy and I sat at the kitchen table with half a sandwich in our hands. David shoved Laura in and entered, followed by Kyle.

"Don't just stand there, let us in," David yelled. "Where's the food?" All were in a good mood.

"Hello," Cassy yelled back. "If by food you mean beer, go check the pit." Cassy was referring to the hole under the tree root where a cooler held the ice.

"I'll get it," Kyle said and disappeared.

A moment later Kyle reappeared with five cans of beer. The sound of tabs opening was synchronous.

"Cheers!" David called out. Cheers were heard all around. "How was town?" David asked.

"It was fabulous," Cassy replied. "It was Flin Flon. Fabulous means better than Snow Lake, that's all." Cassy laughed. "It was boring. I did a bit of office work, ran a bunch of chores for Barry. I got food and beer and gas. That's it. I didn't have any fun. Would have been way better if we all could go in."

"Yeah, well, I suppose we'll be out of here in another couple weeks or so," David added. "So can't complain".

"Well, actually I have some news. Barry says we're staying, indefinitely. The company got more money and he wants to get as much work done as possible. If he doesn't spend the money, we might lose it, and we might lose some claims." Cassy explained.

I felt like this was a punch in the gut. I wanted my freedom, and I wanted to take Cassy with me when the job was over. Now, I was staying. Cassy was staying. I felt trapped here. Everyone else seemed happy. Laura cast a look my way. I knew she was wondering what was going through my mind. I couldn't have looked happy. I sighed, quietly, and left the tent. I went to my tent and sat on my bed. I put my beer down and thought to myself. What would I do? Was this a pivotal point in my life or was this going to be a cop out? I wasn't going to stay, not indefinitely, not any longer. I picked up a pen and paper and started to write a note.

Laura, dear Thora, you know I adore ya. Today's my day, and not tommora.

Better to leave happy than sour, and I've made a decision to be happy. I'm going to ask Cassy to leave with me, tonight, on the train. I'll be jumping a freight car up the top of the Northwest Arm, where the road crosses the tracks. I'm taking Cassy. Hopefully it goes to Winnipeg. We'll catch a bus to Vancouver from there. When we're gone, you can tell the guys, and Barry. I'm glad you all have work here for quite a while. Take good care. Wish me luck. Titus.

I folded the letter and placed it in an envelope with Laura's name on the back. I intended to sneak it to her, but she poked her head in the tent.

"You OK?" she asked.

I smiled at her. "Yeah, I'm great," I answered. "Come on in." I slipped the envelope behind my back. "I just had to take a moment and digest the news."

"Something's wrong," she said. "I know you're not happy. I saw that look on your face when you left the kitchen."

"True," I admitted. "But all's good now. You know when you have that gut ache, that pressure in your belly and then you have a big belch and feel much better? I just had a mental belch, and feel great now. Come on, let's go back." I could tell she wasn't buying it, but she didn't argue. We left and went next door to the kitchen.

"Everything OK?" Cassy asked.

"Everything's fine," I answered. "Drink up. What's for dinner? I'm starved!"

"Kyle has already started the barbeque. I think. I don't smell anything yet. We all want steak. That sound OK?"

"Sounds fuckin' awesome," I said. "Let's make a salad too. I haven't had fresh green stuff in days."

We all started pulling out food from boxes and preparing dinner. Before long, the table was set and a nicely grilled steak placed on each plate along with a good salad. It seemed like a happy, chatty meal, though I was pretty quiet. Normally full of wisecracks and insults, I sat, deep in thought, smiling and nodding at appropriate times.

Chapter 65. Come on!

When dinner was over, we all cleaned up the dishes, not that there were many. It only took a couple minutes. The others all sat at the table, talking. I leaned over and said to Cassy, "Want to take a boat ride?"

"Sure," she answered, and we slipped out. I went to my tent and picked up the letter, then took it over to the next tent and dropped it on Laura's bed. I dashed down to the dock where Cassy was standing, waiting, and we slipped out into the lake. I drove us over to Blueberry Island where we landed on our familiar beach. I took Cassy by the hand and led her up the hill to the cap. She sat down and I sat behind her, my arms wrapped around her.

"I should have asked *you* to go for a boat ride," Cassy said.

"Why?" I was surprised.

"I was worried. You left the tent abruptly after I told you we had more work. Tell me what you're thinking," Cassy softly demanded.

"I was pissed. You know I haven't had a break in a long time. You know I've wanted a change. I didn't want to be stuck in a bush camp any longer. I had plans," I answered her.

"What plans? I know it's selfish of me, but I'm glad the job is extended. The longer the job lasts, the longer I have you," Cassy said.

"But it shouldn't be like that. We can't be together just because we work together. Aren't we more than that?"

"So what are you saying?" Cassy asked.

"I'm saying be with me. Just be with me. Tonight, I choose a new life. I choose a new life with you. I want you to come with me."

"What? I don't understand what you're talking about. Go with you where?" Cassy asked.

"I'm talking about running, far away. I was going to ask you to come with me when the job was over, but now I just want to go. I can't wait around. Your friend came to camp. We had a good talk."

"My friend?" Cassy wondered out loud.

"Ron. He dropped by yesterday. He told me not to be afraid to take risks in life," I said.

I suppose I wasn't very clear about what he told me or how I was conveying it. I could sense apprehension in Cassy. She was not exhibiting signs of enthusiasm.

"I don't really understand what you're talking about," Cassy added. I couldn't blame her.

"OK, listen, I was going to ask you to come with me, out west. We could find a place, start new. I don't want to be a nomad anymore. I love you. I want a stable life. I want all the things we talked about, and I want them with you. Now the job won't end. Maybe it'll never end here. I don't want to wait," I explained.

I continued, "Tonight Cass, I want to grab the freight train, head south. We could ride it to Winnipeg and then go west. I've saved up money, enough to go back to school if I want. Doesn't matter what we do, it's gotta be better than running from one mining camp to another. We could never be together that way." I was rambling now. Maybe I was sounding incoherent or hysterical. I was trying my best to explain what I wanted.

"Barry told me we have enough work for months, maybe for a whole year. I get to meet the V.P. next month. We could end up as permanent employees," Cassy pleaded.

"It's a suckers bet. They always string you along and then nothing ever happens. Look at me, eight years in and I'm nowhere." I sounded bitter.

I think the problem was perception. Living and working in Flin Flon was Cassy's idea of success, not mine. And she had that slime ball Barry playing her, no doubt hoping to get into her pants someday. Fucking bastard!

"Come with me tonight," I said. I was not thinking clearly. I had allowed my judgement to be blurred by a fear of career entrapment.

"Titus, don't. Please. Let's think about it," Cassy begged. I saw fear in her eyes.

"Look," I pointed to the sky over the peninsula. The clouds were a beautiful orangey colour. It was a gorgeous sunset, just like the night we first spent on Blueberry Island. But I wasn't thinking of the sunset, just the time. "It's getting late. Come on!"

I grabbed her hand and led her down to the boat. I quickly cast off and drifted into the tiny inlet, then rounded the island. I twisted the throttle all the way reaching full speed, the wind blowing hard in my face. I was driven. I was propelled, like the boat, to fulfill this mission. I was doing it. I was not just thinking it.

I reached the point where the road meets the lake. I rammed the boat up the sandy shore and leapt out.

After departing, I dragged it up the shore so the others could find it tomorrow. I grabbed Cassy by the hand and we ran down the road toward the train crossing.

Once there I skidded to a stop, dust rising at my feet. I was near frantic. "Come on, come on!" I yelled down the bare tracks, pacing the width of the road along the crossing. "Where are you?" I yelled, my hands flailing about.

Then a sound. I stopped and listened. I looked at Cassy. She did not look happy. I looked back up the tracks, and there up the line, coming around the bend in the forest was the engine. It was a brute of an engine too. The nose was flat with a big scoop on the bottom and windshields up above. The front was a brilliant orangey red, trailed behind by a jagged white stripe and followed by black. The large, white 'CN' logo plastered on the front was clear as day.

The train was slow moving, as I expected. "Yeah! Yeah!" I hollered.

The train rumbled closer and closer until the engine passed. The sound was deafening. I waited for a flatbed car, one that was easy to jump on. All I saw were big box cars. There were several in a row, and then finally a flatbed.

"There!" I called out, looking back at Cassy. "There, that one. That's the one!" I pointed at the car.

Cassy shook her head. "I don't want to go," she yelled to me.

"You gotta. You gotta come with me." I was convinced she would. I just needed to show her I was serious. I had to get on first. She would hop on behind me.

This was it. I was actually starting over. I was making the biggest change in my life since I had left high school. I was potentially changing the entire direction of my life. This was a huge decision. Cassy must know it.

The flatbed car approached. "Clack clack... clack clack... clack clack..." It rumbled along, crossing the dirt road.

I waited until it passed by me and then I grabbed the back end, swinging myself up and onto the platform. This car was only used for a scattering of lumber, so there was lots of room. Once up there, I looked back at Cassy who was standing on the road by the tracks.

"Come on!" I called out and waved her to me. "Come on! Come on!" I reached down with my hand for her to grab onto.

Cassy stood there, tears in her eyes. She shook her head and gave me a small wave.

Now it sunk in. I was at a crossroads, literally and figuratively. Was she letting me go, to be free? Was she giving me my chance to make this change unencumbered? All of a sudden I was consumed with doubt. What was I doing? What was I choosing, the complete unknown over a girl I loved? I had to stop and think for a moment what was really important to me. Could I really leave this princess behind? Could I ever come back for her? There was no time to think. I had been too impulsive. I was afraid of this. Love always has a way of clouding my judgement.

I looked down, frantically searching the ground in front of me. My thoughts were chaos. At this point I didn't know up from down. I looked out. It was steep here, not flat like at the road. I paced up and down the flatbed car looking for a safe place to hop off. I saw none. I panicked and took my chance, leaping off. I sailed through the air. It felt like I was moving in slow motion.

"Clack clack... clack clack... clack clack..."

The train was moving a little faster. I landed on a steep and jagged slope. My feet buckled as they struck the ground and I flipped around, falling head first. I could feel by leg bone snap. A flash of pain struck me, first in my feet, then my body and head. I had come to rest someplace. I saw stars and lights dance before my eyes. A moment later, my vision came back. I felt my head against a rock and my body contorted on uneven ground. I could clearly hear the train carrying on above me.

"Clack clack... clack clack... clack clack..."

I'm sure the conductor of this long, sinewy train was completely unaware of my unscheduled embarkment and subsequent disembarkment. I blinked a few times. I could hear screaming over the sound of the train. "Titus! Titus!" It was Cassy. She was running toward me, looking for me. The long train continued to track south without me.

"Clack clack... clack clack... clack clack..."

Why did I jump off? Why did I doubt my choice? This is what Ron was talking about; taking a risk. But I was afraid to leave. I was afraid to make this change in my life all alone. Perhaps I had become weak or too dependent on these mining companies to feed me and house me and take care of me. But I was so close. I just had to stay on the train. I was so sure Cassy would come with me. I thought this would compel her to leave with me.

"Clack clack... clack clack... clack clack..."

My thoughts turned to Laura and the guys. Did she get my letter? Perhaps she read it and they were in a boat just off shore at the bottom of the lake waiting for the train, looking for me and Cassy to say goodbye. They will be disappointed, I suppose. The train was long and continued rolling by.

"Clack clack... clack clack... clack clack..."

Cassy stopped before me. I could see the shock in her face. She knelt down beside me and lifted me in her arms. I felt comforted that she was with me. She cried so hard. "Titus! Can you hear me? Please, don't leave me." She flung her head back and wailed in grief. I must have looked a terrible mess, a pool of blood on the rock where my head fell, my body twisted. This was far from the heroic and courageous outcome I had imagined.

I found enough strength to speak. "Cassy, I'm sorry. I couldn't leave without you. You know I love you."

Cassy looked pale. She said, "Titus, I love you too. I should have come with you." I could feel her trembling. "Titus? Titus! You'll be OK. Hang on."

My eyes closed and I saw the scene from up above. It was as if I was really up there. I felt as light as a feather. I could see the vast, green forest stretched out as far as the horizon. The lakes shimmered in the evening glow. I saw a boat out in our lake. Perhaps that was Laura and the boys, watching for me. Birds and dragonflies sailed around in glorious play. And down below, I saw myself, a weak man held by a beautiful woman. It was actually a peaceful sight. I soared higher and higher. There went the train, the last car, weaving a trail down the tracks to another place.

"Clack clack... clack clack... clack clack..."

My pain slowly subsided. My senses began to dull. I didn't feel so bad anymore. I didn't really feel anything at all. As my body grew numb and the rumbling din of the train faded away, I, the titan of Schist Lake, forever left this world, cradled in the arms of Cassy.

About the Author

Matt Egner grew up in Nova Scotia and Eastern Ontario. From an early age he developed a love of science and exploration. He completed a Master's degree in Geology and worked for many years in mining and exploration camps searching for gold, copper, nickel, platinum and diamonds. Exploration camps were a normal part of life for ten years before moving on to other endeavours. Today, Matt lives in a sleepy town in Eastern Ontario.

Glossary

Fucking the dog............	Not working, being lazy
Sulphide.....................	Metallic sulphide mineral
Massive sulphide.........	Rock made of mostly sulphide
Pyroclastics................	Explosive debris from a volcano
Pop Water..................	Club Soda
Basashi.....................	Horse sashimi
Perogies....................	Ukranian dumplings
Foamy.......................	Foam pad for sleeping
Frankum....................	Hardened spruce gum

Copyright © 2015 by Matt Egner

The moral right of the author has been asserted.

All characters and events in this publication, other than those clearly in the public domain, are fictitious and any resemblance to real persons, living or dead, is purely coincidental.

All rights reserved.

No part of this publication may be reproduced, stored in a retrieval system, or transmitted, in any form or by any means, without prior permission in writing from the publisher, nor be otherwise circulated in any form of binding or cover other than that in which it is published and without a similar condition including this condition being imposed on the subsequent purchaser.

Made in the USA
Charleston, SC
05 February 2016